YOU ONLY LIVE ONCE

MAXINE MORREY

Boldwood

First published in Great Britain in 2022 by Boldwood Books Ltd.

Copyright © Maxine Morrey, 2022

Cover Design by Debbie Clement Design

Cover Photography: Shutterstock

A CIP catalogue record for this book is available from the British Library.

Paperback ISBN 978-1-80162-621-7

Large Print ISBN 978-1-80162-620-0

Hardback ISBN 978-1-80162-624-8

Ebook ISBN 978-1-80162-623-1

Kindle ISBN 978-1-80162-622-4

Audio CD ISBN 978-1-80162-615-6

MP3 CD ISBN 978-1-80162-616-3

Digital audio download ISBN 978-1-80162-617-0

Boldwood Books Ltd
23 Bowerdean Street
London SW6 3TN
www.boldwoodbooks.com

For Mum

Love you. Miss you. Always.

1

'So obviously I said no problem.'

'Absolutely not!' I said at exactly the same time.

'Huh?' My brother took a large swig of the revoltingly strong, expensive coffee I got in for his visits and nabbed another biscuit from the jar.

'I said absolutely not.'

'But I've already told him now.'

'Then you'll just have to untell him.' I glanced out of the open bi-fold doors that formed one entire wall of my kitchen-diner, over to where my nephew and niece were playing in the garden. 'Umm. Should he be doing that?'

My brother looked round, rolled his eyes and walked to the threshold. 'Freddy! What have I told you about hanging your sister upside down? Her tooth will come out when it's ready, not by you trying to shake it out.' My nephew and niece looked over at us, from their opposite perspectives. A large sigh escaped from Freddy as he laid his sister on the ground. She hauled herself up, staggered once or twice as though she'd just left a good night at the pub and then ran off to play on the swing.

'Where was I?'

'Uninviting *your* friend to *my* house.'

'He's your friend too.'

I gave Felix a look.

'Well, you know him, at least.'

'I know a lot of people but that doesn't mean I'm about to invite them to stay at my house for an indefinite length of time!'

'It's not indefinite.'

'OK, then,' I said, hand on hip as my brother fished around in the bottom of his mug for an errant bit of biscuit, following some mismanaged dunking. 'How long would he be staying for?'

'Just until he gets himself set back up over here.'

'Which will take how long?'

'I don't know exactly.'

'Would you say then that, at present, the length of time it will take for your friend to restart a business he abandoned years ago is of an undetermined time?'

'Possibly.'

'Which would mean his stay here would be for an unstated duration.'

'I'm sure it wouldn't be long. I mean, no offence, Lils, but you're hardly the life and soul of the party, so I'm sure he'd want to get out and set up in his own place as soon as possible.'

'Then that works out marvellously.'

'It does?'

'Yes. As you quite rightly state, my company would be far below the entertainment level that Jack Coulsdon-Hart is used to courting and, as you say, he would want to set up his own accommodation swiftly. In which case, it's probably best if we skip the whole "he can stay here" step entirely and just go straight to the bit where he buys or rents his own place. Sound good? Great. I'm glad that's all settled. Are you done with that?' I grabbed the empty cup and popped it in the dishwasher before sweeping biscuit detritus from the counter with the side of my hand.

Felix looked at his watch then bellowed out into the garden for the kids to come in as it was time to go home.

'They can stay if they want.'

'They can, but poor, homeless Jack can't? That's not very charitable of you.'

I pulled a face. 'It's not the same thing and you know it. Family is different. Also, he's very far from poor.'

'You know he never touches his family's money. As for the rest, Jack is like family to me. He's the children's godfather, for a start.'

'I know that, but he's not family to me.'

'Kids. Home. Now!' he yelled again when no small people appeared in response to the first holler.

'Good job my nearest neighbours are sheep.'

Felix did a loud 'baaaaaa' and got a few replies in return. 'Seriously? I have more luck getting sheep to take notice of me than my own offspring.'

'You don't know what the sheep said. It might have been "bugger off" for all you know.'

'Always possible. Look, if you find my – there you are! I thought you'd disappeared into the jungle undergrowth for good!' my brother said, ruffling Freddy's hair and picking a twig from his daughter's.

'It's not that bad out there!' I said, feeling somewhat forced to defend my garden.

'Right.'

'It's not!' I protested. 'It's natural. I'm... rewilding. It's all the rage, you know.'

Felix sniffed the air. 'I guess they must be muck spreading at one of those farms nearby.' His gaze slid from the garden to me, one brow slightly quirked.

Freddy gave several sniffs, each one bigger than the last. 'I can't smell anything.'

'Maybe the wind changed, mate. Come on, let's get you home and in the bath. Both of you look like you could audition for *Lord of the Flies*.'

'What's that?'

'A book that you're too young to read just now,' I stated, wrangling my nephew into a coat that had been discarded as he worked up a head of steam charging around the garden.

'Well, don't say that!' my brother huffed. 'Now he'll definitely want to read it.'

'Are there fairies in it?' Ruby asked.

'No, sweetheart. Definitely no fairies.'

'Good!' Freddy said.

'It's not a book for your age group, darling.'

'But I'm good at reading. My teacher said so, didn't she, Daddy?'

'She did, but Auntie Lily is right. This isn't a children's book. When you're older, you can read it and make your own decision as to whether you like it.'

Freddy stuck his lip out.

I crouched down to zip up his coat. 'If you put that lip away, next time you come round, we could have a look on the local bookshop's website and see if there are any new books you might like instead. How does that sound?'

Freddy sucked his lip back in.

'Go and put your shoes on, please. I'll be there in a minute.' The children, having abandoned the wellies I kept for them to wear in the garden, zoomed through to the hallway.

'Alternatively, you could always take them to the actual bookshop,' said Felix.

'Could we please not have this conversation again today?'

'You never want to have this conversation.'

'Exactly. So perhaps that's a clue that I don't want to talk about it.'

'You can't hide away in here forever, you know.'

'I know. I do go out.'

'Barely. And only when you've run out of milk.'

'That still counts as out.'

'No, Lils. It doesn't. Unfortunately, I don't have time to get into this now. I've got to get these two home before Poppy thinks we've done a runner.'

'Give her a hug from me.'

'Will do, but you can give her one yourself on Saturday. Don't forget it's takeaway night. Poppy's mum and dad are having the kids this weekend.'

'So why don't you go out together? Paint the town red.'

'We're doing that Friday night and, since having kids, our stamina for nights out is very limited. Flopping over here for takeaway will be about the limit by then.'

'OK. So long as you're sure.'

'Yep. Any preference on food?'

'Nope. Just order what you like, but it's my treat.'

'Not this time. You always sneak a way to pay. This time I'm definitely paying.'

'Fine. OK. Then I'd like lobster thermidor, with caviar to start.' I paused. 'I'll have to think about pudding.'

'Funny. You do know that I know you can't stand caviar, don't you? Neither have I forgotten that the last time you had lobster, it paid a very hasty return visit.'

'You can be terribly annoying at times, you know that too, don't you?'

'I'm your brother. It's in the contract.'

'Go home, before your wife has time to realise she's been duped and there are far better options than you out there.'

Felix grinned and kissed me on the cheek. 'See ya.'

'Bye, Auntie Lily!' the kids chorused as Felix got to the front door.

'Umm, excuse me, I do believe some people have forgotten something.'

With that, both the children ran at me and flung their arms around me, laughing as they did so. 'Love you!'

I bent down to them, peppering each of their heads with lots of little kisses. 'I love you too. See you soon.'

I waited at the door until the car turned out of sight halfway down the driveway, then closed the front door, trying not to think about the silence that suddenly surrounded me once more.

I knew that moving out of the city had been the right decision after everything that happened, and I still loved this place. I had from the moment I saw it. From outside, it looked wonderfully and authentically Georgian, built by an architect who adored the style as a pet project for a client who had given him free rein. Except that when it came to it, the client decided that wasn't what he was after at all and that in fact he wanted not just the latest technology inside, but also a modern-looking exterior to reflect it. The house, consequently, never lived in, went on the market the day I decided to move from the city. In contrast to the original client, I loved the idea that all the modern amenities and energy efficient technology could be wrapped up in such an authentically period-accurate house. I didn't even look at anything else. This had felt right the moment I stepped in. I'd got a sense of peace and security and the large grounds gave me the privacy I craved.

Felix and Poppy, I knew, had their reservations but, on the other hand, it was far closer to them and the children and shamelessly, I used this excuse to talk them round. Not that they would have stopped me buying it. I'd already paid the deposit by the time I told them, anyway, but it did go some way to easing their anxieties that I'd be rattling around in a big house on my own and that it was a lot to look after. I'd promised I'd get a cleaner and a gardener to help me and they appeared satisfied with that.

Obviously, neither of those things happened. I'd decided that perhaps this would be a good time to take up gardening myself. All sorts of studies had been done showing both the physical and mental benefits of such a pastime and I did try. I just literally had no idea what I was doing. Did I cut that down? Was this dead or was it supposed to look like that? When Poppy gently advised me that I'd just ripped out a plant that likely cost about a thousand pounds and that it wasn't dead, just going into dormancy for the winter, I gave up. Which is why the once beautifully landscaped gardens were now more akin to the rewilding project I'd attempted to get my brother to buy into – unsuccessfully. It really was kind of a mess. I'd have to have another go at tackling it. Swot up on some *Gardener's World* episodes and do my best to channel Monty as I ventured forth with my secateurs. I looked again out at the wilderness – a machete might be more appropriate – but where to even start?

I went back through to the bright and airy kitchen that opened out onto the garden and the fields beyond. One was a paddock that belonged to the property but that was home to two horses owned by someone in the village. Thankfully, Felix had been here when they came asking if there was any chance of using the paddock for stabling. I'd wangled him into dealing with it all apart from setting the price which I'd stipulated as a minimum fee. During the chat, from which I'd hidden myself in the study with the excuse that I was on a deadline (I was always on a deadline, so that day was really no different, but it was a good enough reason to exclude myself from the proceedings), I'd overheard that the lady used the horses for therapy work with disabled children. I didn't need the extra money and the paddock was just sitting there empty anyway, so it made sense to lease it to someone who could make good use of it. The fact that that someone was giving help and bringing joy to children and their families for whom life was a constant struggle made it a no-brainer decision.

I'd wanted to lease it for free but when I proposed this to my solicitor, he went into a long spiel about... the truth is, I'm not sure what he said. After the first few sentences of legalese, my brain switched off and only flicked back on again when I realised he'd stopped talking. I asked him what the absolute minimum was I could charge and still satisfy his terms and he grudgingly gave me one, which I then requested he draw up a contract for. Ideally, I'd have just done everything without the need for anyone else being involved but, as Felix had pointed out, that land was part of my home and it made sense to have terms of use laid out clearly in order to avoid any problems in the future. He was right. The last thing I wanted was confrontation and mess. Felix did point out that it had cost me more to get the contract drawn up than I was charging her for a year's rent, but I reminded him about the children and he'd shrugged, said, 'Fair enough,' and let it go.

In my one flash of gardening inspiration a few years ago, Poppy and I had turned the other field into a wildflower meadow. We'd done it together as a family, clearing the grass and planting the seed. Early signs were encouraging, if a little sparse, but now, three years on, it was well established, and in the summer became a packed riot of clashing colours humming and buzzing with a thriving population of insects and pollinators. The kids absolutely loved it and I found it a source of calm when I took a walk around, just resting against the five-bar gate that separated it from the edge of the garden, surrounded by nature and able to put everything else out of sight and mind.

I'd continued to live in our London flat for over a year following the accident that killed my husband but, instead of getting easier, every day seemed to bring with it another memory of our time together there, constantly ripping open a wound that was already struggling to heal. My brother and his wife had been absolute rocks, visiting and staying with me even when I didn't want anyone around. They refused to leave me alone for long, which was probably just as well. What I thought I wanted and what I actually needed had been, I realised now, two very different things.

Friends initially had called and sent cards but when they visited, or I forced myself to accept invitations, I could feel their discomfort as strongly as my own. They trod on eggshells, being sure not to mention anything they thought might cause upset. They didn't know how to 'be' with me when all I'd really wanted was some sense of normality, whatever that was. They meant well, but none of us enjoyed the evenings, and I think they were relieved when I began to decline the invitations, and I was certainly relieved when they ceased to ask.

I sat gazing out in the garden. The first hints of early spring were tentatively showing themselves, as crocuses pushed up through the grass, replacing the snowdrops that had burst through earlier in the year. There was something reliable about a garden and nature in general. It was one of the many things that had attracted me to this place, even though I knew I had done a poor job of looking after its beautiful grounds. Whatever else went on in life, trees burst into leaf, daffodils danced in great swathes, snowdrops peeped their nodding heads above the ground to signal the start of it all. Even when your life had been shattered, nature's cycle continued and, at a time I found it hard to discern comfort in anything, I did find some sort of comfort in that.

2

Having overstuffed ourselves with takeaway, Felix, Poppy and I sprawled on the sofas in the lounge while my brother surfed through streaming channels to try to find a film we all wanted to watch. Poppy and I had already vetoed several versions of a zombie apocalypse and umpteen superhero incarnations. Knowing there were piles of brilliant screenplays sat out there, withering in slush piles while the movie industry remade the same old thing, was one of the many reasons I'd declared I didn't plan to have a TV when I moved in. The look of horror on my brother's face meant that the decision was soon reversed, and I gave him carte blanche to order whatever he thought was right for the room, after of course specifying I was looking for a television and not a cinema screen.

I now had a TV that I did actually use more than I had anticipated, if only for company, and I had found a streaming service that was mostly documentaries which was often a source of interest and occasionally inspiration, so it hadn't been a total waste. And, of course, I got to watch fun things like the *Toy Story* series with the kids. I'd also sat through a few superhero movies with Freddy while Ruby had often, and quite wisely, curled up on my lap and gone to sleep. But even those films meant I got to spend time with the people I loved and that, I knew, was the most important thing of all, because you were never sure just how much time you would have. My husband and I thought we had decades ahead of us as we'd sat celebrating our third wedding anniversary. As it turned out, we had just minutes.

* * *

Paris had been its usual glittering and romantic self as we'd strolled along next to the Seine that night, making our way slowly to a particular restaurant I'd read about and been keen to try. The place had certainly lived up to the hype and, after a wonderful meal and a bottle of champagne to toast our anniversary, we sat watching the Parisian world go by from the vantage point of our pavement table, sipping coffee. Mike had suggested another romantic stroll past the beautifully lit Eiffel Tower on the way back to our luxury hotel and, bearing in mind the fizz and the coffee I'd been consuming, I'd excused myself for a nip to the ladies' before we left, passing our waitress taking the card machine out to Mike at our table.

I was washing my hands when I heard the noise, a huge bang accompanied by glass shattering and then, for a split second, absolute silence. That was immediately replaced by a cacophony of shouts and screaming. I realised later that one of those screams was mine.

The autopsy showed that the driver of the car which ploughed into the pavement and straight on into the front of the restaurant had suffered a fatal heart attack. He was on his usual route home and, thirty seconds later, would have turned down a small, empty side street. Although he sadly would still have died, he wouldn't have taken an Italian businessman, the waitress who had been serving us, and my darling husband with him. None of them stood a chance. From the eyewitness reports, it all happened so quickly they barely had time to see the car coming before it hit them.

I don't remember a lot about those first few days. There was a hysterical, garbled phone call to Felix which a kind French paramedic who spoke excellent English took over for me, advising Felix of the facts, as he knew them at that moment, which wasn't a lot, but enough. More than enough. The main fact, the only fact, I perhaps somewhat selfishly thought of was that Mike, my husband, was gone. If I hadn't nipped to the loo, I'd have been at that table too, and all I wanted was to turn back time and have stayed. Three years ago that day, we'd promised 'until death do us part'. But I didn't want death to part us. I wanted to go with him. I wanted to have died with him.

It took a long time for those feelings to subside and there were still days they flickered inside me. I realise now how hard it must have been for my brother to have heard me repeating the same refrain over and over again, and I felt awful I'd put him and Poppy through that. They didn't deserve it. But other people were beyond my scope of vision at that point. All I knew was an unending see-saw of utter numbness tipping into pain so deep and so violent I longed for the numbness again.

People tried to help, but I felt like an automaton around them. I couldn't concentrate on conversations. As terrible as it sounds, I had no interest in them. I didn't care about their lives or their holidays or their children. I didn't care about my own life and it was hard to even pretend to show interest in theirs. And when a few well-meaning friends made an attempt to introduce me to a man ten months after Mike's death, I knew I couldn't deal with any of it anymore. Everywhere I looked in London, in the flat, outside in the city, was a memory of something we'd done, or something we'd planned which would now never come to fruition. I didn't need reminders. They were all etched into my very soul and the London I'd once loved had now become painful to look upon because I was no longer looking upon it with the man who'd meant everything. That was the day I decided to leave London and the day I'd found Meadow Blossom House.

I sat in the lounger, a blanket laid over me as I hugged a cup of hot chocolate and looked out into the beginnings of twilight and the wild beauty that was my garden. I really ought to get a gardener in, but the thought of it filled me with dread. The longer I'd stayed away from society, other than my immediate family, the worse I felt every time I thought about having to interact with anyone. As I'd told Felix, I did nip to the local shop when I had to, but I always made sure I went about 6 a.m., as soon as they opened, as there was less chance of running into people at that time. It wasn't that the villagers were unpleasant. Quite the opposite, in fact. They always had a smile and a gentle exchange. Poppy had told me there was a bit of gossip for a while when I'd first moved in. The archetypal reclusive writer, hidden away behind tall gates and high walls. It was, even to me, with a writer's natural fear and distaste of clichés, obvious that I did appear to have turned into one. But it hadn't been intentional and it's not like I never went out – just not very often. Of course, I saw my family all the time here. Although, right now, I wasn't sure that was such a good thing.

Poppy and I had given up on Felix's appalling choices and left him to it. I'd lobbed a pair of wireless headphones at him and he was now happily ensconced in a big, squashy armchair, watching something that from what I could tell by the odd glance made up for its paper-thin plot with oceans of blood and gore. Poppy and I continued our chat about the children, *Bake Off* and what we hoped for from the next series of *Sewing Bee* until Felix's phone began to ring. Wrapped up in the violence of his apocalyptic nightmare, he didn't hear it, so Poppy tossed it over, making an excellent shot of landing it on his full stomach. He let out an 'oof', paused the gore and answered the video call.

'Jack, mate. How are you?'

Poppy and I turned back to our conversation until my brother interrupted. 'Hang on. I'm just going to cast this onto the TV. We can all see you then.'

I looked at him momentarily in horror. 'That TV has a webcam,' I whispered. 'He'll be able to see us too!'

My brother gave me a look that appeared to question my intelligence. 'That's kind of the point of video calls, Lils.'

As I opened my mouth to reply, I was halted by a forty-two-inch high-definition picture of Jack Coulsdon-Hart filling my living room. I'd only seen him briefly a few times over the years, and therefore my strongest memory of Jack remained a night in my late teens at a village party and, although my recollection of that night was somewhat clouded and yet still mortifyingly vivid, he had, if possible, only got better looking with age. Of course he had.

Jack had often been around our house – Felix, loyally, didn't speak about Jack's home life much. I don't think even he was entirely sure of all the facts, but it was hard not to notice that he spent as little time at home as possible. They'd been friends from living in the same small village but had cemented their friendship at university. Felix was bright and worked hard to get into Cambridge. Jack was bright but, whether it was admitted or not, had the extra benefit of having been to Eton and being the son of an earl. This wasn't something he ever talked about and most of the time we all forgot. Until a chauffeur would turn up at our house with the liveried man advising that his mother would like him to return home now. Jack always looked mortified whenever this happened. I'd catch him glancing out of the window occasionally when he came round to hang out with Felix (not that I was looking at him, obviously). When he did catch me looking, he'd give the briefest smile and try to look relaxed. I might have been younger, but I wasn't stupid.

Seeing him on the screen now revived those memories in my mind. The night of the village summer fête was always a brilliant evening. Had it not been for the embarrassment I suffered that night, it probably would have been another teenage memory that drifted into the recesses of my mind. But that night, emboldened by friends and an ill-judged number of piña coladas, I'd approached Jack in what I'd considered a sexy, flirtatious way. Looking back now, and also by the look on his face at the time, it was likely neither of those things. Time and alcohol had erased the exact words I'd used but, oh Lord, it was definitely something ridiculous about how it must be nice to be so tall and be able to reach things on high shelves.

God! I still cringed now thinking about it. He'd nodded and agreed that it came in handy. Then, clearly thinking I was on a roll, I had proceeded to tell him just how good-looking I thought he was, affecting what I assumed was a sexy stance. Again, most likely not. In fact, definitely not, in that Jack Coulsdon-Hart's response to this, after a moment of merely staring at me, was to *pat me on the head*! Yes. He actually patted me on the head, said thank you and disappeared like a spectre into the crowd. Having been rescued by my friends, who had stood watching the whole disastrous situation unfurl, I stumbled to a corner of the field.

'I didn't even warrant a "I can't. You're my best friend's sister,"' I'd wailed, downing yet more cocktails. 'He just patted me on the head like a sodding puppy!' We'd all watched silently when, half an hour later, Jack had left the fete with the prettiest girl in the village. He'd cast a glance towards us, then carried on out of my life. The whole regrettable night was topped off by me spending most of the early hours of the following morning alternating between hugging the toilet bowl and crying.

After that, I had made a point of avoiding Jack, a strategy that had worked exceptionally well. There had been, of course, the brief meetings when the children were christened due to us both being godparents but we'd both spent as little time as possible in each other's company. I'd gone to the church and done my bit but, without Mike, I couldn't face anything more. Thankfully, Felix and Poppy had understood. Or at least, had tried to, and I would always appreciate that. Jack had also made a point of attending both my parents' funerals, despite living abroad. Apparently, he'd also come to Mike's, which I'd thought was kind, but I still had little recollection of that particular day thanks to a mixture of shock, grief and Valium.

I'd put the moment of lust I'd felt for Jack at the fête out of my mind. Until now, of course. But the past was a long time ago. I doubt he even remembered anyway, and I was a grown woman, and a successful novelist. Jack Coulsdon-Hart held no sway for me now as the big handsome face stared out from my smart TV. But, bloody hell, did he really have to be so good-looking? Life really wasn't fair sometimes.

'Hey!' Jack raised a slightly awkward hand at Felix's decision to suddenly thrust him virtually into my living room. For a moment, I thought he looked as uncomfortable as I felt, but the moment passed and I was sure I'd imagined it. Poppy bounced next to her husband and waved happily. Jack's smile was genuine and warm.

'No kids tonight, or they in bed?'

'Grandparents,' Felix advised, 'so we're over at Lils's place, stuffing takeaway and watching hideous movies.'

'You're watching them,' Poppy corrected. 'Lily and I are having in-depth and meaningful conversations.'

'You are not,' Felix scoffed. 'Don't think I didn't hear that comment about how arrogant you think offering a handshake as some sort of prize on *Bake Off* is.'

Poppy drew herself up. 'Well, I know you agree.'

'I do, but that's not the point.'

'Hey, Lily.' Jack interrupted the marital bicker to raise a hand, his striking green eyes boring out of the screen.

'Hello.' I gave him a small smile. 'I'll go and put the kettle on, shall I?' I said, getting up and heading out of the room before anyone could reply. The only company I was used to, real or virtual, was my family. Now Jack Coulsdon-Hart was being beamed directly into my lounge and it felt weird. Not least because somewhere in the very pit of my stomach I felt something I had thought long dead show the briefest flicker of life. Dismissing the feeling as the after-effects of overindulging in Indian takeaway, I pootled around in the kitchen for as long as possible before Poppy came through.

'I'm the search party. Are you coming back in?'

'Yeah, sorry. Got distracted,' I fibbed. 'Here's the tea. Has Felix finished?'

'No, they're still chatting.'

My stomach sank. 'Oh, right.'

'Here. I'll take the tray if you bring the biscuits.'

I obeyed and followed her back into the living room.

3

As I entered the living room, Jack was laughing heartily at, I assumed, something my brother had said. While he was distracted, I took a moment to study him. The intervening years had scuffed off those last few 'eldest son of a distinguished family' edges. It suited him, there were more laughter lines around his eyes now, crinkling as my brother continued to tease him about something. His face was gently weathered. Not like an old salty fisherman, but a healthy outdoorsy look. The slight tan he sported contrasted with the startling green eyes that had always secretly entranced me.

'What are you two laughing at?' asked Poppy.

My brother threw me a grin and my guard flew up. 'I was just reminiscing with Jack about that village fête and how ill Lils was that night. God, I don't think you came out of your bedroom for about three days, did you?'

I glared at Felix. 'I don't remember,' I lied. 'It was a very long time ago. I'm sure Jack doesn't either.' We all looked towards the screen.

'Oh, I'm sure he does.' Felix took a sip of tea and burned his mouth. I found it hard to sympathise in that moment.

Jack's striking eyes looked out from the screen and locked with mine. Immediately I knew. He totally remembered. 'Can't say I do, really,' he said, holding the gaze. 'As Lily said, it was a long time ago.'

Oh God. He remembered everything.

'Congratulations on the new book, by the way,' Jack effectively and swiftly changed the subject, something for which I was very grateful. 'Straight into *The Times* bestseller list, I saw. That's great.'

'Yes. Thanks. Bit of a surprise.'

'I don't know why she's surprised,' my brother said through a mouthful of biscuit. 'They pretty much always do. Early reviewers were raving about it before it was even released. And of course, once the film premieres, that will bolster up book sales too.'

'Only if people like it.'

Felix sighed and took another biscuit. 'Of course they'll like it. How many tickets do you get to the premiere, by the way?'

'I've no idea. It's not like I'll be going, anyway.'

'Oh!' Poppy's face fell. 'Really? I thought we might all get dressed up and have a swish night out.'

I sat on the sofa and tucked my knees up. 'Sorry.' And I really was. 'You know, it's just not my sort of thing.'

'Very little is your sort of thing these days,' Felix mumbled.

I fiddled with my hair, embarrassed that we were having this discussion in front of a virtual stranger, at least a virtual stranger to me.

'So are you still in New Zealand?' I asked Jack in a vain attempt to turn the spotlight off myself.

'Yeah, I'm just at the airport. I fly tomorrow.'

This explained the nondescript background, magnolia walls, with a slightly post-modernist artwork interpretation on the wall to the left of his shoulder vainly attempting to inject some personality into the otherwise bland and soulless room.

'Long flight.' I mentally gave myself a head slap. For someone who worked with words for a living, my conversation skills were as flat as a two-day-old lemonade.

Jack didn't seem to mind. 'Yep. Good job I've got a good book,' he said, holding up a copy of my latest novel.

'Oh!' I was genuinely surprised.

He smiled, and as much as my mortifying encounter with him all those years ago was still etched into my brain, I couldn't help smiling back.

'You seem shocked,' he said, laughing.

'Pleased,' I corrected him. 'I just didn't think it would really be your sort of thing.'

'I guess it's nice to know that I can get to this age and still throw out the old surprise.'

'You're hardly old!' Poppy poked a finger at the screen. 'And don't you dare argue with that because I'm only a few months younger than you.'

He grinned. 'I wouldn't dream of it.'

'Did you decide where you're staying?' Felix asked.

'I've got a hotel booked not far from you for a couple of days. I'm hoping I'll be able to sort out a room to rent in that time.'

I looked up through my lashes at the screen. Was he resentful that I hadn't agreed to let him stay here? He was either a really good actor or he genuinely wasn't bothered.

'I've been in contact with some of my old clients and they seem pretty happy for me to restart with them again, which is good news. I'm effectively building the business up from scratch again, so a mortgage is pretty much out of the question, especially with having been out of the country for so long.'

'Don't you just ring up Coutts, say your family name and receive bags of money?' I asked, partly as a tease and partly as a genuine question. His family was loaded, so why he never took advantage of that seemed a little strange.

'Ha. Funny.' The slightest accent he had picked up twanged occasionally in his words.

'Of course, like I said before, you can always stay here with Lily,' said Felix. 'She's got four spare rooms as it is. And there's plenty of space, so you'd never even have to see each other if you didn't want to.'

I hid behind my mug and planned my brother's demise. The best way to ensure that we didn't see each other would be by Jack not being here at all. I glanced at Poppy and even she looked unsure, knowing I'd already vetoed the suggestion.

'And like I said before,' Jack stated. 'It's not fair on Lily. She likes her privacy and the last thing she needs is me descending on her home.'

'Rubbish. The company would be good for her.'

'I thought you just said that we'd hardly see each other,' I couldn't help adding.

Felix shrugged. 'Well, you don't have to. I'm just saying it wouldn't hurt to actually speak to another human being every now and then.'

'I do speak to other human beings every now and then. I also speak to you, so I've got all the species covered.'

Jack's laugh burst from the screen. Felix turned to him and he straightened his face immediately, although I could still see amusement dancing in his eyes.

'I'm only talking temporarily. It would give Jack a local base from which to build his business. God knows he's spent enough time in featureless rooms and rented accommodation already.'

Had he? Why?

'Just until he's back on his feet.'

'Felix, mate? I know you're trying to help, but badgering Lily isn't the way I want to go.'

'You'd get to see the kids more, being close. And us, of course, always a bonus.' He gave a sweeping gesture as though acknowledging his subjects. My brother could be such a dork at times – but I knew he was also a well-meaning one. 'Plus, you might be able to give Lily some advice about the wilderness currently surrounding this place.'

'It's not a wilderness, it's... private.'

'If it was any more private, the postman would need a machete!'

'Stop exaggerating. It's not that bad.'

Two pairs of eyes gave me an unconvinced reply. I looked at the screen. 'It's really not.'

Jack nodded and gave the kind of awkward smile you do when you have been unwittingly dropped into a family discussion. Not that I thought it was that much of an issue. Besides, the postman had only got lost that once.

Jack gave me that smile again. 'Felix exaggerates. Always has. How do you think he managed to land a hottie like Poppy?'

'Oi!' snapped Felix as the rest of us laughed.

'Felix is right about one thing, though,' I began tentatively. 'Staying here would give you the opportunity to see more of the children. You are their godfather. I know you talk on Skype all the time, but it's not the same, is it?' I knew the kids adored Jack and that Felix especially had missed spending time with his closest friend in person since he'd left the country years ago.

Jack gave a small sigh that had a distinct air of sadness about it. 'No,' he said. 'It's not. But I really do get the feeling this has rather been dropped on you and the last thing I want to do is impose on your privacy.'

'Like Felix said, it's a decent size house. We'd probably hardly ever see each other.'

Jack still looked unsure, and if I was honest, there was currently a tiny little person running around my brain screaming *what are you doing*?

The words had just come out as I thought about the benefits for Felix and his family. But had I really just invited Jack Coulsdon-Hart to stay with me? On the screen, Jack yawned widely, politely covering his mouth with his hand. It was then I realised how tired he looked. Exhausted, even. And what did Felix mean about him having lived in featureless rooms for so long? I knew that, sadly, his marriage had failed over in New Zealand. But from what I'd heard, he'd made a good life out there. It wasn't exactly like he was coming home penniless, plus he was, of course, the heir apparent to a whacking great estate – assuming he hadn't been disinherited. I'm sure Felix would have told me about that, even if I wasn't party to the village gossip in general, something I was actually quite happy about. The current Earl and Duchess of Marsden hadn't been thrilled with their eldest son's life choices, and disinheritance was always a threat they'd held over him, but I got the impression through Felix that if they were to carry through such a threat, it would be more of a relief than anything else. To Jack, anyway.

'Good!' said Felix. 'That's settled. I'll pick you up at the airport as arranged. Cancel those hotel reservations and I'll bring you straight here. That's all right, isn't it, Lily?'

Well, it was a bit late to object now.

'Absolutely fine.' I smiled up at the screen and hoped it looked genuine.

* * *

By the time Felix arrived with Jack a couple of days later, I'd thoroughly cleaned the house from top to bottom, arranged a food delivery to restock all the cupboards and fridge and prepared a large lasagne, complete with salad, in case Jack wanted something to eat after his long journey. Having seen him sitting in the insipid hotel room and Felix's comment about him having spent a good proportion of time in such accommodation, I'd put in extra effort to prepare the room I'd set aside for Jack in a way that made it feel as homely as possible. There was water in a glass carafe on the side, some early blooming fresh flowers picked from my wilderness of a garden in a vase on the dresser, and an assortment of luxury toiletries in the adjoining en suite bathroom. I had no idea of the name of any of the flowers, or indeed if any of them were poisonous. Still, as long as he didn't choose to eat any of them, he should be fine.

If I'd checked my watch once today, I must have checked it a hundred times. My stomach was all in knots, and I couldn't concentrate on writing or any other task, for that matter. Bloody Felix and Poppy. I knew this was a terrible idea.

Later that evening, when Jack Coulsdon-Hart walked through my front door behind my brother, I took one look at his exhausted face and saw there was a whole story written there, one I didn't and might possibly never know. But what I did know was that he needed something more right now than just another soulless hotel room.

Felix dropped down a couple of the bags he'd been carrying and leant over, giving me a peck on the cheek, whispering a 'thanks' as he did so. Behind him, the sizeable bulk of man that was Jack filled the doorway, looking hesitant to come in.

'Come in, come in!' I tried to cover my own nervousness and insecurities with a bright cheery smile and tone. Jack set his suitcase down as I closed the door behind them and then, as I turned back, my gaze caught his and I immediately knew that he saw straight through me. I did my best to keep the smile in place anyway. Fake it till you make it, I told myself, or something like that.

'How was the flight?'

'Yeah, good. Thanks. Kind of long.'

'Quite. Have you eaten?' I asked, leading them both through into the kitchen.

'Just something on the plane earlier, but that's fine, I'm not really hungry. My body clock is all out of whack at the moment.'

'That's OK,' I said. 'I've done a lasagne, but we can have that tomorrow if that's all right with you. Oh! I suppose I should have asked whether you were vegetarian or anything?'

'No,' he replied, laughing. 'Definitely still a carnivore I'm afraid, much to the chagrin of my ex-wife.'

I waited in case he planned to elaborate, but it soon appeared that this was the entirety of the sentence.

'You really didn't have to cook anything for me anyway,' he said.

'No, it's fine. Just don't get used to it.' I gave a quick laugh. 'This is purely a one-off. The rest of the time, you're on your own, although feel free to use anything you need in the kitchen. I've got a shop arriving in the morning so everything should be replenished by then, but if there's anything particular you'd like me to get in then I can do that, so just let me know.'

He shifted his weight, momentarily looking pained. 'I really didn't mean for you to go to all this trouble. I promise it will only be for short time. I'm already looking for places to rent.'

'I know. But that's no reason not to be comfortable now and it's really no trouble. I know you'd certainly do the same for Felix if he was in the same position.'

Felix was nodding in agreement with his back to us as he'd just discovered the cheese straws I'd baked early that afternoon. He pulled a couple out and handed them to Jack. 'Here, try these, they're delicious!'

'Felix!'

'What?' he asked around a mouthful of cheese straw, crumbs spraying out as he did so.

Jack had paused with the cheese straw that my brother had handed him halfway to his mouth. I rolled my eyes.

'Never mind.' I glanced to Jack and nodded at the pastry in his hand. 'You may as well eat them now he's handed them to you.' They both disappeared within seconds, and he made an appreciative noise.

'Those really are delicious.'

'Yeah,' Felix said. 'It's a good job you have an active job, mate. Living with Lily and her cooking could turn you into the size of a house otherwise.'

'He's not living with me,' I corrected, suddenly feeling awkward and needing to clarify the situation, although I wasn't sure exactly for whom.

This time, it was Felix's turn to roll his eyes. 'You know what I mean,' he said, his hand moving towards the tin that held the remnants of my afternoon's baking. I moved it away and put the lid back on. My brother let out a hard-done-by sigh.

'Right, anything else you need, Jack? I'm going to head home.'

'No, thanks, Felix. I really appreciate everything you've done. And you too, of course, Lily.' He smiled at us both.

'I've not really done anything yet,' I joked. 'You might be regretting it all within a week.'

Jack's smile became full wattage. I'd seen it briefly on the screen during the Skype call, but I'd forgotten just what an impact it could have in real life. 'Somehow I doubt that.'

I turned away and began fussing with a tea towel. 'I guess we'll see about that.'

We both said goodbye to Felix, each giving him a hug, and sent our love to Poppy and the children. I closed the bi-fold door behind my brother and turned back to find Jack standing, slightly awkwardly, in my kitchen. It was a big kitchen, but his presence still managed to fill it.

'Are you sure you don't want a drink or anything?'

'No, I'm fine really, thanks. Felix and I got a coffee on the way back from the airport.'

'OK. Perhaps I should just show you to your room so you can start making yourself comfortable, and there's water on the bedside up there if you want it anyway. Is there anything I can carry?'

Jack hoiked the last bag over his shoulder and picked up the suitcase. 'No, I've got it, thanks very much.'

I led the way out of the kitchen and up the stairs, Jack following close behind. I had never been a big jeans wearer, but today I'd changed into a pair, teaming them with a plain T-shirt with cute ruffled sleeves. I tended towards dresses most of the time, but I'd spent far too much time thinking about what I should wear this evening. I'd tied myself up in knots, considering whether, if I put a dress on, Jack might think I'd dressed up for him, and that definitely wasn't the impression I wanted to give. So I'd gone with the casual look. But now I felt sure that had been an error as I was acutely aware that with me leading the way up the stairs my bottom was slap-bang in his eyeline. It's not that it was a bad bum, more that I wasn't used to having it on show as much as it was right now in the snug jeans. I really should have just stuck with the dress and not overthought it. Damn.

Thankfully, we had reached the landing, and I opened the door to the guest bedroom I'd set aside for Jack to use.

'This is yours. I hope it's all right.'

Jack walked in, carefully placing his luggage on the floor and looking around as he did so.

'All right?' he repeated, laughing. 'It's beautiful. You really shouldn't have gone to all this trouble.'

'It was no trouble,' I insisted. 'Nothing I wouldn't do for any guest.' I was suddenly and inexplicably gripped by a need to assure him he wasn't getting preferential treatment.

He levelled the almost hypnotic green gaze at me. 'From what I hear, you're not really overkeen on the whole guest thing apart from your family.'

I waved my hand in dismissal. 'You shouldn't believe half of what my brother tells you. You know what he's like.'

'I do, but I think we both know he's right about that. And, of course, there is the fact that you're known as the reclusive romance writer.'

Turning to look out of the window at the cows in a field two along from mine, I spoke without looking at him. 'I would have thought that coming from a family like yours, you would know better than to believe everything you read in the media.'

He smiled as I turned back. 'Touché.'

'So, through here's the bathroom,' I continued the tour. 'There's some toiletries there, with extras under here.' Briefly opening a cupboard under the sink, I showed him backup supplies. 'If there's anything else you need, just let me know.'

'Lily, this is all great, but you're not a hotel. You don't have to do all this.'

'Like I said, I wanted you to be comfortable. And with that in mind, you look pretty tired, so I'll leave you to rest. If I'm out in the morning, help yourself to anything from the fridge and cupboards for breakfast.'

We both knew it was highly unlikely I'd be out, as there wasn't a blue moon due for ages yet, but I kept up the pretence and Jack went along with it.

'Thanks, Lily. I really do appreciate you putting yourself out like this. I'm aware that this wasn't really your idea.'

'Well, none of that really matters now, does it? You're here and I'd like you to be comfortable. Besides, Felix would never forgive me if I was rude to you and bearing in mind he's one of the few people I see, I kind of have to keep him sweet.' I gave a quick smile, only half joking. 'Goodnight, Jack.'

'Night, Lily.'

With that, I closed the door behind me and went downstairs to lock up, preparing myself for a soak in the bath and a read of my book. When I returned upstairs a short time later, no light shone from beneath Jack's door, and all was silent within.

4

————

The next morning, I tentatively stuck my head out of the bedroom door, listening. When I didn't hear movement, I stuffed my feet into furry slippers and padded downstairs into the kitchen.

'Holy shit!'

Jack, dressed in a T-shirt fitted enough to show a body that was well honed from manual labour, but not tight enough to look like he should be in a boy band, and paired with well-worn jeans and bare feet, looked up from where he was sitting at my kitchen counter, a newspaper spread out in front of him.

'Good morning to you too.' He gave me a smile that I imagined a lot of women had been witness to first thing, having been seduced by it the night before. I put the buffers up against that particular train of thought as I wrapped my dressing gown tighter around me.

'Sorry, it was so quiet I didn't think anyone was down here.'

'Good to know I'm a quiet house guest.'

I quirked an eyebrow. 'Just because your snoring didn't rattle the windowpanes last night and you're capable of reading newspaper in silence doesn't mean I'm going to give you the gold award for best house guest just yet.'

He gave that grin again. I really wished he'd stop doing that. 'It's always good to have something to aim for.' He closed the paper and stepped off the bar stool. 'Can I make you a drink?'

'No, but thank you for asking.' I made my way to the cupboard where my crockery was stored and pulled a bowl out, then headed to the fridge for the yoghurt. 'Did you have something for breakfast? Other than coffee.' I nodded at the empty cup.

'Yeah, I found some muesli in the cupboard. I hope that was OK to use.'

'Absolutely. Like I said, if it's there, use it. Are you sure that's enough, though? I can cook you something if you'd like.'

'Absolutely not.' He laughed. 'I know you were press ganged into hosting me in the first place, so I'm certainly not about to let you cook breakfast for me.'

I squeezed a large blob of golden honey into the centre of my pile of Greek yoghurt and grabbed a spoon from the drawer. 'Can we just agree to move on from the how of you being here, and just accept that you are?'

He nodded. 'Agreed.'

I took my breakfast and climbed up onto the kitchen bar stool, doing my best not to flash Jack any thigh as I did so, placing the bowl before me.

'Do you have plans today?'

'Yes. I've got three appointments to go and see old clients who are interested in taking me back on and another two later in the week. In between that, I need to update my website completely, and I was thinking of designing a flyer so that I could do a leaflet drop around the area to try and draw some more business in.'

'Sounds like you're already well off the blocks. It could be worth you dropping in and seeing Marge at the village shop. I'm sure she'd put one of your leaflets up when you've got them done, and in the meantime, I'm pretty sure there's some sort of local Facebook

village group thingamajig. As you may have guessed, I'm not a
member of it, but Marge definitely will be and I'm sure she wouldn't
mind putting something on there about your garden design and the
services you offer.'

'That sounds great, Lily, thanks very much. I'll definitely do all
that.'

'And obviously Felix and Poppy will be putting out feelers to
anybody and everybody for you. I'm sure before long you'll have
more work than you can cope with.'

'We can always hope, can't we? At least then I'd be out from
under your feet.'

I snapped my head up from my yoghurt, letting a spoonful plop
back into the bowl. 'That wasn't why I was saying it.'

'No, I know. I was just saying.' He gave a one-shouldered
shrug.

It was apparently clear to everyone that I'd been steamrollered
into providing accommodation for Jack's return to England, but I
was beginning to wonder if I hadn't been the only one steamrolled
into this set up. Perhaps he really would rather have preferred the
solitude of a hotel room as he rebuilt his life back on the other side
of the world.

'Have you seen your parents yet?'

'No.' He let out a deep and troubled sigh. 'I was wondering how
long I could put it off for.'

I gave a sympathetic smile. 'I'm assuming your relationship with
them hasn't exactly improved over the years, then?'

'Not exactly,' he replied. 'They haven't agreed with anything I've
done since I was about fifteen years old. They were pretty unhappy
about me getting married out in New Zealand and so, when that
broke down, in their eyes it only confirmed what they considered
the poor choices I had made with my life. As far as they are
concerned, if I'd married one of the many lady-this or lady-thats

they insisted on introducing me to, I wouldn't be in the mess I am now.'

I pulled a face. 'You're not in a mess. Life has a habit of throwing spanners in the works of our carefully laid plans. It's not necessarily anyone's fault, and whether they agreed with your choices at the time, the end result is that you made those choices, and now you're making new ones. I'm sure they just want the best for you,' I added, feeling like it was the diplomatic thing to say.

Jack laughed a cold, humourless laugh. 'They want what's best for the Coulsdon-Hart name, the legacy. And, of course, I didn't even come home with an heir to soften the blow, which hasn't really done much for familial relations.'

'There's still time and then there's your younger brother.'

'I'm not sure whether I'll have kids. At least I get the fun bit now, playing with Ruby and Freddy and handing them back when they're cranky.'

'Yes, it's quite a good deal, isn't it?'

I knew what he meant. Mike and I hadn't decided about children and thought we'd have a few years to see how things worked out. We'd been happy, just the two of us, and then, thanks to the accident, the decision was made for us.

'Ed's pretty keen on having kids but just hasn't met the right woman yet, apparently. My parents would prefer if things were already clear and settled, and obviously I've let the side down, but I'm sure Edward will come to the rescue. He has a knack of getting everything right.' The comment was made with resignation rather than malice. Felix had told me that Jack and his brother were close despite the distance, and I knew he'd been out there to visit. I was glad at least one member of his family was on Jack's side.

'I'm sorry, I shouldn't have asked about your family.'

'I think that classic phrase "we're not upset, just disappointed" is one that could be applied to this particular situation.'

'That's always a good one.'

Jack gave a glimmer of a smile, which this time reached his eyes.

'I was sorry to hear about your parents,' he said. 'They were both wonderful people.'

'Thank you. Some days, it seems a long time and others, like yesterday. It was a shock to have them go so close together, but I suppose it's never the right time, is it? You always want more time with someone.'

'Absolutely.'

'Thank you for coming to both their funerals. We didn't expect that. It wasn't like you were round the corner.'

'They'd always been incredibly special to me. There was no way I wasn't going to pay my respects. You'd already been through such a lot as a family.'

I gave him a smile and looked across at the photo of Mum, Dad, Felix and me that Mike had taken and had framed for us a few months before he died. Within a couple of years, Mum and Dad would both be gone, too.

'I think I spent most of my youth around your house. I was always so comfortable there, and if those cheese straws last night are anything to go by, you've certainly inherited your mum's skill at baking.'

I pushed myself off the stool. 'Flattery will get you nowhere,' I said with a laugh in my voice before realising that my concentration had slipped and my slinky silk dressing gown had just flashed Jack a brief ankle-to-thigh shot before I grabbed it closed. Thankfully, he hadn't appeared to notice. I put my breakfast things in the dishwasher and turned back to Jack, one hand securely on my dressing gown this time.

'I'm sure my parents would have adopted you if they thought yours would have allowed it. Mum was always singing your praises about how lovely your manners were. Clearly, she only ever saw your good side.'

'I only have a good side,' he said with a wicked grin that immediately belied the words he had just said.

'You're forgetting I know you of old. You can't pull those lines on me.'

'People change.'

I couldn't argue with that. People did change. But with a face and body like Jack Coulsdon-Hart's, I found it hard to believe that he now only had a good side. Added to which, somewhere deep down, I couldn't help think that if that was true, it was a crying shame.

'What time is your first appointment?'

'Not until half ten,' he replied, the slightest antipodean twang resonating in the odd word, something else his parents probably wouldn't be thrilled at. Personally, I liked it, it suited him. 'If you've got time, you could show me around the garden and perhaps, when I'm not working, I could help you make it a little bit more manageable.'

I couldn't help grinning. 'You appear to have learned some tact on your travels.'

'I've always been tactful.'

I begged to differ, but as the only way to disagree with him was to bring up the night of my teenage mortification, I vowed to keep silent.

'I know the garden is a bit out of hand and I should have got someone in before now, but I...' I paused. 'I didn't really want to deal with it. And the longer I put it off, the harder it was, and now I'm too embarrassed to get anybody in.'

'Why on earth are you embarrassed?' Jack asked.

'I imagine you've already at least stuck your head out of the door and seen what a jungle it is out there. It was beautiful when I moved here.'

'It's beautiful now,' he said glancing out of the window. 'Just in a different way from how it probably was.'

'Again with the tact.' I laughed. 'But I agree. I know Felix gives me a hard time for it, but I like that wild and free feeling that I get from the garden in its current state. I do realise, however, that it would be better if it was a more managed wilderness rather than the current plant free-for-all it is at present. I did try to look after it. I know it doesn't look that way, but I literally had no idea what I was doing. I'm sure Poppy's told you about the rather expensive plant I dug up thinking it was dead.'

'It may have been mentioned once or twice.'

'Well, I rather lost confidence after that and it sort of grew, quite literally, from there.'

'OK, but everything is fixable. If you have time, we could look together now?'

I agreed.

'Why don't you meet me outside when you're ready and we can assess things properly.'

I hesitated.

'What's the matter?'

'I just think that you're probably going to get a lot more work than you think and a lot quicker than you plan. I know when I did start looking for a designer and help, it wasn't that easy to find a decent landscaper around here. The fact that your previous clients from ten years ago are desperate to have you back says a lot. I just have doubts that you will want to come home from one job to start on another.'

'This wouldn't be a job. This is something I could do in my free time. For fun.' He shrugged his broad shoulders and I tried not to notice the muscles ripple beneath the white fitted shirt. I gave myself a mental slap. I wasn't a teenager anymore, and I certainly wasn't about to start mooning over Jack Coulsdon-Hart again.

'Only if you're sure, but please don't feel that you're obliged to do anything while you're here. And, obviously, anything that you do I will pay full rates for.'

'No, you won't.'

'I beg your pardon?'

'You heard me.'

'I did hear you, which is exactly why I said I beg your pardon.'

'You know that doesn't make sense, right?'

'Yes, it does. It means don't be so ridiculous, of course I'll be paying you.'

'Fair enough.' He spread his hands and rolled his shoulders and tipped his head one way, then the other, loosening the muscles after his long flight. Even with jet lag, he looked hot. It really wasn't fair. I remembered the teenage head pat and the thoughts dissipated. 'By the way, your rent is in an envelope next to the bread bin.'

I snapped my head up to look at him. The green eyes gazed down, challenging me with an unconcerned air.

'I told Felix to inform you that I was not prepared to take rent as it's a favour to a friend.'

'I wasn't aware that we were friends too. That's nice to know. But either way, I'm still not accepting any money for work I do in the garden.'

'Then perhaps I won't let you do any work in my garden,' I said, drawing myself up to my full height of five foot two, over a foot shorter than him.

He grinned widely, the perfect white teeth contrasting against his tan, apparently amused, and I knew for sure that his line earlier about only having a good side was complete rot.

Ten minutes later, I was walking around my garden with Jack.

After a few minutes, he pulled up, and it took me a few steps to realise he'd stopped.

'What's wrong?' I asked.

'You.'

The comment seemed unnecessarily blunt and I folded my arms across my chest.

'I was about to say "and before you get defensive" but I can see from that stance I'm already too late.'

'I'm not defensive. I haven't said anything. Yet.'

It looked like he was trying not to smile. 'You don't need to say anything. Like I said, the way you're standing and the way you're looking at me says it all.'

I made a snort of disagreement.

'Perhaps I should have been more clear. What I meant when I said "you" was that if we're going to do this, you need to stop apologising every two seconds for the state the garden is in. It's easy to see that there's something beautiful here and it's also easy to see how that could get out of hand. It's a large plot. It's a lot for one person to take on, especially if they're not going to have help.'

'It wasn't that I was against having help, as such. I thought I'd be able to manage it and that it would be a good distraction and a bit of exercise, fresh air – all that sort of stuff. But it got out of hand quicker than I was expecting and then the thought of having to explain what I wanted to a complete stranger, when I didn't even know what I wanted...' I let the sentence drift off and gave a shrug to punctuate it.

Jack nodded. 'I get it. But there's nothing to be ashamed of here.'

My face must have said otherwise.

'There isn't,' he reiterated. 'Besides, gardens are always changing and evolving. The garden that was here when you bought the place might have been beautiful, but you have plans to build on that, and make it even more beautiful. Was this here when you got here?'

We'd arrived at the wildflower meadow, which was showing very early signs of bursting into life.

'No. That's my one and only attempt at doing anything with the grounds here. I thought with the name of the house and everything it should have a meadow. But I had help from the family.'

Jack turned back from the meadow, placing his back against the gate and resting the heel of one foot on the lowest bar.

'Why do you think having help is such a bad thing?'

'It's not that I think it's a bad thing. I don't know. It's hard to explain.'

'You want to show people you're capable of doing things for yourself.'

'I suppose. I know people want to help, but after...' I paused for a second, finding the right words, 'everything that happened, I just sort of wanted to do things myself. Doing anything with someone other than Mike felt wrong, somehow. And as I couldn't do anything with him any longer, I decided I had to do it all myself.' I looked around at the overgrown garden. 'I think maybe I was wrong.'

Jack took a deep breath and looked past me into the distance, back towards the house.

'Lily, I can't begin to pretend that I know what you've been through, and I am concerned that you were strong-armed into letting me stay here. If you want me to leave, I will do so with no hard feelings. But if you do want me to stay, I will help you make this amazing space into whatever you want. But only when you're ready for someone to help you do that. In the meantime, I can cut back the worst of it so that you can at least have pathways to walk through and think and enjoy the space a little easier. The last thing

I want to do is force you into anything or make you feel uncomfortable. Like anything, you have to be ready for this change.'

I studied him for a moment. Calm, relaxed, happy in his own skin. It had been years now since I'd last seen him at Mum's funeral and I barely spoke to him, except to thank him for coming. Jack's time away had not only improved his looks but there was a layer of something else now. An insight that hadn't been there before. The chip that he'd always carried on his shoulder about the unfairness of family expectations seemed to have been knocked off, or at least reduced drastically in size. Clearly all was still not happy families in the Coulsdon-Hart country pad, going by the fact that he had asked my brother to collect him from the airport and was staying with me rather than in one of the many, many rooms his ancestral home had to offer. But he'd obviously found a better way to handle it now, and I was glad for him.

I gave a glance around the garden and took a deep breath. 'I'm ready,' I declared.

5

We wandered around the garden together for the next half an hour, Jack naming plants that I immediately forgot, and him asking me what I thought about this or that. Before I knew it, the time had passed, and we were heading back towards the house.

'What do you use that for?' Jack pointed to a small outbuilding with a deck attached to the front.

'Nothing, at the moment. I had planned to make it into an office, but shortly after it was put up, we had torrential rain and storms and the thought of having to leave the house at all, even just across the garden, didn't really appeal to me. So I chose to stay in my slippers and work in the house.' I shrugged. 'It's not like I have to get away from anybody or find some quiet space.' I gave a glance back towards the outbuilding before returning my gaze to him. 'I have these good ideas, and then they turn out to be not so great after all. It's a bit of a white elephant now.'

Jack looked at the building for a long moment. 'Let's leave it for a while and see how we go. You might come up with a better idea for it.'

I gave him a disbelieving look and turned back towards the

house. He fell into step beside me. 'This really is a beautiful place. I can see why you chose to move here.'

'Felix and Poppy weren't convinced, at least at the start. To be honest, I'm still not sure they're entirely convinced, but I like it.' I studied the back of the house, shading my eyes against the strengthening sun with my hand. 'It probably is too big for one person to rattle around in, but I knew I wanted land around the property and it was pretty hard to find a two-bedroom with this sort of acreage.'

Jack gave a shrug. 'You knew what you needed. This place obviously felt right when you came here, so you did what you had to do. Other people may have our best interests at heart but, in the end, these important decisions have to be our own and we know what feels right. What are you smiling at?'

'You.'

'Dare I ask why?'

'I don't know. I just never really had you pegged as the philosophical wisdom-giver type.'

He gave a brief incline of his head. 'To be fair, I was probably less so before I went away, but life happens and you learn and you change.' He gave me a quick glance. 'Hopefully for the better.'

'I suppose that depends on what life throws at you. I know I've changed, but there are those who would argue not for the better.'

Jack gave a small nod but remained silent. I wasn't sure what to make of that.

'I suppose you'd better be getting to your first appointment. Don't want to be late.'

He checked his watch. 'You're right. Do you know the name of a good taxi firm around here?'

'There's someone that Felix uses but I can't think of the name at the moment. I'm sure I can find one. What do you need a taxi for?'

'To get to my meeting. Felix is going to help me try and find a car tomorrow. I didn't really expect to be able to set up any meetings quite this soon, so I'm a bit unprepared.'

'Well, you couldn't turn it down. Don't worry about the taxi. My old car is in the garage. You can use that for a while if you like. It's only sitting there anyway so would do it good to be driven properly. I should sell it really – something else that fills me with dread.' I pulled a face. 'It does run, though. I take it out once a week or so and bomb it round the drive a few times. It's quite good fun, actually.'

He looked down at me, grinning. 'A clandestine rally driver. You're full of hidden secrets, aren't you?'

'Ha, hardly. Anyway, the offer is there. It would probably do it good to have a proper run.'

'That would be great, if you're sure.'

'I am. You just need to give me some details so I can get you on the insurance. We can do that now and you'll be ready to go.'

Ten minutes later, my old car was insured for Jack to drive. I pulled it out of the garage while he went to change for his meeting and had just finished giving the windscreen a quick clean when Jack appeared.

'You... umm... look nice.' I tucked the cloth behind my back and wound my fingers within it, twisting it tightly until I risked cutting off the blood flow. Jack looked way more than nice, and I wasn't prepared for the effect that seeing him in the fitted gunmetal-grey suit would have on me. His tanned skin was set off perfectly by the crisp white shirt and subtle pale blue tie.

'Look OK?' he asked, an endearing hint of uncertainty in his voice.

'Absolutely. Definitely. Really good.'

Shut up, Lily!

I put both thumbs up to make sure I'd played a full hand of awkwardness.

He tugged at one of the cuffs before his hand moved to fiddle with the knot in his tie.

'I'm not sure. It's so long since I've worn a suit. It feels really weird.' He began to run a finger around his shirt collar. I caught his hand.

'Stop fidgeting, you look very professional.' *And super hot!* I cleared my throat and attempted to clear my mind. 'But you're going to mess it up if you keep fiddling with everything.'

Jack's gaze drifted down to where my hands still held his. My eyes followed. I let go of his hand with a jerk as if it was burning me.

'Sorry.'

He gave the smallest of movements with his head. 'No problem,' he replied, smiling. 'Are you always this bossy?'

'It's usually only me here, so it's kind of hard to boss yourself around. Anyway, I'm not bossy, I'm just trying to help you.'

'Which I greatly appreciate.'

'You could have fooled me,' I mumbled under my breath.

He laughed then, deep, warm and low, throwing his head back as he did so, his even white teeth shining in the spring sunshine. It was a nice sound and I suddenly realised how quiet it usually was here. Not that I didn't like the quiet, but a small part of me acknowledged that having Jack's company this morning had been enjoyable. It didn't hurt that he was very easy on the eyes, but he'd gained a depth of character since I'd known him last. Or perhaps I never really knew him. There was more to Jack Coulsdon-Hart than I thought, and I was glad I could help him out. I didn't know exactly what had brought him back home, but if he was looking to build his business up again then he obviously planned to hang around. I'd been lucky that my family had banded around me when I needed help. Jack had family but clearly not the support. He'd always been there for Felix, and Felix had always been there for me.

This was a way I could thank Felix for the unfailing support he'd given me. I waved Jack off before turning back to the house and heading for my study.

I was just preparing some salad to go with dinner when I heard a car coming down the driveway. A few minutes later, there was a knock at the back door. In the fading light of the early spring evening, I could see Jack silhouetted against the glass. I beckoned him to come in.

'You don't have to knock.'

'It seemed the polite thing to do.'

'Don't be daft, you're living here now. I mean, you know, temporarily, obviously.'

Was that a smile?

'Obviously,' he repeated.

'I meant to give you some keys last night, actually, but it got late and I forgot. I've put a spare set there for you now.' I pointed to them on the table. 'Have you eaten?'

'I haven't but I can do myself something. You don't have to cook for me.'

'I know. Don't get used to it, but there's food here now and you look like you've had a long day so wash your hands and take a seat.' He did as he was told.

'How did it go today?' I asked as I dished up steaming lasagne oozing with white sauce and melting cheese.

'That looks amazing!'

'Thanks. I hope you like it. There's some salad to go with it, and some garlic bread.'

Jack laughed that deep, rich laugh. 'If you want me to leave, this probably isn't the best way to achieve it.'

'I don't want you to leave. I mean... not immediately. Not until you're ready. I hope that wasn't the impression I gave you. Anyway, it's only lasagne.'

'It's delicious is what it is,' he said, taking another large forkful. 'And no, you didn't give me that impression. It's just that it's not exactly a secret you like your privacy. You're a little bit of a mystery around here, aren't you?'

'Am I?'

'The reclusive writer who lives up at the big house? Oh, yeah.' He loaded salad and a couple of slices of garlic bread onto his plate.

'Oh God.'

Jack shook his head gently as he finished his mouthful. 'Don't worry about it. People are always looking for something to talk about.'

'I know. I'd just rather it wasn't me.'

'Sorry. I shouldn't have said anything. I didn't think.'

'It's all right,' I said, letting out a sigh. 'But let's talk about something more interesting.'

'You are interesting.'

'Hmm. How did you get on today?'

Jack proceeded to tell me how well the meetings had gone. He'd even squeezed in an extra one and already had three clients on the books, and through the village grapevine had another two meetings lined up next week.

'That's great!' I said, genuinely thrilled for him.

'Thanks. I'm really pleased too. I knew it was a risk coming back here and trying to start again. I had a decent amount of clients before but I can't expect them all to need my services.'

'I'm sure there are plenty of new people here since you moved away. And there seems to be much more of an interest in gardens and gardening and outdoor spaces in general these days. I have a good feeling about it.'

'Is that so?' he said, leaning back in his chair.

'It is. Now, are you ready for pudding?'

'I'm not sure I have room,' he said, patting his stomach and laughing.

'Nonsense, of course you do. You have to make up for barely eating the last day or so. There's never much to those airline meals, certainly not for someone of your size. Besides, if you're going to be working in this garden, plus the work you're already building up, you're going to need the energy. You can always say no, of course,' I said putting the plate of steaming sticky toffee pudding and custard in the centre of the table, an innocent look on my face.

Jack looked up at me, the corner of his generous mouth tilting up one side. 'Oh, yeah. I could always say no,' he said and picked up a spoon.

The next morning, I wandered out into the garden, still slightly bleary-eyed, my hands curled around a cup of herbal tea and my feet tucked into functional, but admittedly ugly, welly shoes. The good thing about living on your own is that you don't have to worry about looking glamorous, or even normal. I turned the corner and walked slap-bang into a fast-moving Jack. He moved even faster backwards as he tore off the T-shirt which was currently soaking up the hot tea I'd just poured down it from his body.

Oh. That's right. I didn't currently live alone, and here I was with scary bed hair, a dressing gown that had seen better days, legs that definitely needed a shave, and welly shoes. Opposite me stood a tanned, currently half-naked Adonis. I stared at him for a moment. I was never great for conversation first thing in the morning but today had an added level of difficulty. At least, right at this moment it did.

'Put some clothes on!' I blurted.

Jack was still batting his chest with his T-shirt. 'I had some clothes on until you chucked boiling water over me!'

'It wasn't intentional, and I only have it at ninety degrees for herbal tea.'

He gave me a look that suggested he didn't think either of those made much of a difference right at this moment and strode off towards the house, returning a few minutes later wearing a fresh, clean T-shirt.

'Sorry,' I said. 'You gave me a fright. I didn't expect to see anyone out here this early.'

'It's fine. You gave me a third-degree burn so I guess we're even.'

I pulled a face at him, and he relinquished the hint of a grin.

'Are you all right?' I made a gesture that sort of encompassed his chest area while trying not to look at said chest area, although the image was most likely burned into my retinas forever now.

'Yes. I'm fine. It was just as much my fault. I didn't expect you to be out here this early either and I wasn't looking where I was going.'

'What are you doing out here, anyway?'

He looked down and smiled. 'Come with me.'

'I bet you say that to all the girls.'

He laughed. 'Not these days. Come on.'

Just around the corner lay a huge pile of greenery and brown stuff that had once been green. Behind it, a tiny part of my garden no longer looked like an out-of-control mess. I was immediately transported back to the moment that I'd come to view the house, falling in love with the building, the garden and the tranquillity it promised. A wave of emotion swept over me, and I turned away from Jack so that he couldn't see the tears threatening in my eyes.

'Did I do something wrong?' His voice sounded pained.

'No! Oh, gosh, no! Not at all. It looks amazing. Thank you.'

'So why are you crying?'

'I'm not!' I returned in a voice that sounded exactly like I was crying.

I felt Jack move closer to me. He bent down, his cheek almost touching mine as he leant forwards over my shoulder. 'Fibber.'

A small laugh escaped, easing the tension for both of us.

Jack straightened up behind me. 'You sure you're OK?'

I nodded. 'Yes. And thank you for this. I think I thought it was all lost, but you've shown me perhaps there's something redeemable here after all.'

'I like to think there's always something redeemable, even when it looks like all hope is lost.'

I turned around to face him, forgetting my bed hair and all the rest of it for a moment. 'Who are you and what have you done with the real Jack Coulsdon-Hart?'

Jack threw his head back and laughed. 'I really did leave a bad impression on you, didn't I?'

'So long as you don't pat me on the head this time, I'll give you the benefit of the doubt.'

'Yeeahhh,' he said, drawing out the word. 'I didn't handle that very well, did I?'

'Oh my God! You do remember! I knew you did.'

He grinned. 'I do, much to my chagrin. I just didn't think you'd appreciate me bringing it up in front of Felix and Poppy the other night.'

'No, I wouldn't have, so thank you for that at least.' I turned back to the house. 'I still can't believe you patted me on the head.'

He laughed again. 'No, neither can I. I was normally much more suave than that. You threw me.'

I gave an unladylike snort. 'I knew it'd be my fault.'

6

'Are you always up this early?' I asked, accepting the mug of fresh tea Jack presented me with when I returned downstairs, having changed into something more suitable for company.

'It varies,' he said. 'I think my body clock's all out of whack at the moment. Jet lag and stuff.'

'Stuff?'

'Lots on my mind, I guess.'

I took a sip of my tea.

'Spit it out,' Jack said with a grin.

I swallowed the tea. 'Pardon?'

'The question, not the tea.' He smiled. 'You're clearly dying to ask something, so just ask me.'

'No. It's none of my business.'

'I have descended on your home, invaded your privacy with very little notice, and probably even less choice if I know Felix, so I think you're entitled to ask a few questions.'

'OK,' I said, taking the chair opposite him at the table. 'How come you left England?'

'My parents were driving me mad, trying to marry me off to lady this or that, telling me what my life should be, how my life should be and who I should live it with. I couldn't take anymore so I booked a ticket to the furthest place I could think of, closed my business and took off. Probably not the wisest decision but...' He shrugged. 'I couldn't deal with the pressure anymore.'

'Sometimes you just have to get away from everything. I understand that.'

He tilted his head slightly. 'Yeah, I think you're one of the few people who can understand.'

'Do I get another question?'

He gave me that grin again and I really wished he wouldn't keep doing that. 'Why stop at one?'

'Why are you back in England?'

'I missed it. I loved it out in New Zealand but I'm older now and I guess I missed home. Once my marriage broke down a few years ago, I felt there was nothing to tie me there anymore. I've been thinking about coming home for a few years, but my wife was very against it, and I could understand that. All her family and friends were out there, her career. She had no reason to move and I was losing my reason to stay. We'd been growing apart for a while anyway, and I think it had come to its natural end.'

'I'm sorry.'

'Don't be. She met someone else within six months and got married again.'

'Yes, but you didn't.'

He gave a brief smile. 'That's true. But never say never, eh?'

'I'm sure there's a lady so-and-so somewhere out there for you.'

'Oh, I really hope not.'

'You wouldn't get married?'

'Like I say, never say never. I'm just not interested in that aristocratic lifestyle.'

'You are still going to be an earl one day, Jack. Unless you're planning to renounce the title? Can you do that?'

He shrugged. 'I try not to think about it most days.'

I pulled a face. 'Always a good strategy – ignore it and it might go away.'

'Still the smart-arse, I see?'

'It seems you bring out my aptitude for it.'

'I do my best.'

I rolled my eyes, swiped the mug from in front of him and got up to put them in the dishwasher.

'We need to talk about rent.'

'No, we don't,' I said, my back still to him.

I heard the chair scrape on the floor and when he spoke again, his words were closer. 'Yes, we do.'

I turned to object and caught my breath as Jack was closer than I thought.

'You're doing work in the garden for me,' I said, not looking at him as I squeezed out of the space.

'That hardly makes up for what I'd be paying for rent and food.'

'Of course it does. It would have cost me loads to have somebody come in and do what you've done already, especially someone of your calibre, but this way, I don't have to have strangers in my house. That makes it even more valuable to me.'

'I'm a stranger.'

'No, you're just strange. It's two different things.'

His laughter filled the kitchen, warming it through, reverberating through my chest as it did so.

'Do you have any more meetings today?'

'I'm starting work at Mrs Wembley's at two o'clock this afternoon. Probably be there until about five.'

'Great! Diving straight in.'

'Yes. But until then, I'm all yours.'

I raised an eyebrow. 'Lucky me.'

He shook his head, his lips curling in a smile. 'Thanks for the tea.'

'You made it.'

'I thought I probably should after I sent your first one flying this morning.'

'In the future, perhaps we should both agree to take a little extra care with where we're going whilst you are here.'

'Deal. I'm going to head back outside.'

'No, you've done enough, especially if you're working this afternoon as well. I don't want you wearing yourself out before you get to your paid job.'

'I'm fine,' he assured me, one hand on the door handle. 'The exercise does me good and I love the work.'

With a quick wave, he was off, striding across the garden and into the wilderness.

I watched him go, his words tumbling around in my mind. Judging by what I'd seen this morning when he ripped off his scalding T-shirt, the one thing Jack did not need was exercise. From where I was standing, his body looked pretty damn perfect just the way it was.

* * *

'So?' Poppy asked, looking out to where Felix and Jack were spinning the children around in the garden. 'Do you still think he's hot all these years later?'

'Of course not,' I said, dismissively. 'It was just a teenage crush. Pretty much all the girls in the village had one on him at one time or another.'

I could feel her eyes boring into me as I kneaded the biscuit dough. 'What?' I asked without looking up.

'It's OK, you know?'

I pushed a lock of hair that had come away from my clip back from my forehead with the side of my hand.

'What's OK?'

'To have feelings for someone else. Mike wouldn't have expected you to stay alone forever. It's the last thing he would have wanted.'

'Surely it's more about what I want now, though, isn't it?' I replied, sharper than I intended.

Poppy sat back.

'I'm sorry, I didn't mean to snap at you. I just don't want you or anybody thinking there's more to this than there is. Yes, Jack is good-looking – I'm not blind, but neither am I interested in another relationship. And bearing in mind the state he saw me in the other morning, I think we can pretty much categorically say he's not interested in a relationship with me either.'

'Oooh? What state did he see you in?' Poppy leaned back in.

'Calm down.' I laughed. 'I was half asleep and forgot he was here, so I wandered out into the garden without brushing my hair in my ratty old dressing gown, hairy legs and those little welly shoe things.'

'You never know, that might be his sort of thing,' Poppy replied, a mischievous grin on her face.

'I don't think a leopard changes its spots that much, do you?'

'I don't know, but I do know he's done a lot of growing up while he's been away.'

I thought back to the philosophical words spoken in previous days and couldn't help but agree. However, there was still no way I would entertain any thought of having a relationship with Jack Coulsdon-Hart. I had my routine, I had my books, and I had my family. That was all I needed. I'd tried something else in the past and I wouldn't – couldn't – go through that pain ever again.

'Are you happy?' Poppy watched me rolling out the dough on the cool surface.

'Yes, of course.'

And I was happy. Wasn't I?

* * *

'Darling! You absolutely must go!' Zinnia, my agent, was waving a finger at me, this one bedecked with a large sapphire ring, through the screen.

'No, I absolutely must not, Zinnia. I don't do these things. Remember, we talked about this. Several times.'

'I know, darling. It's really not your thing and I do understand, honestly. But this is different. You have to see that? This is a premiere with big Hollywood names. You can't turn that down.'

'I can and I think I did – several times.'

'Yes, well, I didn't pass that on, obviously.'

'Can't you just go instead? Nobody cares about the writers anyway.'

'Well, they do in this instance, because Bella Dupree raved so much about your book even before she bought the rights. Probably shot the value of them right up, so you really ought to say thank you.'

I gave Zinnia a look that told her that was unlikely to happen. I was of course grateful that my book had been picked up and made into a major Hollywood movie. Beyond grateful. But neither was I about to bow and scrape to the golden great and good to thank them for even noticing me. Without people to write these stories, actors would be out of a job, so I figured it all balanced out in the end.

'It'll be great publicity, darling. I know you're not a great fan of it,' she said, ever the mistress of the understatement, 'but this could be really important for your career. There are new writers coming along all the time. You know that, and I know you have a loyal readership, but we do have to keep on top of it all. Bella picking up on this book could bring a whole new demographic to your readership and it's important that we capitalise on that.'

'I agree. I just don't agree with the suggestion that me parading at a premiere will help.'

'Darling, darling. Sometimes one just has to be seen. It's all very well cultivating this reclusive romantic image, and that's fine. That's worked for us as well, the air of mystery and all that.'

'It's not an image, Zinnia,' I said, doing my best to stay calm.

'No, no.' She waved a hand conversationally, every finger sporting a large ring, each a different colour and all catching the light, shooting a rainbow of colours across her desk. 'You know what I mean, but we can't rest on our laurels. This is a great opportunity and if you do want to continue as you are, we have to work at it.'

'I'll think about it, OK?'

'Marvellous, darling. You've got the tickets, haven't you? I'll get the publishers to send a car and book you a suite at the nearest luxury hotel.'

'You don't need to do that. I can—'

'Must dash. So glad you're going to do this.'

'I didn't say I was...' I let the sentence drift off as Zinnia had long gone.

Shit. I really, really did not want to go to a flashy premiere in London. I didn't want to go to the village shop, so why on earth would I want to go to the West End?

* * *

'Take Jack with you,' Felix shrugged when I mentioned my dilemma the next day.

'What? No! Why would I do that?'

'Company. At least, that way, you wouldn't be on your own. I mean, I know the publishing people and your agent will be there, but I don't know, maybe it would help to have someone along too who you can relax with.'

'I'm not sure I can relax with him any more than anyone else. And I know I'll probably end up standing there like a lemon with nobody talking to me and it's really just not my scene.'

'You can't stay in your house for the rest of your life, Lils. This will do you good. Give you a chance to dress up, get out.'

'In case you hadn't noticed, those two things aren't high on my list of priorities these days.'

'Perhaps they should be,' said Felix.

'What's that supposed to mean?'

'It means that you can't stay here shut up in this house for the rest of your life just because Mike's gone.' His voice was uncharacteristically sharp. 'I'm sorry, Lils, I don't mean to hurt you, you know that's the last thing I want to do, but it's killing us to see you just existing here. You were spared that day, so maybe there's a reason for that.'

'I didn't want to be spared!' I said, banging the worktop with my hand so hard it hurt. 'I can't tell you how many times I've wished I'd never left that table and not have to deal with any of this. I wouldn't have had to bury my husband and stand awkwardly at parties while people looked at me and didn't know what to say or spoke about me behind my back.'

'Nobody did that.'

'Yes, Felix, they did. Less than a year after Mike's death, I overheard somebody saying that it was really about time I moved on!'

He looked at me. 'It's a lot more than a year now, though, Lily.

No one is saying you have to make a habit of going to parties, but you've achieved an amazing thing here. You've had a book adapted into a major Hollywood movie and you should be proud of that.'

'I am proud of that.'

'So, show people. Show people who the amazing woman is behind this brilliant book. Like your agent said, it's good publicity, and that's never a bad thing, especially not in a competitive world like the one you operate in. You have to keep your name out there and what better way than to appear at a function like this?'

'I don't know, Felix. I know it makes sense, it's just...'

'Scary?'

'A bit.'

'Way out of your comfort zone?'

'So far past it.'

He gave me a hug. 'I never want to upset you, but I think you need to do this. And I agree, going somewhere where you don't know anyone is scary. So, like I said, take Jack, he could do with an evening out.'

'Take Jack where?' We both turned round at the sound of the deep voice. Fresh from the shower, with damp hair pushed back from his forehead, a loose T-shirt and jersey shorts with bare feet, Jack looked the epitome of relaxed, not to mention sexy. I really didn't want to notice the 'sexy'. If he looked this good in a T-shirt and shorts, how good would he look in a tuxedo?

'How do you feel about accompanying my sister to a film premiere?'

Jack slowly shifted his gaze to me. 'I think that would depend on how Lily felt about me accompanying her.'

'It wouldn't be a date,' I said hurriedly. Perhaps, I realised, a little too hurriedly. 'I mean, not that that would be a bad thing for someone else, obviously.'

'Obviously,' he repeated.

'It's just that I seem to have got roped into going and I'd rather not look like an idiot standing on my own.'

'How could I turn down an offer like that?' Jack replied with a smile.

Felix looked at me and shook his head in despair. 'I need to get home. I'll leave you two to it.' He gave me a quick peck on the cheek, clapped Jack briefly on the shoulder and headed out the back door.

At least he didn't leave us in an awkward moment or anything...

7

'It wasn't my idea,' I started suddenly. 'And I wouldn't expect you to take it up anyway. I'm still trying to get out of it myself. If there's any way I can, I will.'

'Why?'

'Because it's not my thing.'

'Being amazingly successful and celebrating it isn't your thing?'

I flicked a glance to him. 'You know that's not what I meant.'

'Then what do you mean?'

'The whole publicity show around it all. Movies are all about the actors and the directors and sometimes the producers. Nobody cares about the writer.'

'Isn't that even more reason for you to show your face at the premiere? Try and make a change in that direction for both yourself and other writers.'

'I don't think me turning up is going to make much difference.'

'Everything has to start somewhere. You're a well-known name and who's to say you wouldn't give inspiration to a struggling writer watching the coverage, seeing you there and thinking, yeah that's where I want to be? She can do it so I can do it. You already inspire people, Lily. This is just another step on from that. If you don't do it for yourself, then do it for your fans and writers all around the world.'

No pressure, then.

'I do realise that I'm very privileged to be in this position, and that other writers would be falling over themselves to have this opportunity. It's not that I don't appreciate it all.'

'I know,' he said easily. 'And I also know how difficult and scary the prospect of going to something like this is for you.'

I pulled a face that suggested he had no idea.

'I do,' he said this time with more emphasis on the two words. 'It's clear in every fibre of your being that you really don't want to go. That you're scared of going. But you can't go around scared of life forever, Lily.'

'I'm not scared of life,' I snapped back at him.

He said nothing but the green gaze was fixed on me, daring me to argue further.

'You wouldn't understand.' I moved to push past him, out of the kitchen, but his hand reached out, catching my wrist gently but firmly, halting me in my tracks.

I looked up, ready to ask him what the hell he thought he was doing, but his expression stopped me. There was a softness to it that I wasn't expecting, and it stilled my words.

His eyes locked with mine. 'So help me understand,' he said, his voice quiet and gentle. Almost imperceptibly, his grip tightened, and I felt a wave of something rush through me that I hadn't felt in so many years. Something I had doubted I'd ever feel again. Something I wasn't sure I ever wanted to feel again. My body pulsed and my mind raced.

'I... I can't,' I said, pulling away. I wasn't entirely sure what it was I was saying that I couldn't do. I sneaked a look at Jack, easier now that there was space between us. Still calm, still relaxed. The only thing Jack Coulsdon-Hart wanted from me was an explanation as to why, according to him, I was scared of the world. But my mind, or perhaps more accurately my body, had got carried away and gone charging ahead of itself. I gave myself a mental slap and told my imagination to keep the romance and spice for my novel writing where it belonged and not interfere in my real life.

'I'll be here when you're ready,' he said.

I kept my back to him, looking out onto the garden, more of which could be seen after dark now, thanks to the subtle lighting Jack had begun installing out there.

I didn't answer.

'And if you do want someone to come with you, assuming you decide to go to the premiere, purely as moral support, of course, you know where I am.'

'Thank you,' I said, before turning and leaving the room.

* * *

I added several vegetables and a couple of fruits to my basket, thinking that I ought to shop here more often as the produce looked far better than that delivered from the supermarkets. It would be good to support local businesses, too. It was just a shame it involved actually leaving the house and seeing people. Thankfully, the shop wasn't busy, and I was nearly done so would soon be back in the safe cocoon of my car to drive home. There had been nobody at the till when I'd come in, so I'd managed to avoid one conversation already.

I stopped at the small selection of books and magazines that the village shop stocked and nosed at them briefly. I was about to move and head towards the till when I heard two women out of sight begin talking.

'I hear the lord of the manor is back.'

'Old Charles? I didn't realise he'd been anywhere.'

'Not Charles, you daft wotsit. The prodigal son, Jack.'

I turned, knowing I should make my presence known before anything else was said, but somehow I was unable to.

'Oh, is he now?'

'Yes, haven't you heard? Living with Miss Lily up there at the Meadow Blossom House, apparently.'

'No, really? I've not seen hide nor hair of a man since she moved in there, other than her family. Such a shame about what happened. You can hardly blame her for closing herself away. It must have been so traumatic.'

'Jack always did have a way with the ladies. And he's only got better looking, if that's possible. You can hardly blame her for falling for him. I just hope he doesn't leave her broken hearted. She's had far too much of that in her life already.'

The other woman made a sound of agreement as I looked down at my hands to see that the knuckles were white as they gripped my wicker basket. I should go to the till. But then they'd know I'd overheard and it would be hideously awkward. But I couldn't hide in here all day. Bloody Felix. I should have known that there would be gossip if Jack stayed with me. I hadn't even considered that until now.

'He did leave a trail of broken hearts behind when he left. My niece pined over him for nearly a year.'

'She wasn't the only one.'

'I wonder why he's back?'

'Maybe old Charles is on the way out?'

'Do you think?'

There was silence for a moment, and I could only assume the first woman was shrugging her shoulders.

'Unless it's love that's brought him home? Maybe they've been having a long-distance romance. Her brother's his best friend, you know. Has been for years. He used to spend a lot of time at their house so they must have got to know each other back then.'

'I never heard of them courting, though, did you?'

'No, I doubt he was particularly interested in the quiet ones.'

'I don't remember him being that picky at the time. Anything to boost his ego.'

'Oh, now, Marge, that's a bit harsh. A few years younger and you'd have been queuing up too.' Two cackles of laughter broke out, punctuating the sentence.

'I don't think he was all that happy at home. Can be funny, these aristocratic lot, can't they? She swans in here from time to time, his mother, acting like lady of the manor.'

'She is lady of the manor, Marge.'

'You know what I mean.'

'I don't blame him putting all that distance between them. Can't imagine he had much of a warm upbringing. Maybe that's why he went looking for comfort in the arms of as many women as he could.'

I tipped my head back and looked at the ceiling, wondering how long realistically I could stay here. I didn't want to overhear this conversation, and wished I'd left a long time ago. The longer I stayed, the worse it was getting. I took a deep breath and made for the till.

'I wonder—'

I registered the brief shock on both the women's faces before they hurriedly tried to cover it as I emerged from behind the shelves.

'Hello, dear. Nice to see you here. Find everything you needed?'

'Yes, thank you.' I smiled.

'Celebrating anything nice?' Marge asked as she rang up the champagne I'd picked out. It wasn't a great brand, but it was the best that the village shop stocked and right now I really wished I'd left it on the shelf. The truth was it was for champagne jellies that Felix and Poppy adored but, having already overheard their conversation, I could only imagine the thoughts now racing through both their heads as to what me buying this bottle of champagne meant.

'No, not at all. It's for making champagne jellies with. My family love them.' I decided to go with the truth, although I had my doubts as to whether they'd believe a word of it.

'Lovely!' Marge said as she rang the items through.

I made a show of looking down to get my purse out, but I didn't miss the brief exchange of looks between the two women as I did so.

They totally didn't believe me. Well, there was little I could do about it now. Hopefully, by tomorrow, they'd have found something else to gossip about.

It was a few days before I saw Jack, other than briefly. Word had got around that he was back and available for work. I had a feeling that word had got around he was available for other things as well, and that might have been another reason for his absences. It didn't bother me. In fact, I was quite glad of it. If it was known he was seeing somebody else, the gossips would have less inclination to talk about me and I could go back to my quiet life.

'You don't have to leave me food out every time, you know?' Jack's deep voice made me jump. I'd been dishing out shepherd's pie into individual portions, freezing a couple and putting a couple aside to be reheated for dinner time, my mind elsewhere as I turned over a plot dilemma in my head. The spoon clattered to the floor. Jack reached it before I could and moved to the sink to rinse it off before handing it back to me and then quickly cleaning the floor where it had landed.

'Thanks,' I said taking it from him and continuing with my task.

'Did you hear what I said?' he asked.

'Are you complaining?'

'Of course not, the meals are always delicious, but that's not the point.'

'What is the point?' I asked, moving him aside as I finished up and bent to get the labels from the drawer behind him.

'The point is you don't have to cook for me. That wasn't the agreement.'

'It wasn't not the agreement, either. And we've had this conversation.'

A soft rumble of laughter wafted itself around me. 'You have an answer for everything. You always did. I wasn't surprised when I heard your writing had really taken off. You always seem to have the right words.'

'I'm not sure about that but, as far as this is concerned, I'm cooking anyway. The only thing it means is that there's one less portion in the freezer, which is neither here nor there. You may as well eat it. It's better than you having to cook when you come in late or eating a ready meal.'

'I'd still feel better if you let me pay for my bed and board.'

'Only if you let me pay for all the work you're doing outside. Plus the shelf you put up in my study, and don't think I haven't noticed that the utility door isn't creaking anymore. I find it hard to believe the garden shed painted itself either.'

'The paint was there,' said Jack.

'Yes. The paint's been there for the last two years. And now it's actually on the shed, which is where it was supposed to be, saving me time if I were to do it myself, or money if I had to pay someone else to do it. Stop banging on about paying me rent. I think we're even.'

'I still think I'm getting the better deal, but I'm not going to win on this, am I?'

'Nope,' I said. 'And I'm glad you finally realise that so that we can move on. Are you ready for dinner or are you going out?'

'Nope. No plans.'

'I was just going to dish mine up, but you can eat later if you like.'

'I'm happy to eat with you if I'm not in your way.'

'Of course not. Take a seat.'

'Can I get us some drinks?' Jack asked.

'That would be good, thank you.'

He opened the fridge. 'Champagne? Something to celebrate?'

'Don't you start.' I gave him a brief smile as I put the two plates down on the table.

'That sounds like a story,' he replied, returning the smile with a fuller one of his own.

I glanced up at him, my eyes shifting to the champagne and then back again.

'Oh, sod it, why not? Don't open that one, though. There's a nicer one in the cooler underneath.' I pulled two champagne flutes from the cupboard and set them on the table as he pulled out a bottle of Veuve Clicquot from the cooler, opening it like an expert and pouring the golden fizzing liquid into the two glasses.

I picked up my fork to begin eating, before noticing that Jack was holding up his glass. I returned my fork to the table, and I picked up my own glass.

'It seems someone does have something to celebrate, then?'

'There's always something to celebrate if you look hard enough.'

I wiggled my head in a maybe yes, maybe no kind of fashion.

Jack looked at me patiently. 'Right now, I'd like to make a toast to you.'

'Me?'

'Yes. You. For opening your home to me and making what could have been a very difficult transition so much easier. Especially when I know you could probably have brained Felix for making the offer on your behalf.'

'Who said it was on my behalf? It might have been my idea all along, for all you know.'

He really did have a great laugh and I loved the way it filled my kitchen with warmth and joy. My determination to keep a straight face lasted all of two seconds.

'It was pretty obvious from your face on the screen that night that it definitely wasn't your idea.'

'Rubbish, you don't know me well enough to judge that.'

'You'd be surprised. I spent an awful lot of time at your house and watched you grow up.'

'Oh, pfft. You didn't even notice I was there. Your eyes were always on the next pretty girl.'

'Maybe they were,' Jack said, evenly. 'Can I make this toast now?'

'Be my guest.'

'To you. For all that you are.'

His eyes didn't leave me as he spoke and I felt the heat creep up my chest under his gaze and the attention, neither of which I was used to. I saw a flicker of something I guessed to be amusement flit across his face before he tilted his glass to connect with mine, the crystal ringing clear before he lifted his own to his lips and took a sip. I, on the other hand, drained the glass.

8

Jack watched me put the glass down and without a word refilled it.

'Thirsty,' I said by way of an explanation.

Eager to move the focus away from me, I asked Jack to tell me about his day, which morphed into him telling me how the rebuild of his business was going and the people he'd met so far, as well as the plans both they and he had for moving forward. In between this, he complimented me several times on the dinner, of which he had now had second helpings.

My plate empty, I sat listening to him talk, loving the enthusiasm that radiated from him when he spoke about his work. It was easy to see the joy that it brought him, and it was a shame that his family had never supported him on his choice. Inevitably, the conversation drifted around to this very point.

'You still haven't seen them, then?'

'No, although I can only put it off for so long. I think they were hoping I'd have got this whole "gardener" business out of my system by now. They were pretty horrified to find out that I was still happily toiling in the earth.'

'What is it that they don't agree with? You're a respected garden designer who trained at Kew, for goodness' sake. You can't get much better than that. You've made a huge success of it all and it makes people happy.'

He laughed without humour. 'Making people happy is the last thing to be considered when it comes to my family. Tradition, appearances, doing the right thing – that's all of importance. Whether people are happy or not is way down the list of considerations.'

'OK, in which case, you are doing the right thing. The right thing for you.'

'Oh, my dear girl,' he said thickening and emphasising his original cut-glass accent until it was almost a pastiche of his own father's. 'How little you understand these things. Yes, it's about doing the right thing. But the right thing for the family, not you personally.'

'New traditions are born all the time,' I said, taking a sip of my third glass. I did a double take at the glass. Was it really my third? How did that happen?

'Not in the Coulsdon-Hart estate, they're not.'

'I think it's a shame. They've missed out on you for all these years. People don't live forever.'

'No, they don't. I don't think they feel they have missed out on me, but I do appreciate you saying it.'

'Then it really is their loss if they can't even understand what they've missed.'

'Are you complimenting me?' One side of his generous mouth raised in a teasing smile.

'Don't be ridiculous. I know you of old, and I'm well aware that you don't need any more compliments than you already get.'

'Who says I get any?'

I almost snorted my champagne. 'Valiant attempt at modesty, but let's just take it as written that we both know you were always the village heart-throb, and if the gossip I overheard the other day is anything to go by, nothing's changed. Obviously none of them know what a pain in the arse you really are.'

He gave me an even look. 'Is that so?'

'Yep. As you said, you spent a lot of time around my house growing up, being Felix's best friend and my parents liked you, although God knows why.'

'Because I'm delightful, obviously.'

'Well, you had them fooled. But I didn't need warning to stay away from you. The trail of broken hearts around the village streets was enough. Plus, you were just so sure of yourself.'

'Quite the opposite, actually.'

'What do you mean?'

'I don't think I was at all sure of myself. I knew who I was supposed to be, and what I was supposed to be, but I don't think I really began to discover who I was until I moved away to London to pursue the life I wanted, very much without the blessing of my family. It was still a struggle then and things only became clearer when I moved abroad and had the absolute freedom to explore the person I could be, the person I wanted to be. As for the rest, you're probably right. And I don't blame you for not being interested in me, apart from that one night at the fete.' His eyes twinkled mischievously in the low light.

I sipped my drink and disappeared behind the glass momentarily as a means of escape.

A lazy smile appeared on Jack's face as I did so. 'But the rest of it? That was all bravado. I'm surprised Felix hasn't told you. He worked it out years before. I think that's why we were such good friends and still are now. I never had to pretend with Felix. I could just be myself, and when I acted too much of a dick, he would tell me.'

'That definitely sounds like Felix. I'm glad you've found yourself now.'

'Me too.'

'So when are you going to go and see your parents?'

'I think I've put it off as long as I can. I'm going to have to bite the bullet and just go.' He quickly finished his drink in a gulp before replacing the glass on the coaster. Splaying his hands out on the table, he studied them for a moment before looking back at me. 'I don't suppose you'd consider coming with me, would you?'

'Me? Why would you want me with you?'

'Moral support?'

'I'm not sure I'd know what to say to them.'

'That makes two of us. It's OK if you don't want to. Believe me, I really do understand!' he chuckled.

I lifted my glass, thinking, as I took a sip of the cool amber liquid, the bubbles tickling my nose. Jack had agreed to come with me to the premiere, assuming I decided to go, with little protestation, and that was a much bigger deal than just going to a house. All right, it was a bloody big house, but it was still someone's home rather than the circus of a major film premiere. As usual, the thought of leaving the security of my four walls wrapped itself around me and slowly knotted itself in my stomach. But he was asking me a favour, and I didn't feel I could turn it down.

'OK, I'll come.'

Jack had been studying his long fingers, still resting on the table. At my words, his head snapped up and the intense green eyes, wide with surprise, met mine.

'You don't have to look quite so shocked.' I laughed. 'I'm not that bad.' OK, I was that bad, but that didn't mean I had to admit it outright.

'No! I'm just... fine, I am shocked. But in a good way. In a really good way.'

'Nice save.' I tilted my glass towards him in a gesture of acknowledgement.

'You really don't have to do it, you know?'

'I know.' I pushed my chair away from the table and got up, taking the plates with me over towards the dishwasher. As I began to stack, Jack came to stand beside me, resting his hands for a moment on mine. A buzz of electricity rushed through me at the touch, and I stepped away in what I hoped was a subtle manner.

'Sorry, I didn't mean to make you jump.'

Apparently not subtle enough – but if Jack was going to take that as the reason for my movements, then that worked too.

'I was just going to say I'll do that. You've done enough today.'

'It's fine, I'll just finish this—'

Jack took the plate out of my hands, placed it on the worktop, then, with his own hands resting gently on my upper arms, he steered me over to the other end of the kitchen-diner where I had a cosy sofa, stacked with cushions and a blanket.

'Sit,' he said.

'I'm not a dog!'

'Sit, please?'

I did as he asked and watched him cross back to the kitchen in a few strides and, within moments, he was back at my side, my champagne glass once again topped up.

'I shouldn't be drinking this much on a school night.'

'I promise I won't tell.' He flashed a grin that, had I been writing the scene, I would have described as devilishly sexy, but obviously that description would not do here in the real world. He returned back to the kitchen, humming quietly, quickly finishing off the chore I had begun. As he did so, I gazed out into the garden, feeling contentment and calm wash over me, the background noise of Jack pottering around the kitchen somehow adding to that contentment. As I sat there, my eyes alighted on a row of what I thought was lavender edging the path that ran down to the studio building I'd bought and never used. I'd had the building put up by the contractors and the path created but that had been the extent of the landscaping.

'May I?' Jack stood to the side of the sofa.

I shuffled up a little. It was a slightly snugger fit than I'd anticipated, my hip now resting against Jack's. I took a swig of champagne and tried not to think about it.

'Did you put plants in along the path?'

Jack took a sip from his own glass before looking round at me, a rather sheepish expression on his face.

'I did. Sorry, I got a bit carried away. I should have asked you.'

'No, I like it. Are they lavender?'

'Yes. I thought it would be nice to introduce some to bring in more pollinators. And then, if you do decide to use the building, you'll get the scent from them if you brush the flowers on your way.' He glanced back at me. 'You're smiling, so I'm hoping that's a good sign.'

'It is. Funny enough, that's what I'd thought about doing. But obviously, like the rest of it, I hadn't got around to the actual mechanics of the task. Thank you. But you do need to let me know how much I owe you and give me your bank details, so I can transfer the money across.'

'I don't want any money for them. I get them at wholesale price, anyway.'

'That's not the point. It's still money that you've laid out on my behalf.'

'As was the meal that you cooked tonight. We can't keep counting. Let's just call it even.'

'It's not even if you keep spending money on me.'

'It's not on you,' he said, turning a little to face me. 'It's on your garden. That's different.'

'Is that so?'

'Entirely.'

I gave him a look and rested back against the sofa. 'How's it going, anyway, work, I mean?'

'Really good. Better than I could have expected.'

'Do you have enough room upstairs to do everything you need to do? Paperwork and so on?'

'Yeah, it's good.'

A thought had been swimming about in my brain over the last couple of days and it now came to the surface. 'I've been thinking.'

'Oh?'

'The studio is all kitted out with heat, light, power, et cetera, and it's just sitting there unused. Why don't you take that over as an office? Then you could separate your work life and home life.'

'I couldn't do that. I'd be effectively renting two places off you then and somehow I doubt you're going to take money for that either.'

'Don't be silly. I'd rather it was used. It's a bit of a white elephant just sat there as it is.'

He shifted in the seat again, brushing my thigh with his own as he did so. I kept my focus on the garden.

'Are you really sure?'

'I am. The only thing I would ask was, if you're going to have clients come in, whether we could sort out some sort of screening material, whether that's plants or willow fencing or some other thing that I saw on *Gardener's World*, just so that it wouldn't be quite so easy for them to look over towards the house, or the rest of the garden. I know that sounds ridiculous, probably.'

'Of course it doesn't. It's your home. It's natural that you, or anyone, would want to protect their privacy. But don't worry, I wouldn't hold any meetings there, but I can still put some screening up if you'd prefer.'

'No, that's OK. Although perhaps we could plant around it a bit, soften the edges. That sort of thing?'

He grinned. 'Great minds think alike. Anything in particular you had in mind?'

'You're the designer.' I laughed.

'That doesn't mean you don't have good ideas. As you said, you were already thinking about the lavender.'

'True. OK, I quite like some of those tropical looking plants, you know, with the big leaves? But it might be nice to have some colour dotted around down there too. Does that make sense?'

'It does. I'm sure we can achieve that pretty easily.'

'But only if I pay for the plants. That's the deal,' I said, giving him my hardest Paddington stare.

'You drive a hard bargain.'

'Don't you forget it.'

He clinked his glass against mine and rested back against the sofa, filling the space, with almost the entire length of his body now resting against the side of mine, but there was no tension in it. He was completely relaxed and something about that seemed to permeate its way into me, unfurling the knots of earlier and making my own limbs feel loose and rested. Of course, that could just be the champagne. Whatever it was it felt good, and for once I tried not to overthink and just absorb and sink into the moment.

9

The next morning, I woke up fully clothed under my duvet with no recollection of how I got there. Rolling over, I looked at the clock. It was nearly half past ten and I should have been at my desk an hour ago. I sat up quickly and immediately regretted the movement, a hand going to my forehead as the inevitable hangover from last night's champagne made itself known. Jack Coulsdon-Hart was a bad influence.

Half an hour later, I'd showered, washed my hair, tentatively eaten some breakfast and was now sitting at my desk, gazing out of my study window. There were hints of blue in the sky, but a steady spring rain was falling and, through the slightly open window, I could hear it tap-tap-tapping on the leaves. It was a gentle, soothing sound and I sat listening to it for a few minutes, taking it all in before I fired up my laptop and dived back into my current work in progress.

I wandered in and out of the kitchen a couple of times to get much required cups of tea and a snack but, having hit a good stride, the next time I looked up, twilight had settled over the garden, and my stomach made a loud growl. Closing the lid of my laptop, I stood up, stretched and wandered over to the full-length patio doors that lead out into the garden from my study. Looking across, I could see a light on in the studio. It seemed that Jack had already started to set up shop down there, and I was glad. There had long been a niggle at the back of my mind that I'd spent a lot of money on something that was just sitting empty after my original plan didn't work out, so it was good that it was finally being put to use. I switched the light off in my study and pootled out to the kitchen to find something for dinner. A short time later, Jack entered through the back door.

'Hi,' I said, pulling a pizza from the oven. 'I was just about to call you. Do you want some of this?'

'Looks great. I'll just wash my hands.'

'I saw the light on down there. Are you settling in OK? Is there anything you need?'

'No, it's great! Are you definitely sure you don't want to use it for work?'

'Positive,' I said. 'I like listening to the rain but I'm not such a fan of scooting down the garden in it. I'm cosy in my study.'

'I'm pretty used to working in the rain, so I'm sure a quick jog to the office won't do me any harm.'

'That's true. I'm not really sure why I got it, to be honest, because I like my study. I have my sofa there, all my books, all my research material. I didn't really need the outbuilding, but you see all these gorgeous garden offices and I guess I got caught up in having the space, and what I thought I needed.'

'Easy enough to do,' he replied, drying his hands on the towel. 'I think we all get caught up like that from time to time until we find out that what we actually need is the opposite of what we're doing.'

I felt like we might stray into dangerous territory, so I gave him a brief smile then plonked the pizza down on the table. 'Enjoy!'

'Had a good day?' he asked in between mouthfuls.

'I have, actually. It got better as the hangover wore off, of course.'

He gave a quick shrug of his eyebrows. 'Yeah, perhaps we shouldn't have opened that second bottle of champagne after all.' His grin contrasted with his words.

'I would like the record to state that that was your idea.'

'Fair enough.'

'Can I ask you something?'

'This sounds ominous.'

'No, not really. I'm just sort of wondering... how exactly I got to bed last night. It's just that I don't remember going up the stairs and I never sleep in my clothes.'

'That would be me. You nodded off down here and I couldn't wake you. Admittedly I didn't try that hard, you looked so peaceful, so I took you up.'

'Oh! You didn't need to do that. You could have just left me here.'

'I could. That's true. I just figured you'd get a better sleep in your own bed.'

He was right. I'd nodded off down here before and woken up part way through the night, chilly, with a crick in my neck.

'I hope that was OK. I didn't want to take any liberties and it took me about twenty minutes to decide what to do in the first place. I thought this was for the best, but it was literally a drop and run scenario.'

'You don't have to make me sound quite so much like a bag of old potatoes,' I replied, laughing.

'You're quite chatty when you're asleep, did you know that?'

'Oh God, am I still doing that? Mike used to say I spoke more at night than I did in the day.'

'I think he might have been right.'

'What did I say? Nothing too embarrassing, I hope.'

'Most of it I couldn't understand.' He paused for a moment, wavering.

'Oh no, what is it?'

'Nothing bad.' He touched my arm reassuringly. 'You mentioned his name.'

'Who?'

'Mike.'

I felt something fall in the pit of my stomach. 'Did I?' I asked softly. 'Did you hear what I said?'

He shook his head. 'No. You just said his name.'

We sat in silence for a few moments.

'I shouldn't have said anything. Now I've upset you.'

'No, really, you haven't. I'm glad you told me.'

Jack looked at me, a question in his eyes.

'It's been such a long time. Mike's been gone over ten years now and sometimes I worry that the memories are fading. That they're no longer as sharp in my mind as they once were.'

'You'll never forget him. Clearly he's on your mind a lot, even when you're asleep.'

'Yes. Do you believe in soulmates?'

'I think I do, yes.'

'Do you think you only get one per lifetime?'

'No. I don't. And I think they can come in all forms as well. I think you can have platonic soulmates as well as romantic ones.'

I studied him for a moment.

'What?'

'I don't know. I suppose I didn't really expect to hear that from you.'

'That's because you still think I'm the person I was, or at least pretended to be, when I went away. I guess, at that point in my life, I hadn't thought too much about soulmates or settling down. Like I said before, I thought I was doing what I should be doing, but looking back now, I think perhaps I was searching for the attention that I didn't get at home.' He gave a dry laugh as he dragged his hand across his forehead. 'God, that sounds pathetic when I say it out loud, but hopefully you won't judge me too harshly.'

'I'm not going to judge you at all. As you said, we do what we think we should do at the time. It's easy for others to tell us what they think we should be doing or for us to look back with hindsight, but we don't have all the information at the time, and we just have to act with what we have. Perhaps you needed to get all that out of your system for you to meet the right person and have something meaningful when you went abroad.'

'Yeah, maybe. Why did you ask about soulmates?' The lighting was soft, and Jack's voice matched the setting.

'I don't know. Mike and I used to talk about it occasionally.'

'And what did he think?'

'He was very logical. Scientific. He didn't really believe in anything that you couldn't explain, or touch, or see.'

'But he was madly in love with you. Anyone who saw you together could see that.'

I lifted my gaze from where I had been playing with the corner of the napkin. 'Thank you.'

Jack shrugged. 'I mean, he obviously believed in love, even though that's not tangible. It's a feeling.'

'I never thought to ask him. I guess he felt he could make an exception for that.'

'I think he knew a good thing when he saw it and he wasn't about to let science or logic get in the way.'

I smiled to thank him for the kind words, twisting a lock of hair around a finger. 'It's always afterwards you think of all the things you wanted to talk about, or ask, isn't it?'

'I think, a lot of the time, we assume we still have plenty of time to ask those questions.'

'That's true. But we never really know how much time we have, do we?'

'No, we don't,' he said. 'I guess that's why, if we really want something, we just have to find a way of getting it, or at least of trying to get it. Then you're never left with the what if.'

'Is that what brought you back to England?'

'Partly, I think. And partly I just wanted to come home.'

'And how do you feel now you are home?'

'Like it was the right decision.'

'That's good,' I said and meant it. I got the feeling there was still more about Jack to discover, but I knew I wanted him to be happy.

'I saw earlier that there's a documentary about Jane Austen on tonight. Were you planning on watching it?'

'I was, but if you want to watch something else, that's fine. I can go up and watch it on my tablet in bed.'

Jack laughed. 'It's your house, Lily. If there's a viewing conflict, it should be me who goes up to my room, not you.'

'I don't mind. I quite like being tucked up in bed, all cosy.'

Jack didn't answer for a moment, instead standing and taking the last few items off the dinner table and transferring them across to the dishwasher. Having stacked the dishwasher and closed the door, he turned back to me. 'How do you feel about having company to watch the documentary?' he asked.

I looked up, surprised, but Jack seemed to misunderstand my expression and, suddenly panicked, he blurted out, 'Down here, obviously. Not in bed!'

I stared at him for a moment, trying not to smile. 'Are you blushing?'

'Don't be ridiculous,' he said, turning away.

'Goodness me. What would all the young maidens of the village think now? I didn't think you even had the capability to blush!'

He turned back to face me. 'Having fun, are we?' There was a hint of smile on his face which he was doing his best to suppress.

'I am actually, yes. Thank you for asking.'

He gave me a tight smile, but I could see humour in the green eyes.

'I didn't think Jane Austen was something you'd be interested in.'

'Ah, see, that's where you're wrong. There's more to me than meets the eye.'

To be fair, that which met the eye was more than enough attraction for most people. Adding depth of character and a sense of humour to his attributes was making things a little unfair.

'I distinctly remember you dissing the inimitable Jane in my teenage years. Something for which I may never be able to forgive you.'

'Never is a long time.'

'You clearly have no idea how deep my love for Jane Austen runs.'

'I'm beginning to get an idea, but I did read some of her books when I was abroad.'

'You did?' I said, pushing myself up straighter in the chair. 'And what did you think?'

'Much to my chagrin, you are right. I love them. She's a brilliant writer. I take back everything I said in previous years. I think I only ever said them to try and get a rise out of you anyway. I knew how much you adored her.'

'That was kind of a mean thing to do.'

'Agreed. But it was the only way I could get you to talk to me. Most of the time, you just ignored me when I'd come round.'

I felt my colour rise. 'I'm sorry. I never meant you to feel ignored. I just... I don't know. You were this titled heart-throb of the village, and I was just me. I never really knew what to say and, truthfully, I didn't think you'd notice if I was there or not.'

'I noticed.'

'OK. But not the way I wanted you to notice, I suppose. Only at the time, obviously!' I added, hastily.

'Of course,' he nodded.

'Anyway, I think that was all part of being caught up in the fervour of teenage hormones. I never had a desire to be just another notch on your bedpost.'

'I don't think you could ever just be a notch on someone's bedpost.'

'Believe me, I could. Not that I realised that at the time.'

Jack's face grew serious. 'Then they were an idiot.'

I gave a small head tilt and grinned. 'I agree. They were, but you don't have to flatter me, you know. I'm not going to throw you out.'

He cleared his throat and pushed a hand back through his hair. 'Best to be safe,' he said, grinning.

'I prefer honesty.' I grinned back. 'Don't forget, I already know you. You don't need to try and impress me. Anyway, what time is that documentary on?'

Jack glanced at his watch. 'About five minutes.'

'OK. You go and find it on the TV and I'll make a cuppa. Tea or coffee?'

'What are you having?'

'Just answer the damn question, Jack.'

'Coffee then, please. Thanks.'

'OK, I'll bring it through.'

10

That night, as I sat in bed, I reflected on what a pleasant evening it had been. Having my family's company was one thing, but the evening spent with Jack had been different. There was conversation, silence at times too but it was an easy silence, with neither of us feeling a need to fill it. It had been a long time since I'd experienced that easy comfort, and the truth was I didn't think I'd ever feel that way again. Perhaps subconsciously I'd told myself I *should* never feel that way again, and it was this thought that churned around in my stomach now. I liked Jack, but I wasn't romantically inclined towards him. I appreciated that he had movie star looks and a body to die for, but it was like appreciating art for its beauty. It was easy to see the attraction, but I didn't want it on my wall.

I'd told him I knew him, but it was clear from the last several weeks that Jack Coulsdon-Hart had changed, and those changes were definitely for the better. Perhaps, like he said, this had always been the true Jack. It's just that before it was buried beneath expectations and bluster and the ability to have his pick of women without much thought. I suppose all of us had changed to a certain extent. Time does that to you. Circumstances do that to you.

Though Jack seemed to have grown out of his experiences. I'm not sure I could say the same.

But I was happy where I was. I had my family, and my work, which I'd been lucky to have enough success with to enable me to buy a beautiful place to live. I missed Mike every day but there was nothing I could do to bring him back, and there were plenty of people in far worse positions than I was. I was grateful for all that I had. I would never stop thinking it had been unbearably cruel to have my husband snatched from me, but I was thankful for the time that we did have together. Nothing would ever dim those memories or that love. Jack might be right when he said the universe may provide you with more than one soulmate, but I wasn't prepared to take the risk. I'd had my heart shattered once before and I wasn't prepared to go through that again.

* * *

'You still up for coming to visit my parents?' said Jack.

I could hardly say no, knowing the premiere was looming, and the relief on my agent's face when I told her there was a chance I'd be coming for a short time had been obvious.

'The publishers will be thrilled, darling. This will give us more exposure and more leverage when it comes to negotiating your next contract.'

I tried not to freak out at the word exposure and concentrate on the fact that I didn't have to stay long, and that I had moral support in the large form of Jack. Assuming he didn't disappear off with a starlet/model/both. I hadn't actually considered how many beautiful people I'd be surrounded by, and decided it was best not to go down that road.

'I said I would.'

'I know. It's just that I think it's fair to warn you—'

'Oh God. This sounds bad. Is it bad?'

'If you stop panicking for a moment, I'll tell you.'

I sat down immediately and looked up, feeling my eyes wide as I waited for the news.

'My parents felt the best thing to do, having not seen their eldest son for several years, was to make a gathering of it. It seems they've invited a few people.'

'How many is a few?' I asked.

He was shifting his feet and making a conscious attempt not to let his gaze meet mine. 'Mmmfty or so,' he mumbled, suddenly incredibly interested in the poker resting on the fireplace.

'I'm sorry. How many?'

He let out a sigh. 'Forty or so.'

'That's not a gathering.' I shot up. 'That's a bloody party!'

'Two hundred is a party in their eyes.'

'Oh God. That's a lot of people.'

'To be fair, there'll be a lot more than that at the premiere.'

I shot him a look and he held up his hands. 'Sorry. I was just saying.'

'I realise that, but having to deal with a large gathering there is part of my work. This is supposed to be moral support for you, to reunite with your family, not visit with half the bloody county.'

'That's a bit of an exaggeration.'

'For someone who rarely leaves their house, believe me, it feels like the entire county. I was being generous.'

'Point taken.'

I began chewing the corner of my lip.

'You don't have to come. I'm sorry. I only just found out about this. It's not what you agreed to. I promise it will have no bearing on me coming to your event. I already agreed to that, and I won't go back on that.'

I looked out of the window at the twilight settling around the garden and countryside beyond. Stars began to glitter in the sky and somewhere the remnants of an earlier bonfire drifted wisps of smoke and the faint smell of embers floated through the still open window.

'No. I agreed to come, and I will. You volunteered to support me. It's only fair I stick to my promise too. How bad could it be?' I forced a laugh which I immediately swallowed as I looked back at Jack and saw the expression on his face.

Oh wow. That bad...

* * *

'Master Jack. How very good to see you.' The butler's smile seemed genuine, his bright blue eyes contrasting with the exceedingly tidy short white hair, parted on the side and kept close to his head with what I strongly suspected was Brylcreem.

'Hello, Dawkins. It's good to see you.' Jack held out a hand and, after a moment of surprise which he adeptly, and very profession-ally hid, the man beamed as Jack shook his hand enthusiastically, covering them both with his left. 'Really good to see you. Didn't know if you'd still be here. It's good to see a friendly face. Yours might be the only one of those I see tonight.' He winked and the butler shook his head.

'You've been much missed, Master Jack. I can assure you of that. By everyone.'

I stole a glance at my companion. He looked unconvinced, but I liked the man for doing his best to help.

'This is my friend, Lily, Dawkins.' He leant closer to the man and, in a theatrical whisper said, 'Moral support.'

'Hello.' I smiled.

I was rewarded with a warm smile and a formal but delightful little bow. 'A pleasure to meet you, Ms Lily. I believe you are young Felix's sister? Is that right?'

'It is. How did you know that?'

'I remember your family dropping Master Jack off from time to time. Occasionally you were with them, and I never forget a face.' He gave another kindly smile before calling to another member of staff who took our coats. Reluctantly, we nodded our goodbyes to Dawkins and made our way through towards the sounds of laughter, glasses and talking.

'I've never met a real live butler before.' I giggled suddenly.

Jack stopped and turned, looking down at me. He looked gorgeous beyond words tonight and the truth was the embers of long-abandoned flame had burst into life and threatened an entire inferno the moment I'd seen him walk in in his tuxedo, clean shaven and dark hair freshly cut short. I'd stood there for a moment, mentally throwing an entire reservoir over myself before he spoke.

'You look beautiful,' he'd said. At which point, I'd lost the power of communication, nodded, and waved my hand in his general direction and made a finale of a thumbs up. Yes, a thumbs up. And no, I can't quite believe it either. Mortifying.

'Ready?' Jack said, pausing as we drew closer to the noise.

'Not really, but we're here now and I'm not going to let you enter the arena alone.'

He smiled then and I sent out a telepathic emergency signal to call the fire crews back. *It's fine. You're just not used to it. You've been alone a long time and he's a good-looking man. But it's Jack. Just Jack.* But the last bit didn't seem to be helping. In fact, if I admitted it to myself, which obviously I wouldn't, that bit just made it worse.

'Thank you for doing this.'

'It's fine. As you say, good practice for the film thing.'

'Exactly. If you can get through this, you can get through anything.'

'You're not helping.'

'No. I've just heard that back in my head and it didn't come out exactly as I'd hoped. I'm going to shut up now. I just wanted you to know how much I appreciate you being here.' His gaze drifted over me, the emerald green, bias-cut dress skimming over the minimal curves I did have and enhancing them. It was such a long time since I'd dressed up, I'd had no idea if my evening outfits would still fit or look odd. But this was a classic style and never dated, and thankfully it still fit. Wearing heels again felt weird and took a bit of getting used to, although it did bring me that little bit closer to Jack's face – something I was undecided as to whether was a good thing or not. 'You really do look stunning.'

'I'm already here. You don't need to flatter me now.'

He gave a small shake of his head. 'Not flattery. I'm not into that these days. Just speaking the truth. And the truth is, you look beautiful.' With that, he placed one large hand on the small of my back, and we entered the room together.

There was a momentary hush as first one person noticed Jack's presence, and then another. I was infinitely glad of the warm, solid feel of his hand. The attention was certainly disconcerting for me, so I could only imagine how strange it must be for him.

In a sudden swish of movement, a woman I recognised as Lady Coulsdon-Hart emerged through the throng and made her way over to us, elegantly and in no hurry.

'Brace yourself,' Jack muttered out of the corner of his mouth, and I tried not to giggle.

'Jack, darling, I'm so glad you could make it.'

From what I understood, this gathering was specifically in Jack's honour, so to suggest that he wouldn't make it was an odd thing to say. I couldn't work out whether she was actually glad or whether it was a dig at his long absence, disguised as a perfectly innocuous remark.

'Mother.' He smiled, kissing her cheek and accepting the somewhat brittle hug she offered him as her husband came to stand next to her.

'Jack.' He nodded.

'Dad.' Jack nodded back.

Good Lord. It was obvious to me now why Jack had spent so much time during his formative years at our house. You're away for years and this is the warmth of the greeting you receive?

'I wasn't aware you were bringing anyone. Aren't you going to introduce us?' His mother gave me a smile with all the warmth of an ice lolly.

'Of course. This is my friend, Lily. Lily, my mother.'

His mother held out her hand and I wasn't sure if I was supposed to shake it or kiss it and curtsy. I opted for shaking followed by a quick 'pleased to meet you' and then repeated the action with his father.

'Lily?' The earl looked at his wife, then back at Jack. 'Isn't Lily the name of the woman whose house you're staying at?'

'That's right,' Jack confirmed.

'Oh, darling.' His mother laughed, pulling him away a few steps but still clearly within earshot. 'If you didn't want to come alone tonight, I could have found you a far more suitable partner than your landlady.'

'Mother!' Jack did his best to extricate himself from the hand she had laid upon his arm without making a scene and stepped back beside me. His jaw was clenched, and his hands were now rammed into his pockets as anger and embarrassment mingled on his handsome features.

'I'm not his landlady,' I said in a voice far more confident than I felt. 'Jack's an old friend, and I have a spare room, so he's staying with me until he gets back on his feet. Just one friend helping out another.' I gave what I hoped was a disarming smile, but I doubted Lady Marsden was about to recall the artillery anytime soon.

His mother smiled at me. There was certainly no need to worry if they ran out of ice for this party. All they'd have to do was get Jack's mum to look at the glass for the temperature of anything near it to plummet. I stood my ground with as much warmth as I could muster, unwilling to play the same game. I wasn't about to stand there and let Jack, or myself, be treated like a nobody. It made sense now – if they'd been my parents, I probably would have moved to the other side of the world as well.

'I'm going to get us some drinks,' Jack said, once more placing a hand on the small of my back. 'I'll catch up with you later.' He gave his parents a tight smile before gently steering me away towards a bar area manned by two impeccably dressed members of staff.

'What can I get you, sir?'

'Whiskey. Irish. Double. No ice. Thanks,' Jack ordered in a rapid-fire manner before turning to me.

'Sorry, I should have asked you first. That was rude.'

'Not a problem. You need it more than me. I'll just have an orange juice, please.' I smiled at the young woman behind the bar.

Within a couple of minutes, we both had our drinks and made our way to a quieter part of the room. Jack took a large swig of his drink, appearing to enjoy the burn of the liquor as it went down. 'I don't even know where to start in apologising for my mother.'

'You don't need to. I can handle her. I might not enjoy socialising, but that doesn't mean I'm going to be trodden on when I do go out, or let my friends be embarrassed on my behalf.' I looked up at him and winked. He smiled for the first time since we'd entered the grand old house.

'You're full of surprises.'

'Am I really?'

'Yes.'

I opened my mouth to reply but was cut off by the approach of an uber-glamorous woman, wearing six-inch heels and what was clearly a couture outfit that accentuated and made the best of her slim figure.

'So this is where you're hiding.' The cut-glass accented words were followed up with a full-lipped smile that had definitely had some help from a cosmetic surgeon.

Jack turned away from me to greet her. 'Persephone. How lovely to see you. Looking stunning as always.' He took a step back so as not to completely exclude me from the conversation. It was hard to tell from his face as to whether the compliment had been genuine, but it was clear her delight at seeing Jack was definitely real.

'Oh, Jack.' She batted him on the arm, leaving a hand to rest there for just that little bit too long. 'You always were such a flatterer.'

She turned to me. 'They say flattery gets you nowhere, but I'm afraid it gets people everywhere with me.' She laughed a high, tinkly laugh and curled her arm around Jack's bicep a little more.

Jack, in contrast, was studying the bottom of his glass intently. Clearly there was history here and I had to admit to being intrigued as to what kind, and how deep it ran. As a writer, I was inherently interested in people, how they worked and how they thought. My self-imposed isolation had put rather a damper on my ability to do such things and I realised now how much I had missed watching the interaction between others and the inspiration that could be gained from it.

The woman stuck out her hand. 'Lady Persephone Forbes.' She smiled as she took my hand and shook it. 'I'll introduce myself, as clearly Jack's not going to do the honours. Honestly. It's just as well he's so good-looking, otherwise he'd never get away with half of the things he does.'

I gave a noncommittal smile. 'Lily Thomas.'

'Wonderful to meet you, Lily. I hear Jack is staying with you?' It appeared that news travelled fast at this party.

'That's right. He's helping me redesign my garden, too.'

'Oh! How lovely and... helpful. He always was good with his hands.' She squeezed the bicep and looked doe-eyed at him. I turned away towards the rest of the party for a moment, trying to smother the smile that was threatening to break on my face. It appeared that Jack Coulsdon-Hart's lothario history was coming back to haunt him. I knew I shouldn't really laugh, but my one attempt at trying to seduce him had resulted in a pat on the head in front of all my friends, so although I wasn't prepared to stand and let his mother run either of us down, I also wasn't beyond enjoying a little bit of his discomfort at the hands of one of his many ex-girlfriends. Lady Persephone turned away from us momentarily to call a couple of people over. Jack ducked his head towards me. 'Don't think I can't see you smirking over there.'

'I don't know what you mean,' I replied, looking directly into those striking eyes and keeping an innocent look on my face.

He gave the tiniest shake of his head. 'And don't think you can fool me with that expression either. You're clearly nowhere near as artless as you look.'

I placed a hand on my chest and made a shocked 'O' with my mouth. The flicker of a smile played around his lips, which I believe I had once very drunkenly declared to be sensuous. Looking objectively, they probably still were, but it was kind of hard to look objectively at a man as beautiful as Jack Coulsdon-Hart. He moved again so that this time his lips almost brushed my ear as he whispered, 'You don't fool me...' into my hair before straightening and turning back to where Persephone was trying to get his attention.

'I'm going to get myself another drink.'

'I'll come with you,' Jack said, making an attempt to escape, but

Persephone was one step ahead of him. 'I'm sure Lily won't mind getting yours. You can't just disappear for years on end and then not expect to be fêted at your own homecoming party.'

'It's not a homecoming party.' Jack tried valiantly but his objection was resolutely dismissed, and several others joined the small throng that was now beginning to surround him, edging me out as they did so. Whether that was intentional or not, I couldn't tell, but I could see Jack's brow crease as it happened and his hand reached out, catching my fingers as I made a move to walk behind him and head towards the bar. I squeezed his fingers in a mixed gesture of support and reassurance. Reaching up on my tiptoes, I rested a hand on his shoulder to balance myself and whispered in his ear that I was OK. He turned his head, met my eyes and gave return squeeze of my fingers before I let go and headed off to get a drink.

11

'Whoever left someone as beautiful as you sitting on their own deserves to lose you. They obviously can't have heard that the prodigal son is returned and, by the looks, is back to his old tricks.'

I exchanged a look with the barmaid I'd been chatting to before inclining my head slightly towards the speaker. 'I'm pretty sure I can handle myself against Jack.'

'Brave words. Can I get you a drink?'

'Just an orange juice, please. Isn't it rather unkind to speak about your older brother in such a way?'

He turned, surprised. 'And what makes you think I'm related?'

'Because I know you are, Edward. I grew up in this village a long time ago.'

'It can't have been that long ago,' he said smoothly, and I laughed.

'I see the cheesy lines run in the family, although Jack's travels have improved him on that front.' Edward took a seat next to me, looking at me as if studying a specimen under a microscope.

'I was sure I knew all the pretty women in the village, so how did you escape my notice?'

'Just lucky, I guess.' I grinned, thanking him for the juice and taking a sip. He paused for a moment before letting loose a hearty laugh.

'And unlucky for me, it would appear. Perhaps, as I seem to be a disadvantage, you might tell me your name.'

'But it's so much more fun this way.'

He laughed again and made to step off the stool. 'I will beg if I have to in front of all these people.'

'Don't think for a moment I won't pour this drink over you if you even try.'

'Oh, I don't doubt it for a second, but please, tell me your name.'

'Surely you recognise Lily Madison, little brother.' Jack slung an arm loosely around his brother's shoulder. 'You had a big enough crush on her growing up.'

Edward's eyes widened. 'Lily Madison?'

'The same. Although it's actually Thomas now.'

'Oh. You're married.'

'Yes. Well.' I cleared my throat as I tried not to notice Jack nudge and frown at his brother. 'Widowed, actually.'

'Oh God, yes, of course. I remember hearing about it now. I'm so sorry. You must think I'm a completely insensitive idiot.'

I smiled and briefly touched his arm, reassuring him that I was fine. He gave me an awkward smile. 'No wonder you weren't impressed with my chat-up lines and the upper-crust accent.'

'Yes, I'm afraid you'll have to find someone who doesn't know all the old Coulsdon-Hart tricks for that.'

'The night is young, little brother.'

'The trouble is most of the women around here have had their hearts broken by this oaf and no one wants anything to do with me purely because I have the same surname. Honestly, he ruined my life.'

'If it makes you feel better, he didn't break my heart.'

'Really? That's very interesting.' Edward looked up towards Jack. Jack pulled a face.

'Nope. I think we all had a little crush on him, but that was just par for the course. Teenage hormones and all that, but once you grow up, you want something a little more... substantial.' I looked up at Jack, smiling sweetly.

He parried my look. 'I've told you I can see straight through that sweet outer casing. There's a hard, harsh woman hiding in there.'

'I don't believe a word of it,' Edward defended me gallantly.

'Did you really have a crush on me?' I asked.

'Oh God, yes. Huge.'

'Why did you never come and say hello?'

'I was quite shy back then, if you can believe it. And, of course, I had this one's shadow looming over me like Rudolph Valentino most of the time. A couple of the girls I did ask out only went out with me so that they could get to Jack. I sort of gave up after that. I did plan to ask you out at the fête one year, but then I saw you going up to Jack.'

'Oh God, did you really?' A fresh wave of teenage humiliation washed over me.

He looked at me from under his lashes. 'Yeah.'

Jack stuck his nose in his whiskey glass, keeping his eyes averted.

'You know he turned me down, right?'

'What?'

'I only did it because I'd had far too many cocktails. I'd have never gone up to him sober.'

'Making me feel great over here.'

I waved Jack's protestations away and looked back to Edward. 'You should have asked me. It would have been nice.'

'You turned her down?' Edward turned to his brother with a confused expression. 'But I thought you said—'

'Shall we talk about something else?' Jack broke in. 'Have you managed to persuade Father to bestow the title on you instead of me?'

Edward raised a weary brow. 'What do you think?'

Jack rolled his eyes and took another swig of whiskey before Edward turned back to me.

'How did I really not know that you were back in the village?'

'She keeps herself to herself because she doesn't want to be bothered by oiks like you.' Jack filled him in and got an elbow to the ribs as a reward.

'He's right, to an extent. I live in Meadow Blossom House, but I don't go out much.'

'I thought that was owned by some weird old writer woman.'

Jack dragged his hand across his eyes as a huge grin spread across my face. 'That weird old writer woman would be me.'

'No, no. This is someone who is really successful apparently. Can't say I've heard of her but not really the sort of thing I read.'

Jack leant down and rested on his brother's shoulder. 'I'd stop now if I were you, mate.'

Realisation dawned on Edward's face. 'Oh God. It is you, isn't it?'

I nodded.

'But someone told me you were old. I mean, not that you're old, but the woman that lived there. I mean I assumed... maybe I did just assume. Oh hell.'

'I did tell you to stop,' Jack reiterated.

'It's fine,' I said, laughing. 'I'm sure there's all sorts of rumours around the village about me, but because I tend to stay behind my four walls, I don't hear them, so it doesn't bother me.'

'It shouldn't bother you even if you did hear them,' Jack said.

'No. True. But it's even easier to ignore things if you don't know they exist in the first place.'

'She does have a point,' Edward agreed. 'Am I forgiven?' he

asked. I liked Edward. I always had, although he was definitely the quieter of the two brothers, and I hadn't had a lot to do with him growing up. Now I rather wish I had. He was fun and sweet, and he was good-looking in a quieter, less showy way than his older brother. Not that Jack could help that, but he had certainly made the most of his looks and where they could get him in his earlier years.

'Of course you are. Although I'm not sure I can forgive you the cheesy chat-up line from earlier.'

'No, I agree,' he said. 'That was unforgivable. I don't blame you on that front. Nerves get the better of me sometimes.'

'I think you're probably best just being yourself.'

'I'll remember that.'

'So, I'm guessing by the fact that you were trying out chat-up lines on Lily that there's no special someone in your life at the moment?' said Jack. 'What about that girl you messaged me about?'

'Turns out she wasn't the love of my life after all.'

'You did declare that after only two days of knowing her.'

'I'm passionate. What can I say?'

'That's one word for it.'

Edward gave his brother a side-eye glance and took a sip of champagne. 'I take it you've had the pleasure of meeting my parents?'

'Oh yes.'

'Mother pointed out I didn't have to bring my landlady as my date and that she had plenty more suitable women up her sleeve,' said Jack.

Edward looked mortified and I grinned, giving a small headshake.

'I told you she won't give up. She went positively purple with apoplexy when you wrote and told her you were married. Seriously, all the staff took cover – as did I! Of course, once the news of the divorce came through, she was going around telling everybody that she'd known it wouldn't last and that it was only a matter of time before you saw sense.'

Jack gave a long, deep sigh and leaned towards the bar, conversing with the barman as he got another drink.

'Do you get this pressure too?' I asked.

'Me? No, not really. I'm only the second son, so I don't really count, unless he gets bumped off, and then there will be a rush to get me up the aisle as fast as possible.' He nodded his head towards where Jack was laughing with the barman over something, distracted from our conversation.

'How do you feel about that?'

'Which bit?'

'Either. Both.'

'I don't really think about it. I used to be quite jealous of Jack with all the luck he had with women flinging themselves at him, but I also felt a bit sorry for him. His life was never quite his own. You shouldn't have to flee to the other side of the world to get away from your own parents. I don't think he really wanted to go, but it was always meet lady this, or I've arranged for you to have dinner with lady that. I can see that he felt he had no other choice.'

'You missed him, didn't you?'

'Dreadfully. But, for God's sake, don't tell him. His ego is big enough as it is.'

'Don't tell him this, either, but I think his ego has shrunk a bit in his time away.'

'What are you two gossiping about?'

'Believe me, nothing very interesting,' Edward quipped, flashing a conspiratorial look at me. 'How's the business going?'

'Good, actually. Better than I could have expected. Quite a few clients have come back to me, and various other ones have recommended me to friends and family. Lily's brother, Felix, and his family have been amazing, spreading the word far and wide, and that's brought in some extra business. I even have a proper, if temporary, office.'

'Do you? That's great!'

'I do. Lily has a studio in her garden that she wasn't using and was kind enough to make it over to me until such time as I can set myself up somewhere away from under her feet. Having somewhere to go really makes it feel like a proper commitment, like it's really coming together.'

'That's great, Jack. I'm really pleased for you. I know the parents have their issues with your decisions, but I just want you to know that I don't.'

'I know that.' Jack smiled. 'I've always known that.'

I took a sip of my drink and looked out of the window to where the garden was artfully lit, a large double fountain sprayed water into the still night, the droplets catching in the beams, shimmering like little fireflies over the pond in which it sat. It was clear that Jack had missed his little brother just as much as Edward had missed him, although I doubted either of them would ever say such a thing to the other.

The sound of crystal being tapped by solid silver rang out across the large room, bringing everyone to a hush. The earl nodded to his wife and stepped back. He might have the title, but it was abundantly clear who ran things around here.

'Ladies and gentlemen, we'd just like to thank you all for coming this evening to celebrate the return of our eldest son back into the fold and the comforting bosom of his family.'

Edward's drink went down the wrong way and I patted him on the back hurriedly as Jack shifted his weight and looked down, waiting for a hole in the ground to open up in which to disappear.

'I'm sure,' his mother continued, 'that you would all like to join me in welcoming Jack back and would love to hear from the man himself. Come here, Jack, darling.' She waved regally to where Jack stood rigid, almost vibrating with frustration.

'You have to do it now,' Edward whispered. 'You can argue about it later.'

Jack continued to look down at his feet as if weighing up his options before lifting his head, pasting on a smile and striding towards where his mother stood, then bent and placed a kiss on her cheek exactly as I imagined he'd been brought up to do. He fitted the image perfectly – the handsome man looking every inch the gentleman, not to mention sexy as hell in the tuxedo, but I knew now that it really was all an act, just as he'd told me all the bravado and womanising of his early years had been. It was hard to put on an act all the time. Exhausting, in fact, and I should know. I tried for two years after Mike was killed to pretend that I could get on with my life, live it in the same way as I had before, move on as people told me I should. But all it did was make me even more unhappy. It was like living two lives, being two people, one of whom you didn't even know.

I watched Jack as he made an off-the-cuff but perfectly suited speech for the occasion, making people laugh, and flattering the right ones. In short, doing everything that his mother expected of him, but as he glanced towards me, I could see that inside he was hating every moment. I held his gaze, trying to convey that he wasn't alone, however much it felt like it. He looked away as he finished his speech but then turned again towards me as he raised a glass, and I knew the smile in his eyes was for me alone.

12

'I don't think I could have done that without you,' Jack said as we got out of the car back at the house. It wasn't a long drive, but he'd been quiet the whole time and I hadn't liked to interrupt his thoughts.

'Of course you could,' I said. 'You're stronger than you think.'

'So are you.'

I glanced up at him as I fished the key from my clutch bag. 'Maybe.'

He laughed and I could smell expensive whiskey drift on the still night air. 'No maybe about it. My mother intimidates everyone. Even the vicar quakes in her presence, and he's got God on his side! But you just stood there and defended yourself and me. I'm not sure anyone's ever done that before, certainly not for me, anyway. Any woman I did like whom my mother deemed not suitable, which was most women, ran for the hills after one meeting with her.'

'Yes, but that's different,' I said, waiting for him to come in the door, now that I'd opened it. Caught up in his thoughts, he seemed to have missed that fact, so I reached out and gently pulled him inside.

'Oh? How is it different?'

'Because those women were linked with you romantically. I'm not. She might not like me, but I'm also not a threat and she knows that.'

'I'm not sure she likes anybody,' he said, wandering through to the kitchen and plopping down on the sofa, loosening his tie as he did so that it hung loose around his neck. It really was a good job that nineteen-year-old me wasn't here because even thirty-nine-year-old me couldn't deny that he looked as hot as a rude word right now.

'I assume she must have liked your father, or at least did at some point enough to marry him.'

Jack laughed a hollow laugh. 'You really don't know anything about the aristocracy, do you?'

'Of course I do. I've written several historical romances, you know, and I take my research very seriously.'

'Perhaps you should have told me you wanted to do research that time you came up to me. Things might have gone differently.'

'Ha. You wish.'

Jack didn't reply.

'What do you mean I don't know anything about it, anyway?'

'Marrying for money and titles might seem a bit outdated, but I can tell you, it definitely hasn't disappeared completely.'

'Would you do that?'

'Nope. That's rather been the problem, as far as my parents are concerned. They married "the right people", even though they weren't in love, and know plenty of other people who did the same, so they can't see why I'm so against it.'

'Oh, I see. Do you think Edward would marry the right person, or only for love?'

He rolled his head sideways on the back of the sofa to look at me. His beautiful eyes were heavy-lidded from tiredness and alcohol and, I imagined, a great deal of strain from tonight. Perhaps a little relief too that this part, at least, was over.

'Are you asking for a friend?'

I lolled my knee over to bump against his. 'I'm asking because I'm a writer and being nosy is a necessary trait.'

'Felix told me you prefer to call it interested.'

'He's right, because it's a more accurate description, but you've had several drinks and I was trying to make things easier for you to understand.'

He bumped his own knee back against mine. 'I'm in full control of my faculties, I'll have you know.'

'Good to hear.'

'As for Edward, if you are interested, I think he's already half in love with you, so just give me the word.'

'Oh, shut up.'

He laughed, his whole being relaxed for the first time that night.

'But the honest answer is, I don't know. I don't think he would, but Ed is also keen for a quiet life. He's managed to avoid too much pressure so far by seeing people who generally fit the mould my parents approve of, but obviously nothing serious has come of any of his liaisons yet. I'm sure they'll start dropping hints and making comments before long, if they haven't already.'

'Do you think he'll be as strong as you have at resisting?'

Jack gave a sort of snort. 'I'm not sure running away to the other side of the world counts as being strong.'

'Don't beat yourself up. You did what you had to do for your own sanity. I get that.'

I could feel his eyes on me but stayed looking out at the garden.

'Yeah. I think you do.' His words were soft, and I knew then that he, even if nobody else, understood the steps I'd taken after Mike's death. 'But I guess we can't run away for ever.'

'We can give it a good shot.'

The laugh was deep and rumbled in his chest before I felt him shift beside me. A soft kiss brushed the top of my hair. 'Thank you for coming tonight. I know it can't have been easy for you, but I appreciate it more than you know. Just knowing there was a friendly face there made all the difference.' He pushed himself up.

'There were plenty of friendly faces there.' I grinned, looking up at him. 'All exceedingly glad to have you back in the fold. Persephone, for one. I'm sorry, Lady Persephone.'

'Percy is married.'

'You told me once that doesn't make a lot of difference much of the time in your world.'

'It doesn't feel like my world and it makes a difference to me.'

I made an effort to stand, and Jack reached out a hand which I took, and he pulled me up, which apparently took less effort than he thought as I was suddenly extremely close to his chest, placing a hand on it to steady myself as his own hand went to my waist. The fading scent of his aftershave lingered, and for a split second, I wanted to pause there, breathe it in. But then reality gave me a hard prod.

'Whoops!' I said, a little over-brightly and stepped away, turning as I did so.

'Lily?'

'Yes?' I looked round briefly, but kept walking, heading over to the hob to warm some milk for a drink. When nothing more had been said by the time I got there, I glanced across at him. He was studying his feet. 'Jack?'

His head snapped up. 'Huh?'

'Was there something you wanted to say?'

There was a pause before he shook his head and smiled. 'No. Nothing. Sorry. Not used to alcohol so much these days, but I needed the fortification tonight.'

'It's fine. You're not drunk.'

He laughed. 'I'm not sober, either.'

'This is true. Go on, get up to bed. You look like you're about to fall down asleep anyway. Get some rest. It's been an emotionally exhausting night for you, I'm sure.'

'I don't suppose it was a picnic for you either.'

'We're not talking about me, but I'm fine.' He looked uncertain. 'Really. As you say, it's good practice for the London do.'

'Yeah, I guess. And at least you won't have my mother to deal with at that one, so it should be a breeze.'

'We can only hope,' I replied, before shooing him up the stairs.

Sitting in the silence, sipping my hot drink, I considered the night. In reality, for me, the thought of going this evening had been worse than the actual event. I couldn't speak for Jack but it was obvious to Edward and me at least that he hadn't enjoyed the circus that had been built around his return. Jack was good at putting on a public face. Perhaps it was all part of the upbringing, but I knew from my own attempts at this that there was a limit to how long you could do it for before it either overwhelmed you or you lost sight of who you really were behind the mask.

I had no idea what had been going on in Jack's brain tonight when he'd spoken my name. He was partly standing in the shadows, so it had been hard to read his expression, but I didn't buy it was just the alcohol. There had been something else, but clearly he hadn't been as ready to share as he'd initially thought, and I wasn't about to push. I'd had enough people push me years ago, from every direction, to talk, to get out, to date, in fact, to do everything I had no wish to do. And although I understood all of those wishes came from a good place and caring hearts, it was too much. People have to do things when they're ready. Jack clearly hadn't been ready to share whatever thought was swirling around his mind, but if and when he was, I was happy to listen.

Flicking off the side lamp, I checked the doors were locked and headed up to bed. No light filtered from under Jack's door and there was no sound of movement from within. He'd looked exhausted, so I hoped that a combination of tiredness, relief and alcohol would enable him to get a good sleep.

* * *

I was a little surprised the next morning to see Jack's door ajar and no sign of the man in question throughout the entire house. Taking my herbal tea, I wandered around towards the garage and saw that my old car was gone. I hadn't expected him to have such an early start today, being a Sunday, and with what must have been some form of hangover, even if it wasn't a bad one. Still, he was free to come and go as he pleased. That was the deal and, so long as he felt relaxed and happy enough to do so, that made me happy too.

I ambled back towards the main part of the garden, feeling the delight and calm that it had brought me from the first moment I saw it. The feeling had only increased since Jack had been working on it and, even though he hadn't been here long, the corralling of the most overgrown areas had already begun to make a vast difference to the overall form of the garden.

Looking up into the clear blue sky, I pondered on what to do with myself today. I had thought about some baking, but it was such a beautiful day it seemed a shame to stay inside. Although I'd forced myself out the night before, that didn't mean I was about to launch myself into a round of social engagements, but I did feel an urge to be outside, in nature, and, unusually, further than my garden. I headed back inside and began looking at the map.

* * *

'There you go, love.' The cheery waitress put down a delicious-looking full English breakfast in front of me. I'd decided to head out for a walk and had found a trail on a hiking app that looked doable, not too far to drive to, remote enough to be peaceful but not completely isolated, from a safety point of view. This little café had caught my eye as I was driving and, on a whim, I turned the car into the car park before heading inside and settling myself at a corner table with my Kindle propped up for company. The staff were friendly, but not intrusive, the teapot was huge and the food was home cooked and delicious. Having finished almost an entire pot of tea on my own, I made a quick trip to a delightfully clean bathroom just in case, before I left to go and park up for my walk.

'Thanks, love,' the lady called as she picked up my payment and the large tip I'd left. 'See you again.'

I waved and smiled, and inside, a small thought began to grow that yes, perhaps she would see me again, but one step at a time.

* * *

As I stood at the summit of the hill, I looked across acres of rolling green hills interspersed with the odd farm and breathed in the clean, crisp air. I was lucky enough to live in the countryside but there was something about the air here – perhaps it was the height that I was at – that seemed more pure and felt like it went deeper into my lungs. It had been a long time since I'd taken a walk like this, but it wouldn't be the last. I wasn't sure what Poppy and Felix would think. As far as they were concerned, this was probably still doing things on my own, but at least I was getting out further and I was enjoying myself. It was good for me, fresh air, the exercise, especially with a job where I sat on my backside for most of the day.

It gave me a chance to think, whether that was about life in general or just a particular strand of plot that I was working on in my head. The beautiful views around me inspired me and I took little pieces away from it in my mind to weave into some ideas I had floating around for future novels. I pulled my phone from my pocket and framed up a couple of shots, just as reminders of my day and to look back on when I was writing. On impulse, I sent one to Felix. Of course, there was no signal here and something about that made me happy, but he would get it when I connected once more with civilisation.

Driving home, my phone rang, and I answered it on Bluetooth. 'That's not your back garden!' My brother's voice came over the speaker.

'No, I took myself out for a walk. I thought you'd be pleased.'

'I am pleased. Are you alone?'

'Yes.'

'Was that safe then?'

'There are lots of dog walkers in this area, and I saw plenty of people. I just didn't have to interact with them, so it was a win-win situation, and yes, I enjoyed myself, thanks for asking.' I gave a small eye-roll.

'That was my next question, but I'm sure you've already rolled your eyes.'

It was kind of irritating that my brother knew me so well.

'And I'm glad you got out further than your back garden for once. Actually, I heard this is the second time in as many days that you've been out.'

'News travels fast.'

'Jack told me that you were going with him to his parents' do, but between you and me, I wasn't sure if it was actually going to happen.'

'Well, you volunteered him to come with me to the premiere, so

I didn't really have a lot of choice. It would have been rather ungracious for me to refuse him when he needed support.'

'True, but social things aren't exactly your bag, are they?'

'Definitely not and this was quite an interesting social thing, as you put it. Have you met his mother?'

Felix laughed. 'Oh, yes, the inimitable Lady Coulsdon-Hart. She's something, isn't she?'

'She certainly is that.'

'It's no wonder Jack spent so much time round our house, is it?'

'No, that all became clear last night. His brother seems nice, though. I've never really met him properly before. Not to talk to, anyway.'

'Yeah, Ed's a good bloke. I think Jack really missed him when he was abroad.'

'It was mutual from what Edward said last night. I think he's pleased to have his big brother back in the country.'

'How did it go last night, anyway? How did Jack seem?'

'Like he'd rather be anywhere else but there, but he put on a good front, as was expected of him, I'm sure.'

'Are they still trying to marry him off to the "right" person, then?'

'From all the looks being directed his way, yes, I think that's the general plan. His mother was horrified that he brought his landlady with him.'

'His landlady? Priceless.' Felix let out of roar of a laugh.

'I know,' I said, joining in the laughter. 'I put her right on that account rather swiftly.'

'Did you?' The surprise in his voice was evident.

'Of course I did. You know the arrangement isn't like that and just the way she said it was demeaning to both me and Jack.'

'Still, I'm a little surprised. People don't usually stand up to Lady

CH. She can be pretty intimidating. Especially people who normally barely leave their house.'

'I don't know. Maybe that played to my advantage. It's been so long that I've forgotten when I'm supposed to be intimidated.'

'You should never be intimidated.'

'She did look rather shocked. I don't think she's used to people answering her back, especially common landladies like me.' We both started laughing again.

'God, I wish I'd been there. I'm extremely proud of you, I hope you know that.'

'Thanks.'

'So where is Jack today?'

'Literally no idea. He'd gone when I got up and that wasn't particularly late.'

'OK. I might send him a message and check he's all right after last night. And, Lily?'

'Yep?'

'I really am pleased you've got out today.'

'Then you'll be even more pleased to hear that I had a wonderful cooked breakfast at a little tearoom I passed.'

'Who are you and what have you done with my sister?'

I laughed again and said goodbye to my brother, sending my love on to Poppy and the children, and saying that I would see them in the week, before hanging up and driving the rest of the way home.

13

When I got home, it was to find Jack reading in the kitchen-diner, his long legs stretched out on the sofa, a good proportion of them hanging over the end. Something that smelled yummy was cooking on the hob, simmering under the lid of one of my cast-iron pans.

'Hi.'

'Hello. You look comfy. How was your day?'

'Good, thanks. Have you been out?'

'I have!' I said shucking my coat and walking out to the hall to hang it up in the cupboard before returning to the kitchen.

'Great! Anywhere nice?'

'Just further out into the countryside. I took myself off for a walk and got some proper fresh air and exercise.'

He rested the book down on his broad chest. 'And how was that?'

'What?' I laughed. 'You mean leaving the house again?'

Jack pulled a maybe yes, maybe no kind of expression.

'It's all right. I already had all that from my brother. And yes, I know it's unusual but, in answer to your question, I think it did me good.'

'Did you just walk?'

'I stopped for breakfast and read my book then had a nice long, invigorating walk before finding somewhere to get a much-needed cup of tea, where I read some more of my book and then came home.'

'Sounds like a perfect, not to mention, full day.'

'Full enough for me.'

'You look better for it,' said Jack.

'I'm not quite sure how to take that.'

'Take it as a compliment, which is how it was meant. You looked fine before, just to clarify, but you have a... I don't know... glow about you now.' He waved his hand. 'I don't know. It's just obviously done you good. That's all I'm trying to say.'

'Thanks. What did you do with yourself today?'

'I went back to my parents' and then also took a long walk, which was much needed after Part A of the day.'

'Oh goodness. Did it not go well?'

'About as well as can be expected,' he said, laying the book aside and pushing himself up off the sofa, crossing to where I stood by the hob in a few easy long strides. 'They still want me to take my place at the head of the family and marry the right woman with the right name and the right breeding. I thought being away for that long might give it time to sink in with them that's not what I want or how it's going to be,' he said, taking the lid off the pan and stirring the dish that lay beneath it.

'God, that smells good.'

'Thanks. All that excitement today has probably built up your appetite. At least, I hope so, and I also hope you like it, because I made enough for several meals.'

'You didn't have to cook for me.'

'I know. And you don't have to cook for me either, but when we do it's nice.'

I looked up at him. It was. I realised the more often I sat at dinner with Jack in the evening how much my soul had missed the simple art and enjoyment of conversation with another person. Yes, I had that with my family, but it was regularly interrupted by small children, as family meals often are. Conversation with Jack was easy, sometimes light and sometimes surprisingly deep.

'So how did you leave things?' I took a step back. 'Sorry. This is none of my business, I really shouldn't be asking. I told you I was too nosy for my own good.'

'I prefer to see it as interested,' he teased, the green eyes sparkling with amusement. 'And I like you asking. I like talking to you. You don't judge. You just listen. I didn't realise how much I needed that.' He gave me a brief smile, with the tiniest hint of embarrassment about it. I imagined it was quite hard for someone like Jack to admit that he needed anything, so I appreciated his words twice as much. 'You take a seat at the table, and I'll bring this over. There's a bottle of white wine in the fridge if you want to grab it on your way past.'

I did so, picking up a couple of glasses as well. 'Ooh, swanky stuff!' I said, looking at the label as I walked to the table.

'Well, we don't want word getting around that the eldest son of an earl only brings cheap plonk for dinner.'

'Oh, no. That would never do. Don't worry, I'll be sure to let everyone know that you only ever provide top-drawer choices.'

'If you would be so kind,' he said, a mischievous smile playing on dangerously sexy lips, 'at your next social function.'

'I do have rather a lot of them, as you know.'

'I do indeed, and I'm glad to be able to have this opportunity to steal your company this evening.'

'We are old friends. It would be rude of me if I didn't find a slot somewhere in my heady social calendar for you.'

His eyes twinkled with laughter as he sat down, placing my dish before me as he did so.

'Lentil and Mediterranean vegetable lasagne. I hope you like it. Bon appetit.'

'Oh, crikey, now you're speaking foreign too. I'm not sure my simple education can keep up with Eton and Cambridge.'

He pulled a face that told me not to be a smart-arse.

'Wow, that's delicious,' I said, holding my hand up in front of me as I spoke through a mouthful of food.

The warmth of his smile radiated around me and he appeared genuinely pleased at the compliment. There also seemed a little surprise in his expression, and I wondered how long it had been since he felt he'd received a genuine compliment. That made me a little sad on his behalf, but the smile was there now and something within made me want to ensure it stayed there for a while longer.

'What are you thinking about?' he asked, taking a sip of the wine and watching me over the rim of the glass. 'You look very pensive.'

'Do I?'

'You do.'

'Nothing, really. I was just thinking how nice this is.'

'The dinner?'

'All of it. The dinner, the company, and I was hoping that you feel relaxed here.'

His eyes were down now as he took another sip, but he nodded in response. 'I do,' he said, now concentrating on loading his fork for the next mouthful. 'How far did you walk in the end?'

If I didn't know better, I'd think Jack was changing the subject.

* * *

'Darling!' My agent greeted me on the video call, taking a noisy slurp of coffee as she did so. 'This is just wonderful. Couldn't be better publicity.'

I gave her a slightly bemused look.

'Sorry? What couldn't be better publicity?'

'You and that gorgeous man of yours, the whole love nest thing. And I just wanted to say,' her voice lost its theatrical bent for a moment, 'I really am thrilled for you. No one deserves happiness more than you. God knows you waited long enough for it.'

'I'm sorry, Zinnia. I really don't know what you're talking about.'

She frowned at me for a moment before holding up a newspaper, showing a picture of me at the manor with Jack leaning down towards me, his hand resting at my back. In reality, it been an innocent gesture, him just saying something in conversation over the noise of the chatter surrounding us, but looking at it in black and white, it was easy to see how it could be misconstrued as something with far more meaning. My eyes drifted to the headline:

Is tragic romance author about to finally get happy ending?

'Oh my God. Is that today's paper?'

'It is. Have you not seen it?'

'I don't get a paper.'

'Oh, it's all over the internet as well. I'm surprised you haven't seen it.'

I groaned and dropped my head into my hands. 'I've been beavering away writing all day, I haven't even been on the web. Oh, this is awful.'

My agent gave me a look. 'How is this awful? Firstly, you're clearly out of the house, which is a good step. Secondly, you are with an utterly gorgeous man who looks like he was made for sin and to break hearts. He's one of your iconic heroes come to life. So far, I'm not seeing any downside.'

'He really isn't. He's just a friend from childhood. My brother's friend, actually.'

'Even more romantic – childhood sweethearts!'

'Definitely not childhood sweethearts. You were right about the fact that he knows how to break a heart.'

She raised a heavily pencilled brow in interest.

'Not mine,' I hastened to add quickly. 'But most of the young women in the village and some of the older ones too. I can't believe this. Why can't people keep their nose out of other people's business? See, if I hadn't gone out, none of this would have happened.'

'Darling, you can't stay locked behind those four walls forever. And who cares if people are talking about you? They'll be talking about someone else tomorrow, believe me. In the meantime, this is great publicity for the upcoming film release and your books.'

'This is my life, Zinnia. I don't want it spread all over the papers, especially when it's untrue. It was bad enough when I had my first big success and everyone dug up the circumstances of Mike's death.'

'Just don't read it. It'll blow over in no time. There's always someone else to talk about.' She gave the picture another glance. 'I must admit, I was hoping it was true.'

'Sorry to disappoint you.'

She looked back at me. 'Like I said, you deserve happiness. That's all I meant.'

I ran a hand back over my hair. 'Yes, sorry. I know. I didn't mean to snap. I just hate this side of things.'

'I know. I'll let you get back to your book, and I'll talk to you soon.' She blew me a kiss and I raised my hand in a wave and signed off.

* * *

When Jack walked through the door later that day, I took one look at his face and knew that he'd seen the article too.

'I had nothing to do with it,' I said quickly, my words tripping over themselves as they fell out of my mouth.

He toed off his boots, and crossed to where I was standing, worrying one thumb with the nail of the other. Jack reached out, taking my hands within his own as he came to stand close in front of me. Embarrassed, I kept my eyes focused on the button of his shirt level with my eyeline.

'Look at me,' he said, his voice soft but with an air of authority.

I stared at the button.

'I said look at me.'

This time I obeyed, tilting my head up until I met his gaze.

'I know you had nothing to do with it.' A smile played on his lips. 'I couldn't think of anyone who would be less thrilled about the piece than you, so the idea that you would be behind it is laughable.'

'I am sorry, though. I'm sure it's not helped relations with your family. I didn't even know about it until my agent rang me, telling me what great publicity it was for the new film.'

'Is that what she thinks?'

'Apparently so. Aligns with the epic romance of the book or something. Despite the fact that obviously none of it is true. I'm so sorry to drag you into all this. I'm sure it's the last thing you need right now.'

He tilted his head, making a show of thinking hard, his hands still holding mine. 'Hmm, being romantically linked with a beautiful, successful woman. Yes, I can see how you might think that would bother me.'

In lieu of my hands, which he still held, I bumped my shoulder against his chest. 'Very funny. You know what I mean. Your mum's going to turn purple when she sees this.'

'She's already seen it.'

'Oh God. Has she really?'

'Oh yeah.'

I searched his face. 'Are you in a lot of trouble?'

He looked down at me, eyes focused, face serious. 'I'm grounded for the next month.'

I lifted my hands and pushed against him, releasing us both. 'Very funny. Silly arse. It was a serious question.'

'Well, it shouldn't be. I'm a grown man. I will see whoever I want to see, and that's exactly what I told my mother. Again.'

'But you did tell her that you're not actually seeing me?'

'Whether the report was true didn't really come into the conversation from what I recall.'

'I would have thought that would have been the first thing you told her the moment she spoke to you.'

'Yeah. You would have thought so, wouldn't you? But she does like to go off on her rants and it's really so much effort to disagree or even try to put your point across until she's run out of steam.'

'But you told her then? Once you got a word in?'

'Not really.'

I put my hands on my hips. 'What do you mean, not really? It's a yes or no answer. There's no grey area. You either told her or you didn't tell her.'

'In that case then, no, I didn't tell her. What does it matter what she thinks, anyway? At least she knows you're not my landlady now.'

I threw a look at him across my shoulder as I reached to get something. He gave me a shrug in reply.

'On the other hand, Edward is both thrilled for me and hopes I'm happy but is also disgusted at me for stealing you from him.'

'For goodness' sake. You're both as bad as one another. Can you come and get this off the shelf for me? I can't reach.'

Jack crossed to where I was standing and reached the tin from the cupboard above me easily, handing it to me gently.

'Thank you.'

'My pleasure, dear one. Is there anything else that I can do for you?'

'Yes. You can wipe that smirk off your face and stop being such a pain.'

'I don't know how you can say such harsh words to the hero coming in to sweep you off your feet.'

'I'll sweep you off your bloody feet in a minute if you don't get out from under mine.'

He gave me a formal bow and backed out of the room, chuckling as he did so. I carried on preparing the dinner, still frustrated and upset about the intrusion to my privacy but found, since Jack had walked in, I was unable to work myself into quite the same level of lather that I had been doing. Another perspective and the distraction of company seem to have lessened the initial shock and impact of seeing the newspaper article.

14

When Jack came down for dinner later that night, he approached me, this time more seriously.

'I do understand, you know. I know you like your privacy and that you had a hard time when you first became more of a well-known name as people dug into your past and made news out of your pain. I'm not making light of that. I just don't want you to be so hurt this time around. To try and make you see that this is just gossip and tomorrow someone else will be flavour of the month to talk about.'

'I know. And I do appreciate that. If you hadn't been here...' I thought for a moment. 'Well, if you hadn't been here, none of this would have happened, but also if you hadn't been here then I'd probably have sat and stewed tonight, turning it over and over in my mind until it became the only thing I was thinking about, so thank you.'

'You're very welcome.'

'And I am sorry if you've had extra grief from your mother over this.'

His broad smile warmed the room, not to mention parts of me

that I wasn't going to acknowledge right now, or probably ever. 'Believe me, I can handle my mother these days, and I'm pretty sure you can too.'

'I'd rather not, though.'

'Then that makes two of us. Come on, sit down. I'll serve that. You've had quite the day.'

I flicked a tea towel at his backside and made my way to the table.

* * *

The next couple of weeks went by fairly uneventfully. I did my best to put newspaper reports and internet gossip out of my mind and stayed away from the web as much as possible. Hopefully, as others had said, people had found something far more interesting to talk about by now. I hadn't managed to go out beyond the safety of my garden again just yet. It wasn't that I didn't want to, but there was still something holding me back. I'd had a spurt of bravery, accompanying Jack to his parents' and then exploring wider in the world, but I seemed to have taken a step backwards. The newspaper story about me and Jack had thrown a spanner in the works and reignited some insecurities. Somewhere in my brain a bit of logic was saying, if you keep out of sight, then they won't talk about you. But there was another part of my brain that was hugely frustrated and wanted to kick the first part. In the meantime, I'd baked several cakes, bursting with calories, in the hope that it might spur me on to find the determination to walk it off. So far, however, I'd just ended up doing laps of the garden.

Jack waved as he passed the kitchen window. He wore a peaked cap, shading his eyes from the lowering sun of a beautiful spring day, and I was busy washing salad in the sink as he came in. I turned to say hi, then froze.

'What is that?'

'That's Clive.'

I gave Jack a patient look that probably didn't have an awful lot of patience in it. 'Clive appears to be a golden retriever.'

'Clive is a golden retriever, aren't you, boy?' he said, fussing with the dog who actually appeared to be smiling. Could dogs smile?

'OK,' I began again. 'Let me rephrase this. What is Clive doing in my house?'

'He needs a home.'

'What's wrong with his current home?' I asked, as Jack pulled a small towel from his back pocket and gently wiped Clive's feet, watching as the dog immediately lifted up each paw in turn ready for the procedure.

'His current home is a foster home. He's had a bit of a bad start, poor lad. The breeder didn't want him because there was a problem...' He stopped and then pointed in the vague area of his own crotch.

'Oh God. That's too much information right before dinner.'

'So she was going to put him down.'

I gave him a horrified look.

'I know. The woman I'm working for at the moment runs a small animal shelter. She managed to persuade the breeder to give Clive to her, and she rehomed him. Unfortunately, those people didn't really understand anything about dogs, like their need for exercise in order to prevent boredom, et cetera. Then they wondered why, having been stuck in a flat with no garden and no exercise for five days, the dog, shall we say, redesigned some furniture.'

'So you brought him here to chew mine? Brilliant.'

'No. They took him back to the shelter. The owner has been fostering him ever since, training him, waiting until the right person came along. She didn't want him pinging back and forth into unsuitable homes.'

'I see. I know I did tell you to treat this place as your own, but it might have been an idea to talk to me before you decided to get a dog. Can you get him to stop looking at me like that?'

'Like what?'

'With those big... puppy dog eyes.'

'He's a puppy dog. Those are his eyes.'

'Oh, very funny. You know what I mean.'

'Actually, he's out of the puppy stage. He's two and a half now and really well trained. He's been following me about the last couple of weeks while I've been doing work at this lady's house.'

'Which is all very lovely. But I still think you should have spoken to me before you decided to get a dog.'

'Clive isn't my dog.'

'So he's going back tomorrow?'

'Not exactly. At least, I hope not. I got him for you.'

I sat down heavily on the kitchen chair. 'I beg your pardon?'

'He's your dog. At least, he should be.'

I looked at Jack, looked at the dog then looked back at Jack. 'Did I not eat enough at lunchtime today? Am I hallucinating?'

'Look.' Jack came and crouched down in front of me. The dog followed him and sat obediently beside him. 'He's a great dog and would be company for you. It could help you get back in out into the world. You said you enjoyed doing those walks and what better excuse could there be to have a dog to take on those walks? He'd be company and it forces you out.'

'You said he ate the furniture!'

'That was just one time.'

'One time is enough!'

'It was a long time ago and he was bored. They weren't treating him right. You would. You've got a beautiful big garden for him to run around in and you'd walk him. He'd be in heaven here, and I think it would do you good.'

'No.'

'What do you mean, no?'

I stood up, pushing Jack out of the way, doing my best to hold my temper. 'I mean no. I don't want a dog, and I don't want people making decisions about what they think is best for me without even consulting me. I'm not a child.'

'Nobody said you were a child, but that doesn't mean I don't want to help you.'

'I don't need help.'

'Everybody needs help at one time or another. And you said you enjoyed going out on the walks, but since that stupid article hit the papers, you've shut yourself away again.'

'It's nothing to do with that,' I snapped, feeling the colour rise from my chest as it always did when I tried to tell a fib.

Jack rested back against the door, watching me, and I felt as if he could see straight through me.

'It's not. Look, I'm happy to have you here and it's been working fine until now, but you can't go around making decisions for me, thinking you know what's right for me when you barely know me at all.'

'I know you better than you think I do, not that you make that easy for anybody.'

'What's that supposed to mean?'

'It means you've shut yourself away since your husband died and you locked up your heart as well. There are good people out there and all they want to do is help you.'

'I don't need help,' I repeated.

'Right. So you're just going to sit here on your own, year after year, wasting the life that was spared that day?' He snatched the cap off his head as he spoke. His voice had risen in volume now and his eyes had darkened in anger.

'If I choose to do that, that's my decision. It's got nothing to do with you and you have absolutely no say in it.'

'Do you think this is how your husband would want you to live?'

'Don't you dare bring my husband into this! You don't know anything about him.'

'I know that if he loved you, which he obviously did, he wouldn't want you to be living like this. He'd want you to enjoy the life that you got to keep.'

'Perhaps I didn't want to keep it!' I spat back at him. 'Did you ever think of that? Did you ever think that I wish day after day, night after night, that I'd stayed at that table so I didn't have to experience all this pain, or live like this? I found the person for me and then the world took him away. What was the point of it all? What was the point of all that happiness if it was just going to be snatched away? It would have been better for everybody if I'd just stayed at that table with him instead.'

'Don't say that.' Jack's voice was soft now and he made to take a couple of steps towards me, but I kept the distance by moving backwards. He stopped, getting the message.

'You wouldn't understand. You couldn't.'

'You're right, and I don't pretend to. But you deserve to live, Lily. None of that was your fault.'

'I chose the restaurant!' I shouted at him, roughly brushing away the tears with the side of my hand. 'So it was my fault. If we'd been anywhere else, none of it would have happened. It was all my fault!'

'You can't think like that,' Jack replied, his tone earnest. 'It was nobody's fault. It was just a horrible set of circumstances in which you were caught up. You can't go through life blaming yourself. And no, I didn't know Mike well, but I saw the way he looked at you, and having seen that, I know he wouldn't want you to feel any of that either. You have to let it go, Lily. You have to let that guilt go.'

I walked up to Jack, tilted my head up until I could meet his eyes and addressed him quietly, but with cold steel in my voice. 'You don't get to tell me what to do.'

With that, I turned and walked out of the kitchen, headed straight up to my room, and locked the door.

* * *

Rolling over, I looked at the clock. Half past two. Having left the kitchen, I'd changed into my pyjamas and gone straight to bed, tears still streaming over the row with Jack plus all the memories it had unearthed. I hated arguing with him, but I stood by what I said. Deep down, I knew he had my best interests at heart, at least he thought he did. I'd spent a long time on my own, and maybe I was a little out of practise at the whole compromise thing. I'd had no one else to really consider for the past ten years and, until now, Jack had been pretty easy going. Until now, he hadn't really dived into my private life. Nobody had. That had been locked away for so many years. I hadn't even told my brother the things that I had shouted at Jack tonight. I'd known that, for Felix, hearing something like that at an already difficult time would have been painful for him, and they had done so much for me. Perhaps Jack had a point when he said that I put barriers up. I never used to. But things happen and people change. It wasn't that I didn't want to feel love, only that I couldn't bear the loss of it ever again. In my heart, I knew this solitude wasn't an ideal solution, but it was the only way I could see for getting through it at the time and over the years it had just become a habit.

I fidgeted in the bed and my stomach growled, reminding me that I'd stormed off before eating any of the dinner I'd prepared.

Jack had called through the door at one point, suggesting that I should eat something, but I ignored him and he soon went away. However, as my stomach made another loud grumble, it appeared that the hunger pangs were less easily dismissed.

Pushing the duvet back, I shuffled my feet into slippers and grabbed my dressing gown, wrapping it tightly around me before padding downstairs, making sure to be quiet. From previous experience bustling about the kitchen, it seemed that Jack was normally a pretty heavy sleeper, but the last thing I wanted right now was to have another confrontation.

Moonlight streaked the limestone floor of the kitchen-diner and in the soft light, a golden head raised itself to look at me.

'Oh, crikey, I'd forgotten about you,' I whispered.

Clive's ears twitched and he tilted his head to one side.

'Just go back to sleep.'

He looked at me for a moment more, then rested back against the side of the clearly brand-new bed Jack must have bought him and let out a long sigh.

'I know how you feel, boy.'

As quietly as I could, I made a sandwich and took it over to the sofa, together with a glass of milk.

Clive shuffled in his bed, so that his head was now resting on his paws and looking directly at me.

'Please don't look at me like that. I know you must think I'm horrible. This just isn't the right place for you. You're obviously a nice dog and you deserve a wonderful home. I can't give you what you need. I don't even know what you need, but I do know that I can't give it to you.'

Clive blinked and carried on listening.

'I don't know what Jack was thinking, bringing you home. I'm sure he meant well, but he doesn't really know me, he just thinks he does, and then we end up in a situation like this.'

Clive got up, did a stretch a top yogi would be proud of, made a squeaky little yawn noise and padded over to me, his toenails clicking on the tiles. When he got alongside me, he sat and gently laid his head on my thigh.

'Did Jack teach you that one as well?'

Clive didn't respond.

Letting out my own sigh, I lifted my hand and tentatively stroked the dog's head. His fur was silky soft, and he made a contented sound as I did so.

'Sorry, Clive. I'm not sure if I'm doing this right. I've never had much to do with dogs before.'

Clive shuffled his bum a bit closer to the sofa and my legs, so I guessed I must have been doing something right.

'It's not that I don't want you, particularly. It's just that I've never thought of getting a dog. I've never really been a doggy person, no offence.'

He didn't appear to take any, so I continued.

'People have suggested it before, of course, but you hear such horror stories of puppies chewing this, pooing here, weeing there. I just didn't think I could deal with all that on top of everything else. I hear you had your own little chewing session? Although it does sound like that was more your old owners' fault than yours. I do wonder why some people get dogs if they're not prepared to put the work in and make a suitable home for them. I mean, you're companion animals, aren't you? So what's the point of getting a dog if you're then going to be out at work eight to ten hours at a time? I'm sure you'll make somebody a lovely pet. I just don't think it can be me. You wouldn't like living here, anyway. I mean, I think you'd like the garden. I'm sure there's lots of good sniffs out there and you seem to have taken to Jack. He's here quite a lot, although after the hoo-ha tonight, I'm not sure how long that arrangement will last. But as for the rest of it, I'm pretty sure you'd find it quite boring. I don't really do much. I'm not social at all.'

I bent my head in order to get a better look at the dog's face in the moonlight. He was asleep. Great. I sat there for a while longer, reluctant to disturb Clive from what seemed a very peaceful rest, but eventually my leg went to sleep and I had to move him in order to get up and force some blood back into the system. He gave me a look, rested his nose upwards against my hip and, automatically, I reached down and scratched the top of his head. Content, he then plodded back to his bed, turned round three times and plopped down heavily before drifting back to sleep. I watched him for a moment, feeling calmness resonating from his furry body, the steady rhythm of his tummy going up and down in peaceful rest.

'Oh, no,' I whispered to myself suddenly. 'No, no, no. Don't go down that route, Lily.' I took my glass and plate over to the dishwasher, loaded it in and headed back upstairs, determined not to dream of chocolate brown puppy dog eyes and silky fur.

15

The next morning, when I got up, Jack was already at the hob with what looked like the makings of a very large English breakfast. Clive was in his bed, watching intently, his nose twitching as delicious smells drifted across towards him.

'Morning,' I said, entering the kitchen and heading towards the kettle to make a cup of tea.

'Good morning,' Jack returned, the slightest hint of hesitation in his voice. 'Your tea is there on the side. I've just made it. I heard you moving about.'

'You didn't have to do that.'

Jack turned from his cooking for a moment and I looked up to meet his eyes. I could see he was holding on to his patience.

'But thank you,' I said, remembering my manners. I might still be cross with him but that didn't mean I had to be ungracious as well.

'I thought I'd cook breakfast. You didn't eat last night, so you must be hungry, before you refuse it.'

Don't you just hate it when people are right when you don't want them to be?

'I am a little hungry,' I conceded. My stomach decided to back me up by emitting a long, low grumble.

'That sounds like more than a little.'

I picked up my tea and walked over to the sofa and sat down. Clive padded out of his bed and took up residence next to my leg, his weight leaning against it before he rested his head gently again as he had last night on my leg.

'Looks like someone likes you.'

'Oh, don't even start. Dogs like most people. You still have to take him back.'

Jack rested his head back for a moment, staring at the built-in fan in the ceiling. 'Right. Well, the lady is away this weekend so it will have to wait until Monday. If you've got a problem with that, I'll find a hotel that takes pets for the next couple of nights.'

'Don't be silly. You can both stay here until then.'

Jack looked across at me.

'I mean, obviously you can stay here longer than that, I just meant the dog can stay here till then.'

'To be honest, I wasn't sure whether I would still be welcome after last night's...' he paused, 'discussion.'

'These things happen. You're aware, I trust, that you crossed a line when you thought you knew what is best for me?'

'Sometimes other people can see things clearer.'

I counted to ten and blew out a sigh. 'The dog goes back Monday. You don't make any other decisions on my behalf, and things can go back to normal. Deal?'

'Sounds like you've already made those decisions, so...' He shrugged and turned his attention back to the food sizzling and popping in front of him.

Clive nuzzled his nose further up my leg and gently pressed my tummy with the end of it. 'I know, and I really am sorry.' I leant down over him, speaking softly. 'You are very lovely. I'm just not ready for this. You deserve to have somebody who will shower you with love and sadly I think my days of being able to do that are long past. You deserve so much better than me.'

Breakfast was a slightly awkward affair, with half-hearted attempts at conversation but mostly long silences. Clive looked between us at times as if trying to figure out what was wrong. They do say dogs can be very sensitive and there was definitely tension. To be fair, I was sure even a stick insect could have sensed it.

'Well, I guess I'd better take Clive out for a walk. Unless you want to do it, of course?' said Jack.

'No, thank you.'

'Shame. Looks like a lovely day out there.'

'Which I can appreciate just as well from my own garden.'

'Not really the same, though, is it?' Jack countered. 'And you did say how much you enjoyed getting out for that walk the other week. We could find a dog-friendly café and have a cup of tea afterwards.'

'Which bit of the sentence "I don't want a dog" did you not understand last night?'

'Fine.' He held up his hands. 'There really is no point trying to talk to you, is there?'

'I see the true Jack is showing his colours now. It did seem to be too good to be true that you'd changed that much. Still full of your-self, aren't you? You're like a stick of rock. If they cut you open, it would say arrogance all the way through. Just because someone doesn't agree with you, they're automatically the one in the wrong.'

'Except it's not just me that feels this way, is it?' he snapped back. 'Felix has been trying to get you back into the real world for God knows how many years. I don't know why he keeps bothering. You're clearly so set in your wallowing ways, even all these years later, you're never going to change.'

I opened my mouth to argue, but Jack was there before me. 'I know you went through an awful, awful, tragic thing. But it's like you stopped living that day as well. Some people don't get that choice, Lily. I used to work with a guy out in New Zealand. Fit and healthy as an ox, at least we thought he was, and then one day he collapsed. They rushed him to hospital and found a brain tumour that had spread cancer throughout his body. Absolutely nothing they could do. Suddenly this young, fit guy who had all this life in front of him had it snatched away, just like your husband. Neither of them had a choice. But you have a choice and you're wasting it!' His eyes burned through me for a moment before he turned on his heel and slapped his thigh once, at which the dog trotted up, glancing back at me as he did so.

'She's not coming.' Jack spoke to the dog without looking at me as he pulled on his boots. 'Come on, boy.' Clive gave a small whine as he looked at me.

'Go on,' I said gently, feeling my voice thick in my throat. 'Go and have a lovely walk with Jack.'

Jack opened the door, gestured for the dog to go through, then closed it behind him, leaving a heavy silence in his wake.

* * *

I dropped down onto the sofa and rested my head in my hands, feeling the cooked breakfast which had been so enjoyable to eat, despite the atmosphere, now sitting leaden in the pit of my stomach. Jack had gone too far, whether he admitted it or not, but deep down, I also knew he was right. It was just that nobody had ever been so blunt about it with me before. I'd had heated discussions with my brother, of course, but he knew where to draw the line. Jack seemed to have no idea that there even was a line.

I looked over at the empty dog bed and saw a squashy hot dog with a face tucked into the side of it. Clive must have been cuddling it when I came down last night. The thought made me smile, despite the tear that trickled down my face and dropped off my chin. Walking over to the bed, I crouched down and tidied the blankets and the couple of toys up, making sure it was comfortable for when Clive came back. Knowing Jack, he would walk for miles, so the poor dog would probably be exhausted.

Suddenly the back door opened and I jumped, losing my balance and ending up bum-first on the floor.

'Sorry,' Jack said, looking as though he genuinely meant it and reaching down a hand for me to take to pull myself up again.

'It's fine. I just...' Jack looked from me to the dog bed and back to me again. 'I was just tidying up and I didn't expect you back so soon.'

'I forgot Hot Dog.'

'Pardon?'

'I forgot Hot Dog,' he said, pointing to the toy that I was still holding in my hand. 'I bought it for Clive a couple of weeks ago and he's grown quite attached to it. He doesn't like to go anywhere without it now.'

I smiled in spite of myself. 'You'd better take it, then.' I handed it over.

'Thanks.' Jack turned back to the door, one hand on the side of it. Without looking back at me he spoke. 'I know you probably don't think it, but I absolutely hate arguing with you. I can't bear seeing you cry, and I never meant to upset you. But I want you to live rather than just exist.' With that, he opened the door and was quickly gone.

I heard his boots crunching on the gravel as he walked around to the car and then an excited bark as Clive obviously saw his favourite toy. In the sky, a few wispy clouds decorated the solid blue, and a gentle, warm breeze drifted in through the open window. I stood for a moment watching the clouds float lazily along.

'Oh God, that man!' I cursed as I pulled the door open and ran round to where the cars were parked. Jack was just reversing out but stopped as he saw me, buzzing down a window.

'What's wrong?'

'What's wrong is that you're a huge pain in the arse and I'm wishing I'd never agreed to having you stay here. But secondly, do you have a couple of minutes to wait for me?'

'As you asked so nicely...' He looked back towards the dog in the boot. 'What do you reckon, boy? Should we wait for her?'

I narrowed my eyes at Jack. 'Give me two minutes.'

16

We'd been driving for a while now. I turned occasionally to see Clive looking contentedly out of the back window.

'He's very good in the car, isn't he?'

Jack looked back at the dog in the rear-view mirror. 'He is. He's a good boy, generally.'

There was silence between us for a moment before I spoke again. 'It's not that I don't think he's a lovely dog. It's just that they are a commitment, and I'm not sure I'm ready for that.'

'No, I get it,' Jack said, without taking his eyes from the road, and a distinct lack of emotion in his voice.

We drove on for a while with little conversation and just the background noise of Classic FM playing quietly to break the silence until we turned off the road. I caught the road sign as we began to climb a hill.

'Box Hill? Is that where we're going?' I asked, excitedly.

Jack glanced across. 'Yes. There are some good walks here and I thought you might enjoy the setting.'

'I've wanted to come here forever. Mike and I always meant to come but somehow never got around to it. There's a picnic scene in—'

'Jane Austen's *Emma*.' He smiled at me briefly, but I was relieved to see warmth in it this time. 'I know. I'm afraid I can't quite arrange all the servants and the full spread, but I did get a few things from Marks and Spencer yesterday on the off-chance I could persuade you out, so hopefully that will be OK.'

I felt the smile on my face get wider. 'Our own picnic?'

He nodded, concentrating on the bendy road and the clutch of cyclists in front of him. How they even began to climb up here was beyond me.

'If you're up for it, we could get a roast at a pub later. Obviously depends if you just want to get home, though.'

'Oh! Umm...' I looked out at the bright sky, and the beautiful green countryside surrounding me in every direction.

'Like I said, we don't have—'

'No, I'd love to. But will Clive be able to come in? I don't think I'd feel comfortable leaving him in the car. You hear all these things about dognapping and stuff. I'd never be able to enjoy a meal if I was worrying about someone stealing Clive.'

'No, I know.'

'And this doesn't change my opinion. Just because I'm unable to keep him doesn't mean I want anything bad to happen to him.'

'No, I know,' Jack repeated, languidly. 'The place I was thinking of is definitely dog-friendly so we'd just take him in with us.'

'Oh, OK. That's good. Yes, much better. That sounds lovely, then. Saves either of us cooking and,' I gave a small throat clear, 'it, umm, might be nice to do something like that for a change.' I paused. 'I actually can't remember the last time I did that, aside from my breakfast out a few weeks ago. Felix and Poppy used to suggest going out but I think they just gave up asking after a while. I don't blame them as I always refused to go. I suppose that seems rude, really. I hope they didn't feel that way, as it certainly wasn't meant that way. You don't think they felt like that, do you?' I asked, suddenly a bit agitated about it all.

Jack removed a hand very briefly from the wheel and touched my leg momentarily in reassurance. 'No. I know for a fact they don't feel you were being rude.'

'How?'

'He spoke to me about it.'

'He did?'

'Yes. We've had the odd chat about things over the years. Thankfully for me, distance didn't affect my friendship with Felix. He just worries about you. Although it all got a bit heated between us, he feels the same way as I do – he's just concerned you're not enjoying life as much as you deserve to. They know you're not doing anything to hurt anyone on purpose.'

'But they are hurt? Even if I'm not doing it on purpose.'

Jack indicated left and pulled into the car park at the top of the hill. We drove around to a space and he swung the car in. Switching off the engine, he twisted a little in the seat to face me.

'Do you want me to make you feel better or do you want the truth?'

I heaved a deep breath.

'The truth. I think...'

Jack waited.

'Yes. Definitely. The truth.'

'Yes, they're hurt on occasion when you don't feel able to join them in birthday celebrations out, or parties for the children. They've explained to the kids as well as possible and, at the moment, they know that you won't be there for birthday parties, but I don't know if they'll always accept that as they grow older. That's an unknown, but Poppy and Felix have certainly done all they can to smooth things so far.'

I sat for a moment, staring out towards the trees that were all bursting into leaf, from vibrant lime to deep hunter green. It hadn't occurred to me that Felix had ever felt that something – or more accurately – someone was missing from their celebrations. My stomach churned and twisted.

'Do you think I've been horribly selfish?'

'No,' Jack said. 'I don't. You were devastated and you did what you had to do to try and keep yourself sane. But I do think it's possible to get into a habit, a rut, which can then be very difficult to get out of, partly because we're so used to doing things a certain way, and partly because then doing something different can seem overwhelming.'

'Yes.'

Whether he knew it or not, Jack had hit the nail right on the head. Not that that meant I wasn't still terrified at the thought of social situations. But if I let myself think about it, it hadn't really registered that I was missing out on special moments in Ruby and Freddy's lives. Those were moments I would never get back. I'd missed Felix's fortieth birthday party a few years ago, and Poppy's. As much as I'd wanted to go, I just couldn't do it, but now I knew I should have forced myself. Those nights weren't about me, they were about Felix and Poppy, and I'd missed out on celebrating the wonderful people they were. I'd missed so many opportunities.

It sounded easy. Just stop staying in, go out, accept all the invitations. But I couldn't go from zero to full speed. I'd wrapped myself up in my own security blanket for far too long to just throw it away in one swift move.

'You're doing a lot of thinking over there.' Jack's deep tones broke into my thoughts. 'There's practically steam coming out of your ears.'

I gave him a brief smile, the thoughts still churning.

'Come on,' he said. 'Just forget about it all for now. Come out with me and Clive and enjoy the scenery and the exercise and the glorious day. Imagine Emma and her companions looking out over a similar view all those years ago.' His words made me smile as he referenced one of my favourite books.

'I didn't realise you'd read it.'

'I have a little confession to make. When I used to come round to your house years ago, you often had your nose stuck in a Jane Austen novel and seemed so engrossed, I wondered what all the fuss was about. I mean, obviously I'd seen that there were plenty of adaptations, not that I'd watched any. Anyway, after my wife left, I didn't really feel like being all that sociable either for a while and I took up reading.' He pushed open the door and I followed on my side, meeting him at the rear of the car, where we both changed into walking boots.

'You hadn't been a big reader before?'

'No, not really. Something else my parents despaired of, having spent a ridiculous amount on my education. Obviously, I read all the texts I needed to for my studies, but the thought of picking up a book for enjoyment as you always seemed to? I couldn't really wrap my head around that.'

'And then you started with Jane Austen?'

Jack laughed as he opened the boot. Much to my surprise, Clive didn't spring out like a wind-up jack-in-the-box suddenly released, but stayed put.

'He's not jumping out.'

'Nope. He's been taught not to,' Jack said, clipping the lead onto the dog's collar. 'Come on then, mate.' At this direction, Clive leapt easily from the car, his tail wagging madly back and forth in excitement. He wandered off a little to the length of the lead, towards the edge of bushes, and began sniffing. Jack was patting his pockets.

'You OK? Forgotten something?'

'Just checking I have poo bags.' As if on cue, Clive, in the shade of the bush, squatted and then trotted back to us, looking pleased with himself. Jack handed the lead to me and walked over to the spot, crouched down and tidied up. 'There's a bin just there. I'll be back in a moment,' he said, jogging off. Clive gave a small whine.

'It's all right. He'll be back in a moment,' I said, reaching down to ruffle his chin. He sat, pressed his head against my thigh and waited. As Jack strode quickly back towards us, Clive stood up and did a happy, excited dance at his approach.

'Somebody likes you.'

'Well, at least someone does.' He gave me a wink and gestured for us to set off. I held out the lead for him.

'Can you hold on to him for a minute?'

I looked at him warily, suspecting he might be trying to coax me into getting used to the dog and therefore changing my mind about keeping him. Jack rolled his eyes and waggled his phone at me. 'I just want to check the hike route on the map.'

'Oh. Right. Yes, of course.'

We walked off slowly as Jack familiarised himself with the direction and then held his hand out for me to hand over the lead. 'We can let him off in a minute anyway.'

'Is that OK? He won't get lost or run into a road?'

'No, he's got a really good recall and we're away from the road now.'

'Oh. Right.'

Jack bent down to unclip the lead. Impulsively, I gave Clive's face a little fuss. 'Now, don't you go running off, OK?'

He appeared to listen for a moment then shot off across the field like a greyhound out of a trap.

Part way around the hike, we came to the high spot of Box Hill. People were sitting on the side of the hill, some lying down, eyes closed as they bathed in the gentle spring sunshine. Children ran up and down the top part of the hill with an energy most of us could only dream of regaining, laughing as they did so. Looking across, fields sectioned into squares caught the sunshine, some cultivated, some green with grass, all divided by hedgerows. Beyond them, the odd space of green peeped through dense forest, the deep green of the trees contrasting with the pastel blue sky. A few more clouds had drifted in now, dotting across it as though in a child's painting.

'Isn't it wonderful to think that Jane Austen might have stood here centuries ago and looked upon a similar view?' I said, hearing the dreamy quality to my voice.

'And then used those memories to create a scene that you've read over and over all these years later.'

'Exactly. I think I'll have to start it again when we get back.' I grinned up at him and he returned it. I was glad the tension of before had dissipated, at least for now.

'Can I pat your dog, please?'

We both turned at the voice. A small boy was standing behind us, looking between us and Clive, who was having a breather from haring about the place, discovering new sniffs, and was currently sprawled out on the ground between Jack's feet and mine.

'I told him he needed to ask first,' his mother said. 'And that some doggies are a bit shy of new people.'

'Thank you,' Jack said, taking the lead, after sensing from a quick glance at me that I had no idea how to proceed. 'That's a good plan.' He crouched down so that he was level with the small boy. 'I'm Jack and this is Clive.'

'I'm Tom.'

'Well, Tom, I think Clive will be very pleased to meet you, especially as you have such lovely manners.'

Tom grinned, showing a missing front tooth, then looked back at his mum who smiled back at him and then at me. Jack began to stroke Clive who looked around, saw a new face and wagged his tail.

'He likes you,' Jack said, making the little boy smile wider as he encouraged him to stroke Clive too, which he then did. In response, Clive let out a groan of happiness and rolled onto his back to silently request his tummy rubbed.

'He likes his tummy tickled!' Tom giggled as Clive's tail swished to and fro on the ground in delight.

'He does indeed.'

After a few minutes of fussing, Tom's mum told him they really ought to leave us to get on with our day. The little boy's face and manner showed reluctance, but he did as he was told. Clive sat up as he moved to see what was going on. Tom leant down a little and gave the dog a big cuddle. Clive rested his head on the boy's shoulder and sighed happily. Once he let go, he took his mum's hand and they both thanked us and Clive before walking off. Jack took a treat from his pocket and gave it to the dog.

'You're such a good lad,' he said, snuggling his face.

'Can I ask you something?'

'Yes.'

'Is it me, or when Clive was getting a hug, did it... no, it doesn't matter. It's daft.'

'What? You've started now.'

'OK, it's just that when the little boy gave Clive a hug, it really looked like he was smiling. The dog, I mean. But obviously that's ridiculous. Dogs don't smile.'

'Who says they don't?'

'Well, they just don't. Do they?'

'I think they do,' said Jack. 'Like you said, it definitely looks like Clive smiles.' He glanced down at the dog, who was now engaged in chasing a butterfly. 'And with Clive, he's such a happy dog, that's quite a lot of the time.'

'He does seem a happy dog, and he was so good with that little boy.'

'Yes, he is. If I'd had any doubts whatsoever, I wouldn't have said yes to little Tom.'

'You made his day. Or Clive did.'

'I think Clive had a lot more to do with it than me. Fancy something to eat now?'

'Absolutely! I'm starving after all that exercise.'

'Me too. Let's go and get the picnic out of the car and find a good spot.'

A short time later, we spread out the blanket that Jack had brought, and Clive was lying on his own rug to the side of us. He'd had a little sniff at the food, been told to lie on his blanket, which he had done and got a treat for, and was now happily snoozing in the shade of a large oak tree, its fresh green leaves bright against the blue sky above. Little shafts of sunlight filtered through as the leaves shimmied in the soft breeze, catching Clive's golden fur and making it almost glow.

'Wow. This all looks amazing, Jack. There's quite a lot here for one person, had I not come...' I looked at him questioningly.

He grinned, then looked down, concentrating on spreading brie on some beautifully crusty bread, before topping it with wild rocket and handing it to me.

I took it, giving him a small smile as I did so. 'Don't worry,' he said. 'I'm not trying to seduce you. I'm not that deluded. You've prepared enough food for me since I've been staying. It's the least I could do.'

This was true, but it was nice cooking for more than just me. I did it for Felix and the crew from time to time, but I'd always enjoyed cooking and there was a definite pleasure to be gained from the appreciation of food prepared by somebody else.

'And yes, you're right. This is quite a lot for one person. I admit, I did hope that you would be accompanying us today on our walk. After our...' he paused, 'disagreement, I was pretty certain that you wouldn't, so I'd like to take this opportunity to thank you and say that I'm really pleased you came.' He gave Clive's side an affectionate rub. 'We both are.'

'Thank you. I'm glad I came too. It's been lovely and I'm really excited to finally come and see the area I've read about so often. I have my own picture of it in my mind now rather than relying on adaptation's interpretations.'

Having eaten our fill, Jack and I took a tip from Clive and lay back on the blanket, side by side. Considerately, Jack had thought to bring a cushion each for our heads and obviously I had a book, which was currently resting on my chest as I gazed at my surroundings.

'You OK?' Jack asked.

'Yes, fine, thank you. Just absorbing it all.'

'Good.'

I rolled my head to the side and noticed that his eyes were closed, the long dark lashes throwing shadows on the light tan of his cheeks. His hands rested, one on top of the other on his broad chest, which moved slowly up and down in an even, rhythmic movement. I looked away and then, after a few seconds, looked back. His breathing deepened, soft, slow and even as he drifted into sleep. I found my page and began to read.

When I opened my eyes an hour later, it was to find that my book had dropped off onto the blanket and I'd turned onto my side, as had Jack. My arms were tucked in front of me and one of Jack's muscular ones was slung across me. Oh, crap. Now how did I get out of this?

17

I began to try to shift from my position with the least amount of movement possible in order to avoid waking Jack. The last thing I needed right now was for him to wake up to find us like this. Either Jack would make jokes about how I'd orchestrated it, and tease me when I denied it, which I knew he would be able to goad me into no matter how hard I tried not to be drawn in, or there was the opposite end of the scale, where he woke up and felt horribly awkward and we'd both try to pretend it hadn't happened, while knowing all the while it had. I wasn't sure which was worse. Possibly the second scenario. The teasing at least would get boring and he'd eventually stop. Awkwardness could last a lot longer. The ideal situation, though, was that he never found out, so I continued with my stealth moves, stopping in my tracks, and holding my breath as he made a sound in his sleep and moved again. Unfortunately, his shift in position undid all my work and set me back at the beginning. I needed a new plan.

'Oof!' Jack sat up hurriedly as Clive put his paw and a certain amount of weight on a more delicate part of his anatomy. 'Clive, mate! What you doing?'

'Sorry,' I said from where I was now also sitting up. In the confusion and, probably, shock, Jack had moved so fast I was pretty sure he hadn't noticed anything except where the dog had stood, admittedly encouraged by me with a strategically placed treat that I'd managed to wriggle out from the nearby picnic basket. Yes, I know it was a low trick, so to speak, but desperate times call for desperate measures. 'Don't blame him. That was my fault, I'm afraid. We were playing and got a bit carried away.'

Jack eyed me for a moment, sitting hunched and with his green eyes sparkling even more than usual, but this time I was pretty sure the cause was pain rather than merriment and the unshed tears of a paw to the groin. He gave a tight nod. I did honestly feel quite bad. I hadn't meant for him to be hurt, just a bit uncomfy momentarily in order to extricate myself. Hopefully there wasn't any lasting damage.

'Must have nodded off.'

'Yes.'

'Did you get a nap?' His eyes drifted to the book on my lap. 'Or just read?'

'No, I think I managed a nap too. All this fresh air and good food.'

Jack smiled a little less tightly now and nodded. 'It can do that to you. Throw in some warmth and peace and it's the perfect recipe for a snooze.' He looked up to the sky. 'Those clouds have built since we've been asleep, though.'

My gaze followed his. To the west of us, the wispy white clouds of earlier had grown in both height and volume, filling the sky, shot through with the odd dark streak.

'Is that bad?'

'Could mean there's some rain on the way. They did say on the radio there was a chance of storms later today. Might be an idea to begin packing up and heading back to the car, if that's OK with you?'

'Of course it is.'

'You still up for that roast on the way home?'

I looked down at my stomach. 'If I can find room!'

Jack laughed. 'I'm sure you'll manage. Seriously, this place I have in mind is great. You don't want to miss out.'

'Now I'll have to experience it, won't I? You can't just give that sort of lead-up and then not follow through.'

He grinned. 'You won't regret it.'

'I might do when I can't get my jeans on tomorrow.'

'Oh, pfft,' he said rolling up the blanket as I tided up the last remnants of the picnic. 'We've walked quite a few miles today, so you've burnt it off already.'

'Glad to hear it. Then I shall look forward to it guilt free.'

'As you should. Come on then, Clive. Back to the car.'

Clive trotted happily alongside us, unattached to a lead but as close as he would be with one.

'He's very good, isn't he?'

'He is,' Jack said, glancing down at the dog. The picnic basket swung from one hand and the blanket we'd sat on was rolled and tucked under the other arm. I'd tried to carry one of the things, but he'd wrestled them both off me in the nicest way possible and handed me the dog lead, should we need it. Watching Clive now, it was pretty obvious we weren't going to. Once we were all safely ensconced inside the car, Jack reversed and headed back down the hill onto the main road, in the direction of the pub whose praises he'd been singing.

* * *

He had been exactly right. The roast dinner we had both just enjoyed had to be one of the best I've ever eaten. Golden, crispy potatoes which, when cut open, steamed as they showed their fluffy insides. Light, airy Yorkshire puddings, crisp, fresh veg and perfectly cooked beef, all drowned in delicious, thick home-made gravy. The pudding menu looked just as lovely, but I really didn't have any more space. As it was, I wasn't sure I'd need to eat for the next week. Somehow Jack found room for a sticky toffee pudding, swimming in delicious pale custard, and I succumbed to testing a spoonful, confirming that it did indeed taste even better than it looked. All the while, Clive slept contentedly under the table.

Having to practically roll ourselves out of the pub, we loaded ourselves into the car and headed for home. The clouds of earlier had now multiplied and darkened and, although a faint strip of pale pink hovered on the horizon, the rest of the sky was far less inviting than it had been earlier today.

'I think you might have been right about that rain. It's looking a bit ominous up there.'

'It is. With a bit of luck, we'll get home before the clouds break.'

* * *

We did, but not by much. As we were standing in the kitchen, unpacking the picnic basket, Clive had padded over to his bed and curled up, Hot Dog under one paw, the first few spots of rain began pit patting against the windows. By the time we'd finished, it had become a steady fall. Checking that Clive was comfortable, I told Jack that I was going to head up for a bath, and he mentioned he had similar plans.

'Do you want a glass of wine to take up?'

I smiled. 'That's very lush.'

'I know, but it can be our secret, I promise.' He made a cross your heart sign on his chest.

'Very funny. A Baileys over ice would be nice, though.'

'Good choice. Coming right up.'

'I'm just going to start my bath. I'll pop down and get it in a minute.'

With that, I left the kitchen, grabbing my book on the way and headed up to my en suite, turning on the taps and dropping in my favourite bath essence, at once filling the steamy air with lavender and rose.

'Knock knock,' a voice called from my room.

Heading through the bedroom to where the door stood ajar, and pulling it open, I found Jack standing there with a large glass of Baileys. At its centre was a huge ice cube. I always preferred these to the smaller ones as they took longer to melt and didn't dilute my drink quite so quickly. Not to mention they looked cool too.

'Thanks. You didn't need to bring it up.'

'You were on my route,' he said, smiling softly down.

'Thanks again for today,' I said as I took the drink from him.

'You're very welcome. I'm really glad you enjoyed it. And I'm sorry if I said some things before that I shouldn't have. I'd never hurt or upset you for the world. I know it probably didn't seem that way, but I need you to know that it's true.'

I looked up into the depths of those beautiful green eyes. 'I know it's true,' I confirmed. 'At least I'm sure where I stand with you.'

He gave a soft smile. 'There is that.' He lifted his head a moment, sniffing the air like Clive had earlier when someone had lit a portable barbecue. 'That smells wonderful.'

'It's really relaxing. Do you want some for your bath?'

'Umm, no. No, that's fine. I've got some Radox. That's fine.'

I laughed. 'I promise I won't tell either,' I whispered.

Jack took a step closer, his chest millimetres away now as he tilted his head down. 'How do I know I can trust you not to ruin my reputation as an outdoorsy, tough guy type?'

'You know that's not what people really think, don't you?'

'Huh?' He stepped back and looked surprised. 'They don't?'

I couldn't keep the straight face I'd fixed on. 'OK. They do, but it's actually posh outdoorsy tough guy type.'

He pulled a face at me. 'Great.'

'Oh, don't be so silly,' I said, turning away in order to go and stop my bath, and grab the bath crème. Putting a little more distance between me and Jack for a moment might have also had something to do with it. Believe me, there was no chance the general population had any doubt as to the veracity of Jack being a gorgeous specimen of alpha masculinity and I wouldn't be among those questioning that. Sometimes, when Jack was close, it was easy to feel like a planet being sucked into his gravity field. And I knew that wasn't a good idea. I had my own orbit that I'd been happily, or mostly happily, pootling around in for the last decade or so. I definitely didn't need any celestial moments to come along and wreck all that.

* * *

As I lay back in the bath, surrounded by bubbles and heady scents, I could hear the rain begin to fall more heavily. There was something comforting about being inside, warm and relaxed with the soft wash of rain hushing the sounds of the evening outside. I took a sip of the Baileys that Jack had brought me, before resting it on the small table to the side of the bath. Picking up my book, I began to read.

Between the exercise, good food and a relaxing soak, I was asleep almost as soon as my head touched the soft, expensive cotton of my pillowcase. Three hours later, I was woken suddenly by a huge and extremely loud crack of thunder breaking close to the house. My eyes flew open as I lay there, frozen for a moment, my brain putting together all the pieces as it roused itself from the deep sleep I had been enjoying until that moment. Just as it was doing so, another huge clap resonated and I pushed back the covers, grabbed my dressing gown and headed downstairs.

Clive was standing by the sofa, his tail tucked under, and upon hearing me by the door, he practically flattened me as I entered, launching himself at me, and almost winding his body around my legs. I crouched down.

'It's OK, sweetheart. I'm here. It can't hurt you.' I cuddled him to me. His body shook with fear, making me hold him closer. After some more soothing words, I stood and pulled his bed over to the front of the sofa, holding out Hot Dog for him to take. Clive took him gently and followed my silent instruction to get into his bed. I grabbed one of the blankets and tucked it around him and then settled myself next to him on the sofa, lying down so that I could rest my hand on him, letting him know I was there before pulling a quilt that normally draped over the side of the sofa up over me. Clive gave a couple of whines but, with a few more strokes, seemed to settle.

After a few minutes, Clive sat up again. 'It's all right, boy,' I tried to soothe but he was focused on the door, whining at it. Outside, the thunder rumbled again. It seemed to be stuck right above the house. I pushed back the quilt and followed Clive over, trying to coax him back to his bed with gentle movements and words. Suddenly the door pushed open slowly, and in the bright flash of lightning that accompanied it, from my crouched position next to the dog, I found myself face to face with a pair of muscular legs.

'Hi,' a deep, sleep-roughened voice above them said.

'Hello,' I said, straightening up and, with kind permission of another bolt, saw shorts, T-shirt and what, in my books, would be described as that just out of bed, sexily ruffled look some men do so well. Like I didn't have enough to contend with.

'You OK?'

'Yes, thanks. It's a bit loud out there, isn't it?'

Jack was crouched now, fussing Clive. 'It is. I came down to check on him, but I can see I was slow to the party,' he said, straightening up and leading Clive gently but firmly back to his bed. I briefly lit up my phone to help him see his way.

'I wasn't sure if he would be all right with the storm. I know some animals don't like them.'

'By the looks of it, that includes this one. That was kind of you.' He turned immediately, holding up his hands. 'That sounded way more patronising than it was supposed to. I mean, obviously it wasn't meant to be patronising at all.'

'It's fine,' I said, touching his arm briefly. 'I know what you meant. You can go back up to bed, if you like. I think we're all right here.'

'I don't mind sitting up for a while.' He paused as another loud crack broke over the house. 'It's not exactly like I'm going to be getting much sleep anyway.'

'It does rather seem that way. I can make some hot drinks, if you'd like,' I said, snuggling Clive back under the blanket and tucking Hot Dog in with him.

'Nope,' he said, straightening out the quilt I'd been lying underneath. 'You were obviously pretty comfy under there before I came down. You get back in there and I'll make the drinks.'

'You don't have to do that.'

'I know I don't. But I want to. Come on, in you hop.'

'I'm not five.'

'Oh, just get in, woman,' Jack hustled, with laughter in his voice.

'For that, you can make the drinks.'

'Good. At last, she lets me do something.'

'I let you do stuff all the time,' I said, clambering onto the sofa. Jack gave me a look as I snuggled into a position that was just horizontal enough to be able to drink my drink without choking, once it arrived. Gently, he laid the quilt back over me. 'Comfy?'

'Yes... umm, thanks,' I stammered, caught up for a moment at the tenderness of the gesture, and the softness of his voice. In the darkness of the kitchen, neither of us having yet switched on the light, the simple act seemed to take on a level of intimacy that I hadn't expected – and hadn't experienced – in a long time. I gave myself a mental shake, dissolving the thought. Jack was just being kind and doing the same for me as I had done for Clive a short time before, and I was sure no similar thought had even brushed past his mind, let alone gone through it.

'You OK?' he asked. 'From what I can see in the lightning flashes, you're frowning so hard it looks like your eyebrows might actually drop off.'

'Still got all the smooth lines, haven't you?'

'I'm sure they're still buried in here somewhere, not that I've used them in a long time. Besides, there's no way I'd use a line on you. It'd be utterly pointless.'

'Well, yes, of course. Absolutely.'

He gave the quilt one last tuck, before straightening. 'You know me too well and would see straight through it.' He turned and walked away to make the drinks before I could come up with a pithy – or any – reply. Perhaps there was no reply to be made. Except that I wasn't sure I did know Jack these days. Felix had always been pretty astute, and he must have sensed there was more to Jack than met the eye long ago. And now Jack had discovered who he was, become content and grown. My life, on the other hand, had shrunk and I'd thought I was happy in my little bubble. I *was* happy in my little bubble, until Jack Coulsdon-Hart had walked through my door and back into my life.

18

'You're still frowning.' Jack glanced over from where he was now highlighted by the light above the hob built into the kitchen island.

'Ugh!' I flung myself down and pulled the quilt over my head. 'I remember the days I could frown in peace in my own home,' I said from under the covers.

The only answer was a ripple of deep, warm laughter that filled the kitchen and wrapped itself around me before being drowned out by the storm.

We sat on the sofa, content in each other's company, sipping our drinks. I'd made to move when he came over, but Jack had shaken his head, then put the drinks down on the side table before lifting my feet and sitting down again, resting them on his lap. Turning, he then reached and handed me a cup of steaming hot chocolate, made with full-fat milk and mini marshmallows, neither of which he'd have found in my cupboards ordinarily.

'When did you sneak these goodies in?' I said, before closing my eyes in bliss at the deliciousness. Outside, the storm raged but with both of us near, Clive seemed far more contented. I knew he wasn't asleep, as his ears were twitching, but the rhythmic stroking of his side by Jack's foot kept him settled as we huddled together, cosy and safe.

'It's always good to have emergency supplies.'

'I wasn't aware full-fat milk and mini marshmallows were considered vital for emergencies. I assume the British Armed Forces are aware of this.'

'Absolutely. Where do you think I got the tip from?'

I smiled. Jack had left the light on over the hob and in the low light that reached this side of the diner, I saw him return it. And then it all went dark.

The faint light from the security lights outside that had taken the edge off total darkness earlier now disappeared too as the storm took out a power line somewhere.

'You all right?' Through the quilt, Jack gave my toes a gentle squeeze.

'Yes, thanks. I'm a bit old to be afraid of the dark.'

'Fears often aren't rational and are certainly no respecter of age.'

'Are you all right?' I asked, suddenly aware that Jack was right. Fears had no respect for gender expectations either.

'Yeah, fine.'

'You're right, though. And thank you for asking. I suppose living alone for so long, you generally just end up having to deal with things, whether you like them or not. I'm not a big lover of spiders, but when there's no one else to call upon, you have to find a way, don't you?'

'Clive loves spiders.'

'He does?'

'Yep. Good at catching them, too.'

'Really? What does he do with them?'

'Eats them, usually.'

'That's gross.'

Jack chuckled. 'To be fair, there are far worse things he could eat and he doesn't. At least this is a useful trait, assuming you don't have a pet spider, I suppose.'

I gave an involuntary shiver and Jack chuckled again. 'I felt that.'

'Ugh. I just can't...'

'No, not my idea of the perfect pet either.'

'Each to their own, I guess.'

'Uh-huh.'

We sat in silence for a few more minutes, the house occasionally being brilliantly lit by nature before falling back into pitch darkness.

'Shall I get some candles?'

'I'm quite happy sat here in the dark if you are,' Jack replied softly.

And oddly enough, I was.

'Why don't you try to get some rest? It sounds like the storm is moving away a little now.' The thunder had definitely got quieter and the gaps between the booming claps had lengthened.

'You can go back up to bed,' I tried again.

'I could. But it might unsettle Clive.'

I wriggled onto my side, having slid down again once I'd finished my drink. The dog was finally sleeping, one paw and his nose now resting on Jack's foot.

'Blimey. Rather him than me.'

'Oh, funny. I had a bath in your girly bubble bath stuff, don't forget.'

How could I? The scent of it, mixed with the scent that was just Jack, had drifted on the air to me when I'd opened the door earlier and come face to legs with him. I'd been trying to get it out of my nostrils ever since. Not because it was unpleasant. More because it was most definitely not unpleasant. I didn't need delicious smells on good-looking, hard muscled in all the right places men to addle my brain.

'I can't even see you and I know you're frowning.'

'How can you possibly know that? It's pitch black.'

'Your body's gone all tense and rigid.'

'It has not,' I said, feeling as tight as a snare drum.

'What are you stressing about?'

Ha! You're not getting that out of me in a million years.

'I'm not. It's nothing. I mean, nothing. Because I'm not.'

'Right.'

'Right.'

'Get some rest.'

'How are you going to sleep, sitting up like that?'

Jack gave a wiggle to get comfy, gently held on to my feet when I tried to pull them up out of the way so that I wouldn't be curled up like an ammonite and, from the movement, I guessed pulled a little of the quilt over his chest.

'I've slept in all sorts of places and positions.'

'Why don't I doubt that?'

He gave a low laugh and squeezed my leg so briefly I wondered if I'd imagined it. 'Go to sleep.'

I lay there for a moment, trying to decide whether this was nice or weird or if it was something else entirely.

'Stop frowning and go to sleep.'

My brain was hurting by this point, so I gave up and did as he suggested.

* * *

Twenty minutes later, I was awoken by a somewhat muffled 'Oww', and Jack shifting on the sofa.

'You're not comfortable, are you?'

'I'm fine,' he said, smothering another groan.

'You're clearly not. Come on, up you get,' I said, pulling the quilt away and standing. Clive woke, stretched and then watched us, waiting to see what happened, the odd whine sent out in question.

'You've woken the dog up now.'

'He was bound to wake up sooner or later with all your moaning and groaning. Come on, shift.'

Feeling my way cautiously to the dresser, I pulled out a couple of candles kept there for emergencies, along with the matches, and lit them.

'You go back up to bed. I'll stay here with Clive until the storm passes completely,' Jack suggested, stretching his neck and back.

'It's fine, we can both stay. I mean, if you think that's best.'

We both looked down to where Clive was now practically glued to my leg.

'I'm pretty sure he wants you to stay.'

'OK.' I walked back to the sofa, gently moved Jack to the side and reached into the back, grabbing the frame of the sofa bed and pulling it out into the diner. Tucked inside was a sheet and two pillows. I flicked one side of the sheet over towards Jack as I moved around to the other side of the bed and we quickly made the bed up.

In the flickering candlelight, I saw Jack look across at me. 'Just so that I don't make some awful faux pas here, can you just confirm something to me?'

'Yes, it is for both of us. It's no big deal. You stay on your side, I stay on my side and Clive stays happy. Or you can go back up to bed. Whichever you prefer,' I said, grabbing one of the candles and wandering over to where the light for the hob was still on, despite there being no power. If I did manage to get to sleep, the last thing I wanted was a light beaming out once the power came back on.

'You sure?'

'For goodness' sake, it's just somewhere to sleep. You might take up a certain amount of space, but luckily I'm quite petite. Other than that, I'm pretty sure I can resist you.'

In the candlelight, I could see Jack give me a look I couldn't decipher. 'I'm pretty sure you can too. You always did, apart from that one moment at the fête.'

'Yes, well, that was more to do with the amount of alcohol I'd ingested, rather than a sudden realisation I couldn't live without you. Sorry about that.'

'I'm sure I'll get over it eventually.'

'I'm sure you will. Right, Clive. Come on, lie down. You've got what you wanted. Everyone's here and we need some sleep. We don't get to lie about all day like you do.' He did as I asked and settled himself tidily into the bed, dragging Hot Dog closer with a paw.

'Good boy,' I said, ruffling his head. 'Now you go back to sleep, OK? You're safe now and we're here, so there's nothing to worry about.' Clive nuzzled my hand in response and then plopped his head down.

'For someone who's never had, and doesn't want, a dog, you're doing a decent impression of being very good at it.'

'Don't start,' I said, blowing out one candle and placing the other on the side table next to me before pulling back the quilt. For a second, I hesitated.

'It's just a bed.' His deep voice repeated my own words.

'You're such a smart-arse,' I replied. He, and I, were right. It was. And if it made Clive feel more comfortable, then I could make do.

Jack let out a small, deep chuckle before turning on his side away from me. I got in and did the same so that we were back to back with a decent sized gap between us. I debated momentarily about stuffing one of the decorative cushions from the sofa between us but that seemed like overkill.

'You'd better not snore.'

'I was just thinking the same,' he fired back, although I could hear the smile in the dark.

I now regretted not having the extra cushion to hand so that I could have bopped him with it.

* * *

The dawn broke in epic golden beauty, streaked with red and purple, vibrant and breathtaking, as though last night's storm had washed the sky clean, allowing its colours to be revealed in their full glory. With as little movement as possible, in order not to disturb a still sleeping Jack and Clive, I extricated myself from the bed. Jack appeared not to have moved from the position he'd settled into before I'd blown out the candle a few hours previously, and thankfully hadn't snored.

I moved to the glass doors and took a moment to bask in the glory of the nature that met my eyes. Man could create beautiful things, but nature always had the upper hand.

'There's a sight for sore eyes.' A deep voice broke the silence.

I turned, and the green eyes locked onto mine, causing the familiar flush to begin to creep up my neck. 'The sky, I mean.'

Nodding quickly, I turned back to the garden, mortified that, for a split second, I thought he'd meant something else.

'Yes. It's beautiful, isn't it?'

'It really is.'

A click of toenails alerted me to the dog, and I opened the door so that he could go out and do all the investigation and ablutions he needed to. Much to my surprise, he was soon back in and trotting back to his bed. I watched him settle in and close his eyes, dropping back to sleep almost immediately.

'Looks like someone else is as tired as we are,' Jack said through a yawn, resting up on his elbows and looking over at the dog.

'I'm all right.'

'OK, if I say something, are you going to take it the wrong way?'

'I imagine that depends entirely on what you plan to say.'

'Just promise not to take it wrong.'

Walking over to the dog bed, I laid the little blanket I'd found in a cupboard over him before looking back at my two-legged house-guest. 'How about if I endeavour to do my best not to?'

'Sounds like a deal.'

'Spit it out, then.'

'You look knackered.'

'Right.'

'But in a good way. Obviously.'

'Obviously.'

'Come back to bed.'

I rolled my eyes but couldn't help smiling. At least he was honest. 'I bet you say that to all the girls,' I teased him again.

'Not for a very long time.'

And I believed him.

* * *

'Anyone in?' my brother's voice bellowed moments before he opened the back doors I'd forgotten to lock after letting Clive out and climbing back into the warm bed. Jack had been right. I was knackered and we'd both fallen back asleep almost immediately. Obviously, we were both wide awake now, sitting up next to each other in the sofa bed and staring silently back at my brother, Poppy and both children.

19

'Doggy!'

Clive was up and wagging his tail at the new people, all potential playmates.

'Umm, is he OK with kids?'

'Excellent,' Jack said, sounding just as sleep roughened as he had earlier, and I tried to ignore the flutterings that voice caused.

'Out you go then, kids. Be nice to Clive.' All three of them hared off into the garden as though it was their first taste of freedom in years. Felix and Poppy then turned back to us.

'Shall we come back?' My brother's eyes switched between us, lingering with what I knew was suspicion on Jack.

'No! It's fine. And this isn't what it looks like either,' I said, staring at Felix pointedly. 'Clive was upset last night and wouldn't settle properly. Jack tried sleeping sitting up but that wasn't working, despite his protestations that it was. And the last thing he needs to do is knacker his neck or back whilst he's trying to build up his business.'

Under the covers, out of sight of my family, Jack's little finger brushed mine in thanks. He'd obviously not missed Felix's look either. They might be old friends, but Felix had always been protective of me, especially since the accident. He might want me to move on with my life and probably meet someone, but he'd also be mad as hell if he thought someone was trying to take advantage of me. Jack Coulsdon-Hart had a reputation and, although he claimed to have left those days behind, I could see this from Felix's point of view. He'd just walked in to find his old lothario friend, who he'd effectively placed in my house, in bed with his sister.

'We'll just go and see how the kids are getting on and come back shortly,' Poppy smiled, gently tugging my brother out of the door and closing it behind them.

Jack turned to me. 'I'm pretty sure if looks could kill, you'd be having to bury me in the garden this afternoon.'

'He'll be fine. Anyway, I'm not messing up my garden by sticking your big lump in it. Although maybe you'll make good fertiliser?'

'Thanks.' He smiled.

I smiled back. And then I began to laugh. Once I started, I couldn't stop and, before long, Jack was joining in. The farcical situation, the look on Felix and Poppy's faces and the shock on Jack's. I didn't imagine that it was the first time he'd been caught in bed with someone, but his face had been almost as shocked as theirs.

'I'm glad you think it's funny.'

'Oh my God,' I said, trying to stop. My stomach was hurting now, but I didn't care. It felt good. I felt good. 'Your face.'

'I thought Felix was going to finish me off with a bread knife then and there.'

'He knows better than to mess up my kitchen like that,' I said, lying back, exhausted from the giggling fit.

Jack looked down at me. 'You look happy.'

I looked back up at him, his hair sticking up at odd angles and a dark shadow on his jaw from a few days without a shave. 'I haven't laughed like that since... honestly? I can't remember.'

'Then it's too long.'

'Yes,' I replied softly. 'I think you're probably right.'

'Can I say something, without it seeming weird?'

'You can try,' I said, pushing myself up.

'I had a really nice time yesterday, including all this. Well, maybe not getting a death glare from your brother.'

'He'll be fine,' I repeated.

'Yep, I hope so. But the rest of it. The walk, the meal, camping out here with you and the dog. I don't think I've felt this relaxed in a long time. And I don't think I realised that either.'

'Thank you for goading me into taking the walk yesterday.'

He laughed and bopped me with the pillow as I swung my feet round and placed them on the tiles, comfortably warm from the underfloor heating.

'I didn't goad you into doing anything.'

'Oh, yes you did.' I laughed, over my shoulder. 'You knew if you wound me up enough, I'd do it just to prove you wrong.'

'It didn't work, did it? I mean the proving me wrong bit.'

'Don't be smug,' I said, taking the pillow off him and shoving it at him. 'Now get up and stop making my kitchen look untidy.'

He grinned and briefly touched my hand before hopping out the other side. 'I'll put this back up when I come back down. OK?' Jack said, as he disappeared out into the hall and up the stairs.

'Uh-huh,' I replied, peering round the corner to make sure he'd gone and then proceeded to strip the bed and refold it into a sofa before running upstairs to get changed and clean my teeth.

When I came back, Felix, Poppy and Jack were sitting around the island, apparently once again at ease with each other and watching the kids pelting about the garden with Clive. Jack saw me enter the room first.

'I see you took no notice of me.' He inclined his head towards the sofa before taking a sip of strong black coffee.

I shrugged. 'I can't hang around waiting for you.'

'I was literally five minutes.'

'By which time it was already done.'

'You're impossible, woman.'

'I've told her that before. Many times.'

'Yes, all right,' I said, flicking Felix lightly on the ear as I passed. 'You don't have to join in. I'm used to doing things for myself. That's not a bad quality, you know.'

'So, I hear Clive is going back today?' Felix said.

'Um... well... yes, he was supposed to.' I glanced at the clock. 'Don't you have a client today?' I asked Jack.

'No, I took the day off today as I was kind of hoping to be helping you settle Clive in.'

'Oh. I see.' I looked out to where the three bundles of energy were now playing catch and walked towards the door, opening it a little to watch better and feeling a sudden need for fresh air. Hearing, or sensing movement, Clive stopped and then charged towards me, his tail wagging madly as he ran. Approaching me, he slowed at a pace car makers would be proud of and nuzzled his head under my elbow into my tummy as I crouched. I laughed, rubbing his fur as I sat back and looked at his beautiful face, its big smile accessorised with a large pink tongue. This dog definitely smiled, and I loved it. But I couldn't keep him. It was too much. I knew how much I already felt for him, and I knew how dangerous that could be. Even a good life for a dog was nowhere near long enough... I bent and kissed his head and Clive zoomed back to the kids and continued the game with his new friends.

Turning back, I met three pairs of eyes.

'No. He's not staying. It wouldn't work. But... as he's having fun with the children and had a stressful night, it might be an idea for him to stay today, especially as Jack is going to be here. I mean,' I

said, looking at him, 'you know, as you've taken the day off anyway.'
I gave a shrug to punctuate things.

'Yeah,' he nodded. 'That makes sense. He did have a disturbed night, so it might be good for him to have a settled, relaxed day today before I take him away again.'

I tried not to focus on the last part of his sentence and instead kept focused on all the reasons getting a dog wouldn't be a good idea. There was no denying Clive was a lovely dog and would make someone a wonderful pet. It was just that that someone wasn't me.

'I was wondering if you'd decided what to wear to the premiere yet,' Poppy said, sensing a change of subject might be a good idea right about now.

'Oh God, no. I haven't. I'm thinking about going back to my agent and—'

'No.'

'No what?'

'You're going. You agreed.'

'I know, but—'

'You're going. I need all the gossip on what the stars are like in real life and all the dresses, and stuff.'

'Can't you just buy a copy of *Hello*?'

'You're going,' Poppy said. She was barely five foot and looked like a china doll, but I knew from all the years she'd been married to my brother that beneath that fragile exterior lay a will of iron. It appeared I was going to the premiere.

* * *

'That's it!' Poppy clapped her hands at what felt like the eleventy-seventh dress I'd tried on today.

'You said that about the one before last as well,' I said, facing away from the mirror and craning my neck to look at the back of the dress. 'It's kind of low,' I added, seeing the amount of bare skin exposed back there.

'I know I did but no, it's this one. Definitely. This is it. It's stunning and, oh my God, it looks amazing on you. Very sexy!' She waggled her eyebrows.

'I'm not sure I'm particularly interested in looking sexy.'

'Too bad, because you do. Jack's going to melt when he sees you in this.'

'Hardly. Besides, he'd better not. Knowing I'm going to have someone to talk to there is the only reason I'm actually going at all.'

'And it doesn't help that that someone looks better than most of the movie stars?'

'I hadn't really thought about that aspect.'

Poppy laughed. 'If your nose grows any more, we're going to have difficulty getting you out of this changing room.'

'Oh, very funny. OK, yes, I admit he's good-looking. And I actually think he's got better with age.'

'Like a fine wine.'

'I wouldn't go that far, and definitely don't tell him I said that.'

'Would I?'

'Yes. Besides, neither of you looked that thrilled at the possibility we might have got together the other day.'

'That was just surprise.'

'Felix looked like the thunder from the night before.'

'Yeah, well,' said Poppy. 'You know what he's like.'

'Yes. Always telling me I need to move on. And then, when it actually looks like I might have, he looks like he wants to bury the man in question under my patio.'

'I think his instincts just kicked in for a moment. I mean, we all know what Jack was like years ago. Breaking hearts all over the place. Felix just didn't want you to be another.'

'You two are the ones who are always saying he's not like that anymore.'

'He's not. You must have noticed that from the time he's been staying with you.'

'Well, it's true he doesn't really go out much. Quite a few evenings, we both end up in the snug reading.'

'That's good. Cosy.'

'Yeah, it is nice to have some company, even when you're not talking and... oh, no. Don't look at me like that.'

'Like what?' Poppy's face was a mask of innocence. I, however, knew better.

'Like that,' I said, pointing at her face.

'I'm sure I don't know what you mean.'

'I'm sure you do.'

'Oh, all right, but come on, it's not like it would be the worst thing in the world to happen, would it?'

'It wouldn't be the best thing either,' I said. 'Besides, Jack's definitely not interested in me like that. We're friends – most of the time – and that's plenty for both of us.'

'If you say so.'

'I do say so. Now can you help get out of this dress so that I don't rip it?'

'Are you going to keep it?'

I turned and looked once more in the mirror. The full-length midnight blue satin dress with its bias cut and soft folds of cowl neck looked demure and elegant from the front. The back, however, was another story, with two thin crossover straps securing the fabric as it dipped in a low enough position to be decent but a heck of a lot lower than I'd ever worn before. Added to that were the thigh-high splits each side of the flowing skirt. So long as I stood still, you couldn't see anything, but the moment I walked, there was a distinctive and unmistakable flash of leg. But I had to agree with

Poppy. I loved the dress. It had been such a long time since I'd put on anything this beautiful or glamorous. I had got so used to relaxed, comfy fit clothing that it felt like a different person staring back at me in the mirror. The party at Jack's parents' place had been a smart-casual thing, but this really was a whole other level.

I looked down at where Poppy was perched on a gold-coloured chair in the corner of the lavish dressing room.

'Poppy!' I bent down and took her hands in mine. 'Whatever is the matter?' I dived into my bag with one hand and passed her a tissue for her eyes, which were shining with tears.

'Nothing. Nothing at all. It's all perfect. It's just that... it sort of feels like I'm seeing you again for the first time in such a long time. The real you.'

I squeezed her hand and then we both caught a glimpse of the expanse of thigh I was now showing in my current position.

'Well, you're certainly seeing quite a lot of me. That's for sure.'

'You look amazing. Now, come on, let's get you dressed. We need shoes and a bag yet.'

'I'm pretty sure I have shoes at home somewhere that will do.'

'Nope, no good. For your first proper social occasion in years, especially a glamorous one like this, you need all new things.'

I let out a sigh. 'Then, first of all, I need a huge pot of tea and an even bigger slice of cake.'

20

By the end of the day, I'd spent more money on one outfit than I had in about a decade on everyday clothes.

'Manage to find something?' Felix asked when Poppy and I walked through the door later that evening.

'I went shopping with your wife. What do you think?'

Felix pulled a face. 'Fair point. I did marry a shopping demon.'

'I prefer the term shopping genius,' Poppy replied, placing a couple of bags down with her own purchases inside.

'I stand corrected. I married a beautiful shopping genius.'

'Thank you,' she said, walking over and giving him a kiss. 'Did you boys have a good day? How are the kids?'

'Watching a film in the other room, although it's remarkably quiet.' Felix pushed himself up. 'I think I'll go and check on them. We took them out for a long walk earlier, so I think that tired them out.' He went off and Poppy followed him.

'I know how they feel,' I said, plopping down on the sofa that Felix had just vacated.

'Hard day?' Jack asked from the seat next to me.

'I'd forgotten how much stamina I needed for shopping with Poppy.'

'You got something nice, though, by the sounds of it.'

'I did. I kind of baulked at the price tag, but it's not many times you get to go to a big production film premiere, is it? The last thing I want to do is show myself up.'

'You would never show yourself up.'

'Thanks for the confidence, but to say I'm out of practise at anything remotely social, let alone anything this size, is an understatement.'

'You'll do fine. We'll just have a nice evening.'

'Auntie Lily!' Suddenly, two small children came hurtling down the corridor and launched themselves at me. I heard a muffled 'oof' as something of Freddy's connected with something of Jack's.

'Mind what you're doing,' I said as I gave them both an enormous cuddle. 'We can't injure Jack before he finishes my garden, can we?' I asked, as I gave them a tickle.

They giggled and wriggled and wrapped their arms around my neck as I cuddled them to me. Freddy then wiggled across to Jack and began climbing up on his shoulders.

'Don't you fall off there. I'm not cleaning any blood up.'

As I looked across to Jack, he had his hands firmly on Freddy's legs, sending me a silent promise with his eyes that there is no way he'd let go. I gave the tiniest nod to show I understood before rearranging Ruby on my lap a little more comfortably.

As I cleared my view of children, I was finally able to see Clive, who was now sitting so close to the sofa as to be almost upon it without actually being so. His bum hadn't quite touched the floor in his excitement and his tail was whipping from side to side like some mad duster on overdrive. With one hand wrapped around Ruby, I leant forward and gave the dog a cuddle and a kiss on the top of his silky head.

His day of return to the shelter had been put off, first by one day, then by another, then by a week, and then permanently. I think I'd known from the moment he gave me his first goofy grin that I was already in trouble and then that night of the storm sealed both his and my fate. I loved his company and, even when he was asleep, I never felt alone. I wasn't quite sure how well he'd cope once Jack left, as the moment he came in the door, Clive went absolutely mad, encouraged, I had to add, by Jack. Hopefully he'd be all right. Hopefully we'd both be all right.

'You guys ready for some dinner?' Felix said, having now had a poke around in Poppy's shopping, which she couldn't wait to show him.

'Absolutely famished.'

'Me too,' Poppy added. 'Being a style consultant can be very hard work. What's for dinner?'

'Chilli con carne with rice, guacamole, and sour cream. There are nachos as well, although the kids may have been at them already, and I think Clive hoovered up a few from the floor.'

This was another bonus that I discovered to having a dog. You had an inbuilt vacuum in the event that you ever spilled food. This was all well and good for the odd nacho crumb, but I had discovered it was less of a bonus when the sausages I had just cooked for my sausage sandwich rolled off the plate straight onto the floor and were swallowed in one gulp by Clive.

'Sounds great,' I said through a yawn.

'It won't take too long to heat up, but do you want to go and have a lie down before we dish up?' Jack asked. 'You look tired.'

'No, I'm fine,' I replied through another large yawn.

I could feel Jack's eyes on me for a moment before he gave my leg a quick pat and pushed himself up off the sofa, scooping my niece up on the way past as he made his way into the kitchen end of the room.

'Uncle Jack, can you be a horsey now?'

'Ruby, Daddy said Uncle Jack spent about an hour this after-noon charging around with you on his back. Don't you think you ought to give the horsey a rest now?'

From the look on her little face, Ruby definitely didn't think the horse needed a rest. She wound her fingers together turning from side to side on the spot and nodded anyway. 'OK.'

Jack crouched down next to her, one of his knees making a loud crack as he did so. 'How about five more minutes of horsey before dinner and then you and Freddy go and get washed up. Deal?'

'Deal!' she said, jumping up and down in excitement, her cherubic little face now wearing a wide grin and the bright blue eyes shining. She flung her arms around Jack and gave him a big kiss on the cheek. 'I love you, Uncle Jack.'

'I love you too, chickpea.'

'Can you bend down now? I can't get on.'

'How about we go outside in the garden? The floor's a bit hard for Uncle Jack's old knees in here.'

She was out of the door before you could say tally-ho.

'I want to ride too!' Freddy said, charging out after them. Moments later, Jack was tramping about on his hands and knees with both the children on his back, geeing him up to go faster.

'I think he might be regretting coming back from New Zealand right about now,' Felix said, standing at the threshold of the bi-fold doors.

I went to stand beside him. Jack was a big bloke, but the two children together bouncing up and down were definitely no light-weights. The smile on his face and the deep laughter that rang across the garden, mingling with theirs, gave me the impression that he was enjoying it almost as much as they were.

Hurrying upstairs to change, I pulled on an old pair of jersey shorts instead of my jeans and relished the moment that all women do, the removal of the bra. My top was loose, and I wasn't endowed enough to make it a problem. The relief was bliss. When I came down, Jack was still out in the garden, but obviously tiring. Poppy and Felix were busy setting out bowls and drinks. I stepped out into the garden towards the giggling mass being circled and danced around by Clive. 'I think it's about time this horsey was taken in for stabling, don't you?'

'Noooo! Just a few more minutes.'

'Come on,' I said, leaning over and lifting Ruby off. 'It's time for dinner anyway, you need to go in and wash your hands, both of you. Come on, Freddy.' He dismounted as reluctantly as his sister but they were soon distracted by Clive's antics and ran towards the house with the dog.

Once they were out of sight, Jack collapsed in a heap and rolled onto his back, his arms out at his side like a crucifix. 'I think you may have just saved my life.'

'Well, we can't be sending you to the glue factory just yet, can we?'

He laughed, warm and melodic. 'You say the nicest things.'

'Thanks. I try.' I crouched down next to him, my back to the kitchen. 'Are you sure you're all right?'

His hand moved along the grass and touched mine where it was resting in order to prevent me overbalancing. 'I'm fine. Really. I love spending time with them. I feel like I've missed out on so much. Not such a great godfather, eh?'

'You're a brilliant godfather. Just because you weren't actually in the country a lot of the time doesn't mean anything. People can be just down the road and still not do half as much as you've done for them or take half as much interest. They've always known you were there, and if needed, you'd have been here in a flash. Don't ever sell yourself short by thinking that you haven't been fulfilling that role well enough, because you have.'

'Thanks, Lily. That means a lot, especially coming from you.'

I knew exactly how Jack felt. I *had* been just down the road and still felt like had missed out on so much. He'd had the excuse of thousands of miles' distance, but I didn't. Mine was a choice not to go to nativity plays, or birthday parties or any of the other things that I'd been invited to and felt like I couldn't face. There wasn't really any excuse for that.

'That's a serious expression,' he said, still lying on the grass.

'No, not really,' I said, trying to brush it off.

'Fibber,' he said. 'I know you better than that by now. You can't fool me.'

I gave him a prod in the side. 'Don't be so smug,' I said, trying to stop the smile from breaking on my face. 'Come on, up you get.' I stood up and put down a hand to help him up, which he took. I heaved but not much happened. Placing my other hand over the one already wrapped around his I pulled again, this time really putting my back into it. 'Bloody hell, you're heavy.'

Now upright, probably due more to his own effort than mine, Jack looked down at me and grinned. 'Like I said, you say the nicest things. Shall we go in to dinner?' He offered his arm as though we were at some grand function being held at the manor, where he would be dressed in a tuxedo rather than jersey shorts and the well-washed T-shirt he was currently sporting. His face was so serious, I couldn't help but laugh, quickly covering it to join in with the joke. 'That would be lovely.'

'I do hope it's not turtle soup again.'

'Yes, it does get rather a bore, doesn't it?'

'Perhaps we could have oysters tomorrow? I'll send a note to the housekeeper.' He gave a grin so wicked it could probably challenge the alleged aphrodisiac properties of the oysters.

'You could, but I've heard that the housekeeper is used to her own way of doing things. And you may find that note returned somewhere a little more uncomfortable than your hand.'

Jack threw his head back, laughing as we entered the kitchen, and I pretended not to notice the look exchanged between my brother and his wife.

* * *

'How are you feeling about the premiere now?' Jack asked.

'Nervous but a tiny bit excited too.' I grinned.

He smiled back. 'You're going to do great.'

'Thank you. And thank you again for agreeing to come. I really do appreciate it. Things are a little less scary when you have backup, aren't they?'

'They can be, yes. And you're welcome.'

The house was quiet again now that my family had left. Dinner had been a fun, slightly noisy affair, but I'd enjoyed it. I had found the day shopping with Poppy stressful at times, still unused to dealing with crowds and people in general, but I'd loved having the opportunity to be with my sister-in-law and sharing moments together, even just chatting in the coffee shop as we fuelled up in between bouts of looking for the perfect dress. This was something else I'd missed out on, I reflected. I'd spent all this time thinking I was helping myself, but cracks had begun to appear in that philosophy. I was still absolutely terrified about the premiere and certainly wasn't about to turn into a social butterfly overnight, but I'd have Jack with me for the event. I still didn't think I would have been able to do it alone. I did enjoy the walks on my own, the one I'd done, at least, but I felt so much happier and relaxed going with Clive. It felt like I had social backup if I needed it, and of course, company which was something I'd been sorely short of for much of the past decade.

21

Need help!

I messaged Poppy a couple of days later. The premiere was approaching faster than I'd have liked and, despite spending hours watching YouTube make-up tutorials – time I should have spent writing – I just couldn't seem to end up with anything that looked remotely good enough for a situation this snazzy. Flicking through videos and images of other premieres showing guests with perfect hair, clothes and make-up, not to mention bodies, I began to work myself up into a state. Several times, my fingers hovered over the keyboard, preparing to send Zinnia an email saying I wouldn't be attending after all. But somewhere, in the back of my mind, Jack's words kept echoing. He was right. I had worked hard for this and not many writers got this sort of opportunity. There was no guarantee I'd ever sell the movie rights to any of my other books, just because this one had done well.

Some time ago, I'd been invited to a private screening of the film but, of course, I'd made excuses and declined. Now I wished I'd found some brave pants and gone. What if I got to the premiere and hated what they'd done with the book? Oh God, not only did I need help with make-up, I also needed immediate acting coaching too so that I didn't put my foot in it. But, of course, I could absolutely love it. I stared at the mirror.

'I will love it. It's going to be wonderful,' I said to myself. Clive shuffled a little closer to the chair. Reaching down, I gave his head a scratch. 'That's right, isn't it, Clive? It's all going to be fine.' Maybe if I repeated it enough, I'd trick my brain into believing it. I looked back at the mirror. There was no tricking my brain or my eyes into the belief that I hadn't made a pig's ear of the *evening/smoky eyed look* that the tutorial promised me. This was the fourth time I'd tried, and my face was sore from the constant wiping off and starting again. I'd be out of make-up before I got it right at this rate. As for fake eyelashes, those had quite literally gone out of the window some time ago. I must remember to go and pick them up off the lawn before Clive decided to try to eat them. All the videos made it look so easy but now I knew the truth. They lie!

What's up? You OK??

No.

I replied simply, followed by the exploding brain emoji and then a GIF of a small child who'd found her mum's make-up bag.

Oh... don't worry. I think I've got a plan. Call you in a bit.

I sent a string of hug emojis, stood up and went downstairs to retrieve the duplicitous fake lashes from the garden, with Clive trotting down behind me. Having found them and convinced him that they weren't a delicious treat, I went and got him a real treat and then headed to my office to get back to work.

A couple of hours later, Poppy's face appeared on my screen. I swiped the call to answer and found her beaming out the most enormous smile.

'You look happy.'

'You will too when I tell you what I've arranged,' she said.

'Am I going to like it?'

'You're going to love it!'

'Come on, then.' I grinned at her infectious smile. 'What's the secret?'

'OK, so I'm guessing the tutorials didn't go so well?'

'That GIF I sent?'

'Yep?'

'That was an improvement on the results I was getting. I'm pretty sure Clive could have done a better job.'

'Oh.'

'Quite. I didn't realise how out of practice I was at wearing make-up. Not that I'd ever really worn much before. I don't know. Did it get harder or something?'

'I do think the standards and aspirations got higher. Teenagers now spend so much time perfecting their make-up and hair, thanks to YouTube and influencers, that it suddenly feels like we've been left behind. And that's before you look at the magazines and so on.'

'I really hope you have the answer, then.'

'I do! I've just given an old school friend a call. She's a professional make-up artist now. Works on runway shows and films and all sorts. She's going to come round and do your face for the premiere.'

'Seriously?' I felt my mouth drop open a little.

'Yep.'

'Does she want paying in cash? You know, off the books?'

Poppy frowned. 'Oh! No, she doesn't want payment.'

'Huh?'

'She's doing it for free.'

'She can't.'

'Well, she can, and she is. She's actually a huge fan of your books so was super excited when I asked if she had any time.'

'I don't know what to say.'

'You can say "Darling, Poppy, you're an absolute genius."'

'Darling, Poppy, you're an absolute genius!'

'Thank you. And that's not all. She's bringing her mate, who's a fabulous hair stylist, so you can get the full effect.'

I sat in silence for a moment, both overwhelmed and hugely touched that total strangers would do this. Yes, the woman was Poppy's friend, but still. I knew it wasn't going to be a five-minute job and I now had someone to do my hair too. It felt like a combination of putting on armour, at the same time as emerging from the self-imposed chrysalis I'd wrapped myself in over the years since Mike died.

'You OK?'

'Yeah. Yes,' I reiterated. 'Thank you so much, Poppy. I don't know how to thank you for sorting all this and helping me with the dress and everything. I don't think I could be doing any of it without you backing me up and problem solving all the time.' Tears pricked at my eyes as I realised again just how much I had shut myself off from. The time and experiences I'd missed with those I loved. I knew I needed to make more of an effort with my own family at least. They were all I had, and I loved them so much. They deserved so much more than they'd got from me.

'It's a pleasure, Lils. I mean it. We're just so happy you're doing this. You deserve a special night and anything I can do to help you feel more comfortable in taking that step is absolutely no trouble at all.'

'You'll come with them, though? The stylists?' I asked, suddenly panicked about being asked about colours, styles and shapes and got a vision of me sitting in a chair, staring at them both like a bunny facing down a combine harvester, and the inevitable consequences.

'Of course! You couldn't keep me away even if you wanted to,' she said, laughing.

* * *

'You all right?' Jack asked, early on the morning of the premiere. 'I thought you had the hair and make-up people coming.'

'I do.'

'Right. It's just that you look more like you're awaiting the arrival of a firing squad.'

'It feels a bit like that.'

'It's just because it's out of your comfort zone.'

'It feels like everything is out of my comfort zone lately. I'm not sure I can even see the zone at the moment!'

'You're doing great.' He gave my shoulder a squeeze. 'Bloody hell, your muscles feel like they're welded solid.'

'You don't need to tell me,' I said, reaching up to try to alleviate some of the tension in my neck by digging my fingers in. All that seemed to do was send shooting pains up through my temples, so I stopped.

'Here, let me.' Jack moved to stand behind me. He paused a moment, but when I didn't protest, he continued. Warm, large hands were placed gently either side of my neck before gradually beginning a rhythmic motion, fingers and thumbs applying slight pressure to my knotted muscles.

'How's that?' he asked, continuing the movement.

'So good...'

'Come and sit down for a minute. It will be easier for me to do it that way.'

'I'm sure you have better things to do right now.'

'I'm sure I don't. Come on, sit down. They're going to be here before long and you'll be sitting in that chair for hours.'

He did have a point, so I headed over to a low-backed chair and sank into the soft cushions as Jack stood behind me and once again began the relaxing, soothing motion that was somehow a mixture of both pleasure and pain that felt amazing.

'It feels like it's releasing a bit. Does that feel any easier to you?'

'If I say yes, does that mean you'll stop?'

'Not necessarily.'

'If I say no, does that mean you'll stop?'

'Same answer. Do you want me to stop?'

'No. I don't know about garden design, but you could certainly forge a new career in the field of massage.' I opened my eyes, which had drifted closed, and tipped my head back up to directly meet Jack's. 'I don't know if that came out weird. It wasn't meant to be weird. Did it sound weird?'

'No,' he said, laughing, gently putting his hands each side of my head and tipping it forward again so that he could reach my shoulders. 'I know what you mean, though, so thank you.'

'Dare I ask how you got so good at this?'

'You might be shocked if I told you.'

'Now I absolutely have to know!'

'I don't really want to tell you.'

'With a lead in like that, you can't not now. Come on, it'll take my mind off things.'

'Ha, emotional blackmail. OK, but do know I'm a much better person now.'

'This sounds intriguing.'

'I learned how to do it to impress girls. You know they say their neck, or back or shoulders ache, and I would go, oh, I can help with that, come here. I'd do a bit of massage and ask how that felt and...

you know, one thing quite often led to another. But like I said, it's not something I'm proud of, and actually it's come in useful. Although using the skills on six foot, 200-pound rugby players wasn't exactly what I had in mind when I honed my skills, but if you can help a mate out, then you do, don't you?'

I was considering his answer.

'You're worryingly quiet. I can practically hear you judging me from here.'

'Then you need to get your hearing tested because I'm not judging you at all. I'm just thinking that those were exactly the same words you used on me.'

'Yes, but considering I've now matured as a person, I actually care what your answer is and promise I'm not doing this for any other reward than to see you more comfortable.'

'No, I know. I'm just teasing you. I didn't realise you'd actually learned special skills to enhance your lothario ways.'

Suddenly Jack's voice, deep and soft, was close to my ear. 'You wouldn't believe some of the skills I have.'

I couldn't help laughing. 'And there he is. I knew it was too good to be true that you'd completely matured.'

'Just stating the facts,' he said, straightening up and returning to my shoulders, his strong thumbs pressing gently into my neck and releasing the tension building there. Tension that hadn't been helped by his warm breath brushing against my ear and the unwarranted and unexpected rush of images that suddenly flowed into my head. Jack Coulsdon-Hart might have matured but I had a feeling some of the old Jack remained. And maybe that wasn't a bad thing.

A couple of minutes later, the doorbell rang. I felt the sudden loss of the warmth of Jack's hands and let out a sigh involuntarily.

'Try to enjoy it,' Jack said as I stood and gave the robe I'd been instructed to wear after my bath this morning a quick straighten.

'I will. I'm so thankful to Poppy for this.' The doorbell rang again. 'It will be OK, won't it?' I suddenly looked up at Jack as a barrage of worried thoughts began bowling through my mind. 'He won't want to cut my hair short or something, will he?'

'If he does, and you don't want that, then you say so. It's your hair. Don't let him just do what he wants, and Poppy is here for backup.'

Jack laid a hand gently on my upper arm, gave it a quick squeeze and then headed off to the door. I pulled myself together and followed him a couple of moments later.

22

'Hiiii!' A bubbly-sounding woman of Poppy's age came in, snatching a quick double take at Jack as she did so. She had tumbling waves of electric-blue hair, beautiful skin and barely a scrap of make-up, save a slick of lip gloss, and looked amazing. Following her in was a slim man, of similar age or perhaps a few years older. He was tanned and beautifully dressed in a three-piece suit. Shiny chestnut hair was cut in a short, neat style and I could just see the tip of a tattoo peeking above the crisp collar of his shirt.

'Hello,' he nodded at me and then saw Jack. 'Hello!' he said again, this time with a lot more enthusiasm and emphasis. I flicked my gaze to Jack, who smiled at them both and put his hand out for them to shake.

'Hi, I'm Jack. I'll get out of your way now.'

'Hi, Jack,' Poppy said, giving him a big hug as she closed the front door behind her. 'Any chance of a cuppa before you disappear off?'

'I can do that!' I piped up.

'It's fine, I'll do it. You go off and start getting pampered.'

'Oh, my goodness. This one's definitely a keeper,' the man

exclaimed resting his hand momentarily on Jack's arm and then, feeling the bicep, rested it a moment longer.

'Oh, he's not mine. I mean, I don't keep him. I mean... we're just friends,' I bumbled, knowing that I was now glowing bright red.

I glanced at Poppy with a silent plea in my eyes for some help. She gave me a private smile, then stepped in.

'Jack's an old friend. He's recently moved back from New Zealand, and is setting up his own business again. He's lodging with Lily until he gets settled.'

'And where are you looking to settle?'

'Definitely in this area,' Jack replied, smiling.

'Shame. Well, if you're ever looking for somewhere to stay in London, I'll leave my card.' The man gave Jack a wink and then me a large grin, which I returned. I liked him already. Hopefully I'd still like him by the end of the day.

The lady with the blue hair still hadn't really said anything apart from her initial hi to Jack. I smiled at her and she smiled back, but still nothing came.

'Well, I'm Lily, as you probably guessed.' I held out my hand.

'I'm...' She looked at Poppy for a second as though she temporarily forgotten her own name. 'Sorry, I'm just... I'm such a fan of yours. I'm a little bit star-struck.' She laughed and pushed her hair back from her face with perfectly detailed fingernails. 'I'm Jemima.'

'But I thought Poppy said you worked with film stars and top models and the like?'

'I do, all the time. But that doesn't faze me. To be honest, I'm not really into movies or stuff like that. I much prefer a book and I've always loved your books in particular.'

'Thank you. I'm so glad you enjoyed them and thank you both for coming here today to do this. I can't say how much I appreciate it.'

The man waved away my words of appreciation and took my hand, folding his own over it. 'I'm Martin and this is an absolute pleasure for both of us, darling. We're going to make you look fabulous. Not that you don't already. Just a bit of shoozing up, you know, give you a bit of confidence.'

'That would be wonderful. I definitely need some of that. I've never really done anything like this before.'

'It's really good that you are,' Jemima said, fastening a hairband around my face with all my hair scraped back out of the way. 'I can't wait to see the film, although of course it won't be as good as the book. They never are. I'm going to see it, even though I don't especially like films, just because it's your book.'

'I really hope you enjoy it.'

'Come in.' Poppy led them through to the dining area, which was being commandeered as a temporary beauty salon while Jemima and Martin, hopefully, worked their miracles. Jack was busying himself at the other end of the room, getting out all the paraphernalia for tea and coffee, before wandering over and asking who wanted what. As he walked back, the muscles in his tanned legs were on show in his shorts and both the stylists watched him a little longer than was strictly necessary. I didn't blame them, I might have had a sneaky look myself. Unfortunately, when I looked back, Poppy was looking directly at me and gave me a secret smile which I pretended to completely misunderstand.

'Now let's have a look at this hair,' Martin said, walking around me, feeling my hair, flicking it out and doing various other things I didn't understand. 'It's a good colour, although we could probably brighten it up a little bit.'

'How bright is bright?' I asked.

'Not as bright as Jemima's, don't worry.'

'It's not that. I actually think your hair is beautiful. I'm just not sure that I could pull that off.'

Jemima raised a hand to her own hair and touched it briefly, smiling and thanking me for the compliment.

'But Poppy said you were looking to go quite short today, so we can always start with the cut, and then go in with the colour.'

I sat down heavily in the chair and, across the room, Jack dropped a cup, which smashed into pieces on the floor. I looked at him and he looked at me, exchanging horrified expressions.

'Sorry about that,' he said to me before his eyes flicked to the hairdresser.

'Don't worry,' I said, finding words amongst the panic in my brain.

Just be strong, I told myself. Tell him you don't want it short. And then Martin began to laugh.

'Oh, my goodness, you've gone as white as a sheet! I'm only joking, darling. You've got beautiful hair and Poppy did say you like it long.' He glanced over at Jack, who was now also looking suitably relieved. 'Something tells me someone else likes it long on you as well.'

'No!' Jack began to stammer. 'No, it's not that. It's just I... you know... she... she likes it long and was worried about it being cut. That's all. Nothing else.'

'Ohh, I see.' Martin turned back to me and gave me a huge smile.

I shook my head at him, trying not to smile back. 'I get the feeling you're rather a troublemaker.'

He put his hand on his chest and radiated innocence before giving me a wink. Across the room, Jack swept up the remnants of the bone china mug and tipped them into the bin.

Once everyone had their drinks, Jack gave us a wave and said that he was going to take Clive out for a long walk and then drop him over at Felix's. They were dog sitting for me overnight, although I was hoping not to be back too late tomorrow. The publisher had arranged rooms for us at a hotel near the venue and, although I would have been quite happy to travel back tonight, it might be nice to stay in a swanky hotel for once. It had been a long time since I'd done anything like that. I could have a leisurely breakfast in the room before requesting the car from the publisher to take us back home.

Once Martin cut my hair into an actual style, something it hadn't seen in a long time, but keeping the length as he had promised, Jemima began to show me images of different make-up looks, suggesting what she thought might suit me. Poppy nipped up to my room and brought down the dress so that they could get an idea of the look as a whole. They both oohed and aahed over it. I had explained that it was really all down to Poppy's shopping skills but that I was quite excited to wear it, although I wasn't sure if I would ever be able to remember how to walk in heels that high. It had been a long time since I'd worn those as well.

'They're gorgeous, though,' Jemima said, looking at the strappy numbers Poppy had also brought down. 'They'll look stunning when you get a flash of them from that dress as you move.'

'I agree, and I gather your beau this evening is your delightful butler.' Martin studied the five-inch spikes. 'He is quite tall, so these seem the perfect choice. You're going to look amazing.'

I laughed at Martin's quaint use of the word 'beau'. 'He's neither my beau, nor my butler. Just as well, as that was a nice cup he smashed. He'd be out on his ear.'

'I'm just teasing, love. I know he's the gardener really. It's all very *Lady Chatterley's Lover*, isn't it?' Martin said, squishing his shoulders up in excitement.

I burst out laughing. 'No! It's not that at all! Nothing like.'

'Shame,' he said, grinning widely. 'He'd make a perfect Mellors.'

'More the other way around, anyway,' Poppy added, taking a seat on the sofa and tucking her legs up under her.

'What do you mean?' the hairdresser asked, glancing up from where he was mixing some sort of concoction in a small foil tray with what looked like a paint brush.

'Jack's the eldest son of an earl. When his father eventually shuffles off his mortal coil, that title goes to Jack.'

'Really?'

Jemima was listening now open-mouthed, a finger hovering over the screen from where she had been showing me shades of lipstick.

'Yep. Not that he's thrilled about it.'

'I bet you he'd make a lovely lord of the manor, though,' Jemima said, slightly wistfully.

'I'm pretty sure he'd make a lovely anything,' Martin added cheekily and gave me another wink. 'Now time for colour!'

* * *

'I think I'm going to cry.' Poppy stood beside me, both of us looking into the mirror.

'Don't you dare!' I replied. 'You know what I'm like if someone's crying, and I can't cry in this make-up. I'll never get it the same again.'

'Jemima did put waterproof mascara on though, so that's something.'

'That's true.'

Jemima had done an amazing job, as had Martin. My hair, having lost a couple of inches that were dry and needed to go, now looked healthier but was still long and currently fell in soft waves about my shoulders and down my back. The highlights he had added shimmered as they caught the light, making it look thicker and fuller. Jemima's make-up was picture perfect, literally. I felt like I'd fallen out of a glossy magazine.

'I look like I've been airbrushed! I don't know how she does it, but she's absolutely brilliant. And totally lovely, of course.'

'She's over the moon about that collection of signed copies that you gave her.'

'Yes, I rather got that from the fact she burst into tears. I wasn't sure if I'd made a huge booboo initially, so I was super relieved to see that she was smiling. I wasn't sure what to do for Martin, but I didn't feel I could give Jemima something without doing the same for him. It seems rather vain to foist books upon somebody when they might not even like them.'

'He's thrilled with that boutique gin subscription you got him, though.'

'That was down to you, really, with your detective work finding out what sort of things he liked. Thanks for that, Poppy.'

'I think he'd have been extra thrilled if you could have got him a date with Jack.'

'I think you're right.'

'I'm not sure we could have persuaded your butler to do that,' she said, giggling as we moved to the door.

'For God's sake, don't tell Jack that Martin called him the butler,' I said, opening the bedroom door.

'Your butler?' Jack said, raising one dark brow, a hint of amusement on his full lips.

'I... I didn't realise you were there.'

'No, clearly.' The smile widened.

'Martin was just, um, teasing. You know.'

'Is there anything I can get you, ma'am?'

Poppy sniggered behind me and Jack looked over my shoulder, exchanging a grin with her.

I rolled my eyes and stepped fully out of the room, Poppy following me.

'You look fab!' she said, giving Jack the once-over. 'Very dashing.'

'Thanks,' he smiled and momentarily adjusted his cuffs unnecessarily as if suddenly unsure of the compliment. Fab, however, was an understatement as to how damn good he looked. Freshly shaved, his hair was short, dark and perfect, and that suit definitely wasn't off the peg. It was clearly made to measure from somewhere pricey and I have to say they measured very, very well.

'Are you going out, or have you decided to stay here all evening? What time is the car coming?' Poppy asked as I hovered on the landing.

'Should be any time now,' Jack replied. 'By the way...'

'Huh?' I looked up at him.

'Wow. I've been wanting to say it since you opened the door and then the butler thing was too good an opportunity to miss but seriously, wow.'

Poppy's face broke into a huge grin. 'Doesn't she look amazing?' She was practically vibrating with excitement beside me.

'She does.' Jack's eyes were still fixed on me, his voice soft. 'Absolutely incredible.'

I scratched the back of my neck as I looked off up the landing. 'Poppy's friends are definitely miracle workers,' I said, adding a laugh that didn't quite sound right. My sister-in-law gave me a nudge that was somewhat harder than necessary. 'You're supposed to say thank you,' she whispered so loudly I thought next door had probably heard – and my next-door neighbours were several miles away.

'Sorry. Yes. Thank you. You look very nice yourself.' I suddenly felt like an awkward teenager going to her first prom.

Jack gave me a soft smile and then flicked his arm out, looking at the face of a simple but elegant Philippe Patek watch. 'The car should be here in a couple of minutes. You OK?'

'Fine!' My tone sounded far more shrill than usual, and I felt like a whole raft of butterflies had just taken off inside my stomach and were now bashing against my insides, looking for a way out.

Oh God, was I doing the right thing? Perhaps I should have just started with going to a few more local cafés on my own or something. But no, my first flotations back into society had to be a party held by an earl at the local manor and a major film premiere. I certainly didn't do things by half.

'I'd better be getting off.' Poppy slipped on a light jacket as we got to the bottom of the stairs. 'You both look absolutely gorgeous – and look even better together!' She gave a wicked grin and hugged each of us, air kissing me so as not to ruin my make-up and giving Jack a big smacker on the cheek.

'Thanks for everything, Poppy.' I took her hand. 'I couldn't have done this without you.'

'I'm thrilled to have been part of it all. Felix and I are so proud of you. We know it's hard, but you're doing it and that's brilliant, and it's what you deserve.' She opened her mouth to say something else, but I held up my free hand.

'You have to stop now, otherwise I'm going to cry and I'll really end up looking like the kid in that GIF I sent you, despite all of Jemima's hard work.'

Poppy laughed, a tear rolling down her own cheek. 'OK, OK. I'll stop but I can't wait to hear about it all when you get back.' She blew us more kisses and headed out to her car.

23

'I suppose we ought to get ready to go too. Do you think we should wait outside?' I peered up the drive, turning back as Jack took my hand.

'Just a second. I've got something for you.'

'For me? What for?'

'For tonight. For whenever.' He pulled a small box with the word Cartier on the top from his inside jacket pocket. I looked from the box to his face and then back down at the box.

'I don't understand...'

'Don't worry,' he smiled softly, a gentle laugh in his voice. 'This is just a friend giving another friend a gift to thank her for her kindness in taking him in when he knows she really didn't want to.'

I pulled a face, but the smile broke through. Jack grinned.

'I know it's been an imposition and I've overstepped the mark with certain comments I've made about how you've chosen to live your life, but we seem to have got past that, for which I'm very grateful. I'd always rather be honest with you, but I hope you know that whatever I've said in the past and whatever I might say in the future, I never, ever mean to hurt you. I know this is a massive step for you tonight and that it was a huge step for you to come to my parents' place for that party, but your support that evening meant a lot. I knew you were there and that gave me strength. So, I hope, tonight, that I can do that for you. And this is just a little token of appreciation to say thank you for everything that you've done and for being brave.'

Silence floated between us before I looked back up at him. 'I wish everybody would stop trying to make me cry this evening,' I said, feeling my eyes threatening to fill amid laughter and a strain in my voice.

'Sorry. Definitely not my intention.'

'No, I know.' I smiled up, blinking the tears back. 'Do I get to open this now?'

Without words, Jack opened the box for me. Inside lay the most beautiful platinum necklace. Its simple, elegant chain held a thin pendant from which glittered three exquisite diamonds.

'Oh, Jack,' I whispered. 'It's absolutely beautiful but I couldn't possibly accept this.'

'I'd really like it if you did.'

My eyes drifted back from his to the box. It was stunning, and exactly the sort of thing I would have chosen myself, but I knew it had a far higher price tag than a friendship bracelet from Claire's Accessories.

'Stop overthinking it,' he said, reading my mind. 'You gave Clive a home, a wonderful home. An entire jeweller's shop wouldn't be enough to thank you for that single act of kindness.'

I took a deep breath and nodded. Placing the box on the console table, he removed the necklace and then stood behind me as I lifted my hair to enable him to secure the clasp at my neck.

'Wow. That dress is stunning. I hadn't seen the back properly until now. You need to go shopping with Poppy more often.'

'I'm hoping to,' I replied honestly, as he touched my hands gently to let me know I could drop my hair once more.

'Good.'

I turned to face him, my hand moving up to touch the necklace at my throat. 'How does it look?'

'Beautiful. But see for yourself.' He guided me gently to the mirror by the door, standing behind me as I looked. 'You look perfect.'

'It's absolutely stunning, Jack. I don't know what to say.'

'You don't have to say anything, Lily.'

I turned to face him and his hands slid gently along my forearms.

'Holy shit!'

We both jumped as the doorbell echoed loudly around the hallway, breaking the sudden silence and... whatever else that was. I stepped back. 'I guess that will be the car!' My voice was a little over-bright and I made a mental attempt at reining it back in.

'I suspect it will be.' Jack's, of course, was perfectly normal.

He lifted our coats from where they had been laid over the banister, then opened the door, greeting the driver with some small talk as I checked the house, waiting beside me as I locked up and dropped the key into my clutch bag.

We sat quietly for a while, enjoying the luxurious leather seats of the limousine that the publishers had sent for me. It all felt surreal as we travelled along a dark country road. With no lights outside, the only thing I could see in the window was my reflection looking back at me, and it wasn't a reflection I was used to, not that I didn't like it. It was just different. Very different.

'You all right over there?' Jack's deep tones put the reins on my galloping thoughts.

'Yes, thanks.' I turned to smile at him. 'Just thinking.'

He returned the smile. 'That's what I was worried about.'

'Are you nervous?'

Jack took a deep breath and then let it out slowly. 'Not especially, but I think that's only because I was brought up in a household where social engagements and large functions were part of the norm. Even when I started prep school, most of the boys were from similar, privileged backgrounds so it wasn't until I started mixing with a wider range of people, especially in the village, that I realised my home life wasn't how everybody lived.'

'What did you think about that, when you discovered the majority of people didn't dress for dinner and entertain lords and ladies all the time?'

'Honestly? I thought, well, this is wonderful! That's one of the many reasons I loved coming to your house. Yes, we ate at the table and had that "family time", but at yours it actually was family time. You talked about your days, but it was relaxed. There was no pressure, no one to impress. It was just... great.' He spread his hands, as though unable to encompass all the thoughts he had in words.

'I always wondered if you looked down on us a bit. I said something about it to Felix once, but he dismissed it immediately, saying that you didn't and you weren't like that.'

'But you had your doubts?'

'I did. But perhaps that was due more to my own insecurities than your behaviour.'

'Just for utmost clarification, I never, ever looked down on any of you and never would. If you want God's honest truth, I often wished that I could be part of your family instead of my own.'

I turned to look at him in the low light of the car, shifting slightly in my seat. The movement exposed a sizeable flash of leg, which I hurriedly adjusted in as nonchalant a manner as possible, continuing my conversation at the same time and hoping that Jack hadn't noticed. A hint of smile showed on his face which told me he'd not missed a thing and that my bungled attempt to cover up had probably only made it worse. Perhaps this dress hadn't been such a great idea after all – but I did love it. And why not? My legs were actually in pretty decent shape from the walks I took around my own garden and fields and now, with a dog to exercise as well, I'd noticed some extra tone come back into them. Perhaps it was just one more thing that I needed to chill out about. I returned my train of thought to Jack's original statement.

'You'd really rather have been part of our family?'

'Well, Felix didn't have the pressure on him to marry that I did, and to marry the right person, or pick the correct career, which in essence meant having both my wife and career picked for me. Your parents were interested in what you had to say, what you both thought and wanted to do. My parents are still stuck in an age where everything is ruled by tradition. The aristocracy has moved on, but it feels like sometimes my mother especially is stuck in aspic of a time long gone.'

'I don't think many of us thought about you like that. You were just seen as a privileged, perhaps over privileged, playboy type who could have anything and anyone he wanted.'

'I'm sure it did seem like that, and to an extent it was, apart from having anyone I wanted.'

'Oh?'

He shrugged and I waited for him to elaborate but he remained silent.

'How did your parents feel about you dating girls from the village if they had certain women in mind for you?'

'I don't think they cared. The men of the aristocracy are allowed to have as much fun as they like, with whomever they like, just don't start getting serious about the wrong person. That's the golden rule.'

'Was there someone that you really wanted to get serious with that they wouldn't have approved of?' I thought back to what he'd just said. 'I have to admit, you always appeared as if the word commitment was a complete anathema to you.'

'Partly it was, but some of that was self-preservation. I knew some of the women I went out with were only interested in the possible title that they might one day inherit should we marry, so I went out of my way to make sure, or at least give the impression, that I didn't do serious relationships.'

'I can name a couple of girls who were convinced that they would be able to change your mind.'

'I'm sure you probably can, and I likely know the ones you mean. But unlike my parents, I really did want to marry for a genuine reason rather than title, or money, or any of those superficial motives.'

'Is that what you told your parents?'

'Yes. Looking back on it now, I probably should have been a little bit more circumspect with my choice of wording. Their marriage had effectively been an arranged one and I called it superficial. I might not agree with some beliefs they hold, but I didn't want to hurt them.'

I laid my hand briefly over his as it lay on the cool leather seat.

'I know you didn't mean to hurt them and I'm sure they do too. Sometimes we say things in the heat of the moment and it comes out all wrong. I'm sure, in their own way, they only want the best for you.'

'So long as that best includes Lady Cecily Fullington-Beck, I'm sure they do.'

'Who's that?'

'A very beautiful woman from the social circle they deem acceptable for me to have my pick from.'

'Not your type?'

'She's nice enough. We've known each other since we were kids.

Our parents had plans back then to hook us up, but Cecily rather put a dent in that plan by marrying someone else.'

'Oh, I see! Seems like you weren't the only one who was against the plan?'

'She was pretty happy to go along with it for a while, until she met an extremely wealthy businessman at one of the myriad parties she loves to attend. She's quite the social butterfly is our Cecily.'

'So I assume she's divorced now if they're trying to make it work between you two again?'

'No. Cecily is now one very rich, very merry widow. Her husband was at least three decades older than her and, from what I understand, enjoyed a lot of red meat and a lot of red wine. Cecily will be the first one to tell you that it took longer than she thought.'

'That seems a rather cold approach to a marriage.'

'Like I said, it's more of a business arrangement in certain circles. He had money and apparently quite fancied the idea of being a part of the whole aristocracy circus, whereas she had a title but there wasn't a lot of money behind it, which is quite often the case. Not that that stopped her parents turning their noses up first at the man she was planning to marry because he wasn't from an old family and had made his own money commercially.'

'Surely you can't be serious,' I said, laughing a little. 'That sounds like something out of Jane Austen or Charles Dickens.'

'You'd have thought, wouldn't you? But not in this case. Not really good enough in their eyes, despite the fact that guy had billions. The money brought them round in the end.'

'I bet it did. Do you think she loved him?'

'Cared for him, yes, but loved, no. She told me as much on her wedding day.'

'Noooo, really?'

Jack gave a shrug. 'She sent for me and then asked me if I thought she was doing the right thing.'

'And what did you say?'

'I asked her if she loved him. She told me she had feelings for him but no, she didn't love him, but that she didn't feel that was an impediment to her marriage.'

'What was she asking your opinion about then?'

'I think she was concerned she might be snubbed because she wasn't marrying a title.'

'Did you think that?'

'No, I didn't. That outdated opinion of people in "trade" can still permeate society even today, but money is now far more influential and opens far more doors.'

'So then she was satisfied?'

He shifted in the seat and looked momentarily out of the window.

'Something else happened, didn't it?'

'Nothing of consequence.'

'You know what I used to love most about being a writer, and still do on the occasions that I go out?'

'What's that?' Jack asked, turning back to face me.

'People watching. You can get quite good at it. Picking up on people's mannerisms, behaviour, and so on. Just the way they are sitting can tell a whole story about if they feel comfortable or not with the person opposite them. Naturally, I'm a little out of practise, but I'm still pretty sure you're telling a fib.'

Jack brushed my little finger with the edge of his own as both our hands rested on the car seat between us. 'Seems like you're not that much out of practise, after all.'

'So what else did she say?'

'She asked whether I would be prepared to marry her, as our parents had always planned. If I said yes, then she would stop the wedding that moment.'

'Wow.'

'It was a bit wow, not to mention awkward.'

'I take it you didn't want to.'

'No. I wasn't ready for marriage back then. Yes, I like Cecily and we always got on well, but I definitely didn't have romantic feelings for her.'

'Which you told her?'

'I did.'

'How did she take that?'

He laughed. 'Perfectly well. Told me that she knew that would be my answer anyway but was just double-checking on the off-chance as she knew she'd have more fun in bed with me than her soon-to-be husband.'

'Crikey. And how did she know that?' I asked, laughing along with him.

'Courtesy of far too many glasses of champagne one night and an excruciatingly boring party when I left with her best friend. Women talk, apparently.' He did at least have the decency to look slightly bashful.

'You're such a gigolo.'

Jack threw his head back, laughing. 'A gigolo? I'm not sure about that, but if I was, then I would like to put the record straight by reiterating that this was all in my past.'

'It sounds like Lady Cecily could be a part of your future, if your parents have anything to do with it.'

'My parents don't have anything to do with it. I've made it clear on several occasions that, should I choose to marry ever again, it will be on my own terms.'

'How did that go down?'

'About as well as could be expected. The implication was that my previous marriage, which had obviously been my own choice, had not ended well and so that perhaps indicated that I might be happier and more successful with someone like Cecily.'

'If she's such a rich and merry widow, is she actually looking for a husband?'

'I don't know to be honest. She's been out of the country travelling. I haven't had much of a chance to catch up with her since I got back. We sort of kept in touch and I did see the odd thing in gossip magazines that friends in New Zealand had.'

'What did your friends over there think about you knowing all these rich and famous people?' I asked.

'I never told them.'

'I thought you said that you felt more yourself there than anywhere.'

'I did. More than I ever had before, but I realise now that I was still holding back in some areas. I guess I was worried that they'd judge me or treat me differently or think I was full of it if I name dropped, even accidentally.'

'Ah. I take it they didn't know that you are currently awaiting your crown.'

Jack gave me a gentle prod in the side. 'Very funny. And no, they didn't know my background. I tended to keep it vague.'

'What about your wife?'

'Well, yeah, she did know, but not until a fair while into the relationship, until I knew it was something serious.'

'It was probably only right to inform her that she might one day become a countess.'

'That's kind of what I thought, too.'

'How did she take it? I assume pretty well, bearing in mind she still married you.'

'I guess so. She quite fancied herself as a countess, I think, although I'm not sure she realised how steeped in tradition it is, plus the fact that if the time came, we'd have to move to England. I think she thought that was negotiable, but people believe what they want. She was, however, sworn to secrecy about it all. I really didn't want people knowing.'

'I can understand that.'

'Unfortunately, she considered that vow relevant only during the time that we were married. The moment things got rocky, everybody knew.' Jack pulled a face.

'Oh no.'

'Not ideal, but I got through. With the divorce going on, that was the least of my problems, to be honest.'

'I'm sure. Are you any more resigned to taking on the title if and when you have to?'

'In a way, I suppose. But there's no way I'm giving up my business. I've worked too hard, three times now, to give it up again.'

'Is there any reason that you would have to?' I asked.

'My parents wouldn't be keen. They're still set in their ways – the old ways.'

24

We drove on for a while longer before Jack touched my hand gently. 'How are you doing?'

'Quietly terrified but less so than I would have been on my own. Conversation helps. Distraction.'

Jack peered back out of the window. 'There's still a little while to go yet. What would you like to talk about?'

I splayed my hands out either side of my thighs, realising that I'd been balling them into fists once our previous conversation had finished. They felt clammy, and I was worried about staining the satin of my dress by resting them on my lap.

'Tell me about why you love gardens and design so much – what drew you to that and what your ultimate garden would be,' I said, leaning my head back against the seat and closing my eyes as Jack's deep, melodic voice began to do exactly that.

* * *

'Oh my God.' Outside, a writhing mass of humanity surrounded and spilled out from the theatre where the premiere was to be held this evening. Security guards had already stopped the car twice before allowing us to move further on, the driver having showed the required ID, until we got closer to the entrance. I could see cameras flashing almost constantly and even through the heavy darkened glass of the windows I could hear the shouts and calls from both the crowd and the paparazzi at all the guests as they made their way into the venue. We were still some distance away so goodness knew what the noise would be like once we were right in the centre of things.

'I can't do this.' I turned to Jack in a sudden panic. 'I just can't, it's too much!'

Jack took my hand from where it was once again balled up into a tight fist, so tight that the knuckles and almost the entire hand was white through lack of blood flow. Gently he prised it open, gave it a gentle massage to bring the colour back before folding his own large, reassuringly cool one around it.

'You *can* do this, Lily.'

'I can't. I really can't. Listen to the noise! I can't deal with all this. Please, I just want to go home.'

Jack shifted himself further in the seat and turned so that he was looking directly at me. 'If that's really what you want, then we can do that. We can ask the driver to turn around right now. But it has to be what you truly want, deep in your heart, and not just a temporary, and understandable, anxiety about doing something that is out of your comfort zone. If we go home now, and in a week's time you still think that you did the right thing, then that's fine. But if you think that you're going to have even the slightest regret that you didn't do this, then I think it might be good to just carry on for the moment. I know it's scary, but I'm right here with you, Lily, and I won't leave you. I promise. We can always just try it for a bit, and if you find it still too much, then we can get the car and go home.

You'll still have had a massive achievement, not to mention the opportunity to show just how breathtakingly beautiful you look tonight. It seems a shame to deprive people of that.'

I let out the breath I didn't even realise I'd been holding in a nervous laugh. 'Still got that silver tongue, I see, Jack Coulsdon-Hart?' Finally meeting his gaze but still gripping his hand with a force that I think surprised us both.

'It's always nice to keep your hand in when you have a skill,' he teased before leaning closer. 'Except these days I only say it when it's the truth and, believe me, it's absolutely the truth tonight. You're going to be the most beautiful woman there.'

Laughing helped relieve some of the tension making my body so rigid it was almost painful. 'Now I know you're telling porkies.'

Jack gently pushed a curl back over my left shoulder with his free hand. 'Not at all. In fact, I've never been more serious in my life.'

I took a deep breath, then let it out slowly, releasing the grip on Jack's hand ever so slightly in order to strengthen it once again, silently telling him that I'd heard the words and appreciated them, even if I did find them hard to believe.

'So what would you like to do?' he asked, no pressure in his voice. The decision was entirely mine.

'Let's go a bit further.'

Jack laid his other hand over the top of our joined ones before relaxing back into the seat as we continued to crawl closer to our exit point.

Sooner than I expected, and certainly hoped, we were pulling up and two men in dark suits each opened the car door. In no hurry, Jack faced me. 'You ready to do this?'

I wasn't, but I knew I had to. I'd worked hard for this moment, and although I was terrified, I knew, as Jack had suggested, that if I didn't do this tonight, I would regret it for the rest of my life. I also knew I needed to do this for Mike. He hadn't lived to see me achieve the success that I had today, but he'd always been there cheering me on and encouraging me, helping me believe in myself and basically just keeping me at it. I wish he could have been here to see all this, but hopefully, somewhere, he knew how much I loved him for helping me make it happen.

I met Jack's eyes. 'Yes.' He gave me a wide smile, squeezed my hand and then we each got out of our respective side of the car.

The noise was overwhelming. Between the crowds, spectators and the crush of media all shouting names in every direction, with camera flashes going off almost constantly, it felt like barely controlled chaos. I concentrated on the directions Zinnia had given me to just walk up the carpet and head inside, then give her a call. Somewhere in there, she and a collection of people from the publishing company would find me.

I'd been with Zinnia a long time, but the publishing company was one I'd changed to a couple of years after Mike had passed. At the time, it felt like I needed to change everything. The original company had been a large conglomerate and, whilst the glamorous parties had seemed attractive initially, they'd never especially been my thing, and once Mike had gone, they definitely weren't. I had done OK with them, sitting reasonably comfortably as a mid-list author, but when I read about a new start-up publishing company, something prompted me – perhaps Mike from another plane, which is what I liked to think – to approach them. That was when things really began to take off, and now here I was, in London's Leicester Square, heading towards the red carpet feeling like I was caught up in a very surreal dream.

I stole a glance at Jack as he walked beside me, my arm tucked through his. He looked calm, relaxed, and as though this was something he did every day. It was also hard not to notice that he looked incredibly handsome. It wouldn't surprise me if he got mistaken for a movie star. Suddenly, he seemed to sense me looking at him and the green eyes turned and locked onto my blue ones.

'You're doing great.' He laid his other hand over mine on his arm for a moment in a gesture of reassurance as he bent a little towards me so that he could make himself heard over the clamour that surrounded us.

'OK.' I smiled back at him, gripping his arm probably tighter than was the norm. I could see the door to the theatre now. We were almost there. One hurdle down. It was then somebody recognised me and suddenly my name was being called in all directions, or, more accurately, the pen name that I used.

'Just look up and smile,' Jack encouraged. I retained my grip on him but also did what he said, trying my best to make it seem natural so the internet tomorrow wasn't full of pictures of a terrified-looking author caught in paparazzi headlights. Ahead of me, I saw various people with microphones, dressed in evening dress, speaking into cameras, interviewing various people as they walked up the carpet, faces illuminated by extra lighting on top of the camera. Each microphone had a square tab underneath its head, identifying which channel its holder represented. I recognised a few, but others meant nothing, and I assumed they were perhaps from other countries, or one of the many satellite channels. Not exactly being a TV buff, I wasn't up on these things.

Suddenly someone hurried towards me, calling out my pen name.

'Astoria? Astoria?'

A tall, beautiful black woman in a shocking pink gown with her hair piled on top of her head was gesturing to an assistant, who breathily asked if they could have a few words for a well-known entertainment channel. Even I'd heard of it, so it had to be pretty big.

Jack was hustled to the side, a little behind me. I looked back over my shoulder at Jack, noticed by both the assistant and the presenter.

'If you can just wait there for a moment, sir, we won't be long.'

Jack nodded and stood with his hands in his pockets, before moving to stand behind the camera so that he was out of the way and not just left like a lemon in the middle of the red carpet.

'Hi, lovely to meet you, Astoria.'

'Hi.' I concentrated on breathing so I didn't squeak too much.

'I'm just going to ask you a couple of questions, OK? Great,' she continued, answering her own question. The light on the camera switched on and suddenly both she and I were bathed in what felt like a football pitch floodlight. She didn't seem fazed by it at all, but it felt unnerving to me. I remembered Jack was close by and had now moved so that I could see him. He gave a subtle, reassuring smile which I returned, feeling my pulse rate drop a little as I did so.

'Here with me now is Astoria James, the writer of the hit novel that tonight's premiere is based upon. Astoria?' She turned to me. 'This is the first of your novels to be turned into a film, is that right?'

'Yes, that's right,' I answered into the microphone now thrust close to my face. It swung back towards the presenter.

'And how does it feel to be here tonight? You are famous for being rather a recluse, after all.'

I gripped my clutch bag a little tighter and felt myself get hot, only hoping that the layers of make-up Jemima had applied earlier in the day would be enough to hide my awkward blushes. I knew the woman was just doing her job, even though I found the question a little rude and intrusive, but I suppose that was part of today's world. Everybody wanted to know everything, whether it was their business or not. I didn't think the way I chose to live my life was anything to do with the film, but I also knew that by putting myself out here tonight, I was opening myself up to questions that might not be the most comfortable. Admittedly, I hadn't thought it would be on camera, but there we are. I fixed on a smile and began to reply.

'It's true, I do value my privacy, but a lot of people worked very hard to make my book the success that it has been. I'm very grateful to Bella Dupree for loving the book as much as she does and for championing it into becoming a major film production.'

The woman seemed satisfied with this answer. I'd seen her glance over my shoulder, past the camera. I'd assumed she was looking for the next person to pounce upon and therefore about to wrap up this particular interview. I was grateful it had been so short.

'One more question before you go, following on from that. Are we to believe the rumours that you're about to get your own happy ending with the heir apparent to an earldom?' She smiled a wide smile at me with teeth so brilliant white they were almost transparent.

I didn't know what to say. I had vaguely suspected somebody might make a comment or two tonight but assumed I'd be able to brush them off. I certainly hadn't expected to be ambushed on live TV about the relationship between Jack and me.

I swallowed my fear. *Be brave, Lily.* I smiled at her, remembering that she was just trying to earn a living.

'I never like to give away the ending of any story,' I said, smiling and giving her a nod, signalling to her that the interview was over.

She got the message, smiled and thanked me, continuing with her piece to camera as I walked off. Jack immediately joined me and took my hand. Without thinking, I held tight.

'You did great!' His handsome face was beaming.

'I wasn't expecting the last question. Did it sound OK?'

'You handled it beautifully. Very classy.'

I laughed, looking up at him. 'Coming from an heir apparent, I will take that as a compliment.'

'It was most definitely meant as one.'

25
———

Once inside, I did as Zinnia had instructed, and gave her a call. I also messaged my editor to say that I was inside and where Jack and I were now standing, having thankfully been given a glass of champagne which I'd never needed more.

Within a few minutes, my agent was at my side, air kissing around me and landing a big smacker on Jack's cheek before wiping off her lipstick with a tissue, pulled from a cavernous Gucci bag. In all the time I'd known Zinnia, she had never believed in travelling light, whatever the occasion.

A few minutes later, the attending members of the publishing team also arrived, and for the first time since I'd signed with them six years ago, I was able to give them all a hug. All our meetings so far had been online, as I'd never felt able to head up to their offices or to have dinner meetings. It was wonderful to meet them in person and thank them for all that they'd done over the past years. I introduced Jack and he chatted with them easily, unfazed by all the hustle and bustle that surrounded us as famous faces drifted by. As he said, being expected to attend functions from an early age seemed to have instilled a sense of normality about them into Jack. Right now, I was thankful for his complete calm in the situation, despite Zinnia's cheeky comments about the two of us, which he either smiled enigmatically at or brushed off tactfully in a way that meant neither party were embarrassed.

Over the next forty-five minutes, various people were introduced to me, most of whose names vacated my brain almost immediately due to a mix of excitement, nervousness and the still overwhelming sense of surrealism. Just as we were thinking about going to find our seats, there was a swish of silver and gold and suddenly Bella Dupree appeared in front of me, along with several other people, none of whom I recognised.

'Astoria! Oh my God! It's so good to finally meet you. I'm so excited that you're here tonight. I really hope you like what we've done with the book. I absolutely loved it, as you know, and the moment I finished it, I began reading it again.'

'Thank you,' I said, which didn't seem adequate to balance her kind enthusiasm. 'Thank you so much!' I added. 'I'm sure I will love it, and I'm sorry that I wasn't able to attend the screening previously.'

She took my hand and smiled. 'That's OK, I understand. It can all be a bit overwhelming sometimes, can't it?'

Coming from one of the biggest stars of the Hollywood screen, if anyone could understand overwhelming, it was her.

'Definitely.' I let out a nervous and slightly relieved laugh. We exchanged a private smile and, for a moment, she tightened her hold on my hand before turning to Jack.

'And who's this?'

'Oh, I'm sorry. Bella, this is Jack Coulsdon-Hart. He's my backup for the evening.'

She shook his hand, then turned and grinned at me. 'You have very good taste in backup.'

I smiled, not really knowing what to say, and decided that remaining silent was probably the best option.

One of the entourage leant forward and whispered something in Bella's ear. 'I'm sorry, I have to go but hopefully I'll see you later at the after-party. It really is so good to meet you.' With that, she gave me a huge hug before disappearing back into the crowd in a swoosh of highly expensive metallic fabric.

'Look at you mixing with the rich and famous,' Jack teased.

'Oh, you're a fine one to talk. If you don't behave, I might start introducing you as the Honourable Jack Coulsdon-Hart.'

'You wouldn't dare.'

I looked up and met his gaze, closer to it now with the five-inch heels.

'Do you really want to try me on that?'

A smile tilted one side of his lips upward as he looked back at me, the gaze unwavering.

'I'm in two minds. Part of me thinks you'd never dare, but there's another part of me that knows somewhere in there is a woman who would not hesitate in doing that, just to show me not to take her for granted.'

I gave him a quick raise of my eyebrows, knowing that I would never do that to him anyway. But it was fun to pretend, even though I was pretty sure he knew the truth.

'Would it really bother you?'

'Tonight? Not really. I don't think anyone would even remember.'

'I'm pretty sure quite a few people would. You're fairly hard to forget.'

'Was that a compliment?'

'It was an observation.'

Moments later, we were ushered into the theatre itself for the actual screening. My stomach twisted suddenly with nerves. I'd lived with this book a long time and got to know the characters so well. They felt like friends. I always knew that handing them over in a sale of the dramatic rights meant that they were no longer mine, but I'd never been in the position before to see the outcome of that. Now I was about to and could only hope that Bella's love of the book, and her endeavour to keep it as true as I'd been led to believe she wanted to, had been enough to convince the money men at the studios to do so. Either way, I was about to find out, as the lights dimmed around us and the curtain rose.

* * *

'I know you're really trying not to cry because of the make-up,' Jack whispered close to my ear as the lights came up, 'but I'm hoping those are happy tears you're keeping back.'

I nodded, unable to speak. My worries had been unfounded, and the book had been turned into the most beautiful film, with Bella portraying the heroine of the novel in the best and most sensitive way I could have ever hoped for. My agent and the fabulous team from my publisher all came towards me, clapping and looking as pleased as I was with the outcome, exchanging more hugs and frantically dabbing at make-up in the hope of keeping it in check before filing out.

'What did you think?' Bella rushed towards me, her face suddenly looking younger and slightly insecure. 'Did you like it?'

'I really did,' I replied honestly. 'I absolutely loved it. You did an amazing job and totally captured the heroine as I imagined her when I was writing the book.'

'You really think that? Honestly?'

'I really do. I promise you. Thank you for helping bring my book to life in such a beautiful way.'

Eyes already filling with tears spilled over and she flung her arms around my neck, whispering the words, 'Thank you.' I hugged her back and once again felt what a surreal world I was experiencing. One of the most highly paid actresses in the world was thanking me for telling her that she'd done a wonderful job. Definitely not a position I ever thought I'd find myself in, but one that I suddenly felt grateful for, allowing me to give a genuine compliment to a young woman whom you'd never suspect would require such reassurance. But her expression showed that the simple words I spoke to her resonated and gave her confidence I hadn't expected her to need. Perhaps we all wear a mask at times. The prospect of coming tonight had terrified me and that terror still hadn't completely left me, but this moment made me glad that I had forced myself and that Jack had been so steady and supportive, along with my family.

'You're coming to the party, right?'

'I... err...'

'Yes, she is,' Zinnia answered for me.

'Great!' Bella said, glancing over her shoulder and raising a hand to someone. 'I have to go but I'll catch up with you again there.' I nodded and then she was gone.

I looked up at Jack, feeling the beaming smile on my face.

'Happy?'

'Yes,' I replied, laughing. 'I can't help thinking this is all some sort of dream and I'm going to wake up shortly.'

'Before you do, let's get to that party. I want to make sure I get a dance with a famous author.'

'Oh, shush,' I said taking the arm he offered as we headed out in a small group towards the fleet of black cars that would be whisking people to the various parties. I had no idea which one we were going to, but right now, I didn't care. To my utter astonishment, I was actually enjoying myself. Jack was very much helping that. He wasn't intrusive, never barged into any of the conversations, he just stood there, being polite and making small talk when needed as well as being a silent, steady rock of support for me, and I wasn't sure I would ever be able to repay him for that.

The party was loud, colourful, exciting and eye-opening. The team that had helped make this book what it was, along with Jack, all had far too much champagne, and a wonderful time together. I had laughed more this evening than I had done in what felt like a decade. After Mike died, I didn't think I would ever laugh again, and then on the odd occasion that I did, it felt disloyal to the man I had loved so very much. It was silly to feel like that, I knew that in my heart, but I was unable to let go. And then it was almost as though I forgot how to laugh.

Gradually it had come back, that ability, especially once my niece and nephew arrived on the scene, but there was always a hint of guilt attached to it. But with the advent of Clive into my life, I'd begun to laugh more. His funny, sweet face with that dopey smile and always being so pleased to see me, even if I'd literally been out for twenty seconds dropping something in the compost bin, brought me such joy and release, it was like a dimmer switch had subtly been turned. And tonight, the switch was on full brightness and, for the first time since that awful night, I'd felt no guilt at all. Mike would be proud of me. That's all I needed to think now. Mike wouldn't have wanted me to shut myself away like I had. As much as he'd loved me, he'd want me to be happy, just as I would have, had the situation been reversed – a scenario I'd wished far more times than I could count. Tonight was a massive step but I'd had Jack by my side. I knew I wouldn't be here right now if it hadn't been for him. But I was determined to try harder to do things on my own too. For Mike. And for me.

'You're miles away,' Jack said close to my ear when we were alone, the others having gone off to mingle and star spot.

'I was just thinking about all the people I'm grateful to for helping me get here tonight, including you.'

'You did this yourself, Lily. I certainly didn't do very much at all, if anything.'

'You agreed to come with me, despite being volunteered and therefore not exactly being given a lot of choice.'

'A bit like you with having me stay at your place, then? So far, so even.'

I smiled up at him, accepting the comparison.

'Admittedly, I wasn't really thrilled at the prospect initially, but as it's turned out, I've been glad.'

'Really?' A wide smile spread across Jack's face.

'Really,' I confirmed. 'Without you staying, I wouldn't have felt so comfortable with you, and I know we've had our disagreements, but I've talked to you more than anybody in years. Between you and Clive, I've begun to see what I was missing.'

'I'm glad. I know none of this has been easy for you, and I know it's not a quick fix. I don't expect you to be flashing a chock-full social diary by tomorrow night, but you're taking steps, and that's what matters. You have too much to offer the world to hide from it.'

'Thank you,' I said, not sure what else to say, but deciding that that was probably enough.

'I'm surprised you haven't asked me if I enjoyed the film.'

'I know. Part of me wants to and part of me doesn't want to know in case you didn't like it but would then feel you have to say you liked it for fear of upsetting me.'

'I thought you knew by now I'm not very good at saying things for effect,' Jack said. 'If you can't be honest with someone, then what's the point? Of course, one should always be tactful, but...' He shrugged to punctuate the point, then tilted his head. 'And now you're studying me as though I'm a very rare specimen. What's going through that brain of yours now?'

To be honest, there was a lot going through my brain, or rather being washed around by several glasses of expensive champagne. One of the thoughts was that I was staring at one of the best-looking men I'd ever met. The truth was I liked this new Jack, not just because he was jaw-droppingly handsome, but because he was kind and thoughtful and also because he challenged me. He didn't pander and he certainly didn't take any bullshit.

'I was wondering if you might like to dance?'

A dance floor had been set up in one part of the venue, and it was already beginning to get quite crowded as a DJ, apparently someone extremely well-known but whose name meant nothing to me, was seamlessly mixing one track into another.

'Somehow, I don't believe that was the only thing you were thinking, but yes, I would like to dance,' he said, taking a step closer to me. 'Very much so.'

I couldn't remember the last time I'd danced in public. Normally, I kept my moves to myself, although I now shared them with Clive as I prepared dinner or baked in the kitchen. But here I was, at an after-party of a major film premiere, dancing among faces I recognised from the big and small screen and opposite Jack Coulsdon-Hart. When I made a change, I certainly didn't do it by halves.

As the music shifted to a slower pace, various couples paired up, some of which surprised me, but I did my best not to show it.

'May I have this dance?' Jack asked.

I looked up into the handsome face that now had a hint of seriousness about it and realised he was unsure of my answer. A few months ago, I would have politely turned him down. But now I didn't want to.

I nodded in acceptance and felt my body fizz with excitement as one strong arm slipped around my waist pulling me closer, and the other gently took my hand. He led confidently and skilfully, and as one song merged into another there was a brief question in his eyes. I held myself just that little bit closer to him as an answer and we continued the dance. The music was loud and whenever Jack wanted to speak to me, he had to bend until his lips almost brushed my ear to make himself heard. Every time he did, a fresh wave of excitement rushed through my body in a way that it hadn't done in over a decade.

It was nearly three o'clock in the morning by the time we'd done our rounds of goodbyes, practically falling into the limousine waiting to take us to the hotel, which thankfully wasn't far. The doorman opened the car door, but it was Jack who helped me from the limo and offered me his arm as we walked into the hotel foyer, a shining confection of white marble, crystal chandeliers and subtle gold accents. I was grateful of his strong body next to me, due to both the heels and the copious amounts of champagne I had imbibed during the evening, but also because it felt nice. Walking in tonight, in fact the whole evening spent with Jack just felt *right* but I wasn't ready to acknowledge that, let alone accept it.

The hotel receptionist handed over our key cards, explaining that our luggage had already been taken up earlier, having been dropped off by the driver. She then explained that breakfast could be taken either in the room or downstairs at the restaurant and advised us of the timings. With that, she wished us a good night, and told us that if there was anything else we required, to just call down for it.

We entered the mirrored lift and made our way up to the correct floor. Sneaking a peek, I was amazed to see that both my make-up and hair were still in place, despite a long evening, a warm atmosphere and more dancing than I'd done in years. It was true testament to the skills of the artists my sister-in-law had kindly arranged for me that their work still looked as good now as it had done hours earlier.

We made our way down a silent corridor, and I suddenly had an overwhelming desire to giggle. Jack noticed my big grin and him putting his finger to his lips just made things worse. Thankfully, the room wasn't too far, and he held the card against the mechanism, waiting for the click and the green light before pushing it open and allowing me to go in first, following behind and turning the lock. I'd explained our situation to the publisher, and they had assured me that they would arrange either two rooms or a suite for the evening so that Jack and I could each have our own room. As we'd only been given one number, I assumed it was a suite.

I stopped suddenly and Jack almost walked straight into the back of me, halting himself and putting his hand on my upper arms as he did so to steady himself. 'What's wrong?'

'This isn't a suite.' I turned to look up at him. 'They said they'd arranged a suite so that you and I would be separate. This isn't a suite. This isn't even a twin.' I flapped my hand at the large double bed.

'Does it really matter? It's not like you and I haven't shared a bed before and,' he looked at his watch, 'it's literally just for a few hours. I can go down and try and sort something if you prefer, though.'

He pushed a hand through his hair and, with the other one, undid his bow tie so it hung loose on his shirt as he opened the top couple of buttons. He looked shattered, and I knew how he felt. Who knew how long it would take them to sort out another room, if they even had a spare one available?

'You're right. It's fine. Let's just go to bed.'

'There's a sentence I never thought I'd hear from you.' He gave a devilish grin.

'You're not helping,' I said, taking off my shoes and letting out a sigh of relief and pleasure.

'I know,' he said, coming to stand in front of me. Without the heels, I had to tip my head back further and between the champagne and the tiredness that was definitely now kicking in, I felt myself overbalance. Jack's arms were around me within an instant, steadying me.

'You all right?'

'You're just a long way up.'

'I can fix that,' he said, taking my hand and sitting down on the bed so that we were more eye to eye.

'That's better.'

'Good.'

'I never did ask – did you enjoy the film?'

'I did,' he replied. 'I really did. I thought they made a very sympathetic interpretation of your book. Obviously, the book is better, as they always are, but I was glad to see such a faithful version of your work.'

'You've read the book?'

'I've read all of your books.'

'You have?'

'You seem surprised.'

'I'm stunned,' I said.

'Why?'

'I don't know. I just didn't think they would be the sort of thing that appealed to you.'

'You wrote them. I wanted to read them.'

'You've really read them all?'

'I most certainly have, and loved every one. Now,' he said, standing so that he was even closer, 'you look like you're about to fall asleep standing up, so go and take first turn in the bathroom so you can get to bed.'

Gently, he laid large, strong hands on my now bare shoulders and turned me gently in the direction of the large bathroom we'd passed on the way in. I headed off like a clockwork toy that had been pointed the right way.

'That dress is amazing, by the way. I've been trying to find a way to say it properly since we were back at the house and still haven't, so I'm just going to blurt it out now.'

I looked back over my shoulder and grinned, feeling a rush of warmth at the compliment and the low tone of his voice as he said it, roughened with tiredness.

'Seriously. Sexy as hell.'

My grin got wider and then I disappeared into the bathroom to undo all the amazing work Jemima and Martin had done. Leaving the bathroom free for Jack, I crawled thankfully into the crisp white sheets and was asleep before he'd even closed the bathroom door.

26

When I woke the following morning, for a moment, I thought I'd died. Then I tried to open my eyes and wished that I had died. I was still in exactly the same position I'd gone to sleep in, and got the feeling that I'd passed out rather than drifted off. I let out a large groan as I made an effort to move, with both my head and body objecting to the decision.

'Good morning, sunshine,' a cheery voice greeted me.

I prised open one eyelid to see Jack sitting on the end of the bed, looking annoyingly chirpy and unhungover.

'How come you look like that and I feel like this?' I said in a voice that sounded like I had swallowed the gravel from a budgie's cage. My mouth definitely tasted like I had. Possibly also the budgie.

'Probably because I'm a little bit more used to partying than you are.'

'I thought you didn't do all that any more?'

'I never said I'd stopped altogether, just that I didn't do it as much as when I was younger.'

'You could at least try and look a little less chipper,' I said, swinging my legs out and sitting up slowly before heading off to the bathroom, hoping that a few splashes of cold water on my face might by some miracle take away the thumping head and churning stomach. It didn't, but having brushed my teeth, I at least felt a little more human. I showered quickly, mainly because standing up for any length of time was more of a challenge than usual, and then grabbed one of the thick robes from the back of the door, wrapping myself up in it before shuffling back out into the main room.

'Better?'

'Cleaner, at least.'

'I didn't think you'd feel like going down for breakfast, so I took the liberty of ordering some for the room. I hope that was OK?'

I sat down gingerly on the bed. 'Whatever is fine. I don't think I'll be eating again for some time.'

'You have to eat something, Lily. You need to soak up some of the alcohol. It will help, I promise.'

'It will help me throw up.'

The doorbell to the room rang. I loved that swanky hotel rooms had their own doorbells, although I was less enthusiastic on this occasion as I knew there was a pile of food which Jack was expecting me to eat on the other side of it.

'Just eat what you can,' Jack said, giving a me sympathetic smile and placing two paracetamols in front of me and a bottle of still water with which to take them.

I tucked my feet back under the duvet, squishing myself into a small ball as a polite, uniformed waiter nodded good morning to me and Jack signed the receipt, and gave a tip.

'You'll have to tell me how much you've spent on tips once we get back, so that I can reimburse you.'

'I will do nothing of the sort and neither will you,' Jack said.

'Now, let's see what we can tempt you with. Here, first of all, have some juice. Get some vitamin C into you. Did you take the pills?'

I nodded gently.

'Good. What else?'

'I'm really not sure I can face any of that,' I said tentatively, looking at the plates of food which Jack had uncovered.

'Just a little,' he said, testing the scrambled eggs as he did so. 'These are excellent. It's so hard to get good scrambled eggs anywhere. Come on, just a little bit on some toast?'

He began preparing his culinary suggestion anyway, so it seemed like I was going to get the slice whether I wanted it or not. I didn't, but he was being so kind and understanding that I felt I owed it to him to at least try. Shuffling down the bed to where Jack had got the man to leave the trolley as a makeshift table, I cautiously tried the food he'd put in front of me.

Much to my surprise, I ate more than I thought I would and did indeed feel better. My head still felt like a melon that had been split in two, but my stomach had stopped resembling a washing machine. Well, not completely, but least it was just on the delicate cycle now rather than full spin.

I plodded back into the bathroom to get dressed into jeans and a delicately flowered blouse I'd brought with me as a change from T-shirts. Having gathered together the toiletries I'd left in the bathroom, I returned to the main room, dropped the few extra bits into my overnight bag and zipped it up.

'Ready to go?' Jack asked, lifting two suit carriers out of the wardrobe, one containing his tuxedo and the other my beautiful satin dress. I wasn't sure when I would ever wear it again, but I was glad I had bought it for last night. Somewhere in the woolly space where my brain was supposed to be, a vague memory of Jack saying he loved the dress floated about. I loved the dress too, but the way he had said it had sent shivers up and down my bare spine as I'd walked away from him.

I put a hand to my head. I couldn't think about all that right now. It hadn't meant anything more than that he liked the dress. But I knew, especially last night, I had loved the fact that he did.

'Tablets not helping?' Jack asked, noticing my hand resting at my temple.

'Just making sure it doesn't roll away.' I gave a wan smile that Jack accepted as explanation as he moved towards the door which he opened for me, taking my bag as I passed.

'I can carry that.'

'It's fine.'

'Thanks,' I said, leaning back against the bar in the lift as we travelled smoothly down to the foyer.

'I'll drop the key off,' I said as the doors opened and Jack indicated with a nod of his head for me to go first. I walked towards the reception desk and handed the key cards over to an unengaged member of staff with a smile before heading back to meet Jack. We'd texted the limo service about half an hour ago and thankfully the car was outside waiting. The driver took the luggage, laying the suit carriers carefully on top as Jack opened the door for me and I got in with him following me and closing the door behind him. The day was bright and beautiful, making the journey home a pleasant one, although sadly I missed most of it, as within ten minutes, I was asleep against Jack's side, then didn't wake until the crunching of the car's tyres on the gravel of my driveway woke me.

'Nice snooze?' Jack asked, looking down to where I was still resting on him.

'Yes, thanks,' I said, looking up sleepily and thinking I could stay here all day for more reasons than one. I forced myself towards the door and made my exit into the fresh air, thanking the driver as he handed over the luggage to Jack, and tipping him myself, pulling the money from my jeans pocket where I'd prepared it earlier. He drove off slowly and disappeared up the drive and out of sight as I let us in the door. It seemed strange that there was no Clive to bounce up and say hello.

Jack put the bags down and closed the door behind him. 'It's not the same, is it?'

'No,' I said turning to him. 'It's not. I don't like it.'

'Do you want me to go and get him now? You could have a bit more rest, if you like. I won't be long.'

'I can't sleep the whole day away.'

'Why not?'

'It's a waste.'

Gently, Jack put his hands either side of my head and dipped his forehead to mine.

'You're allowed, Lily. You had a late night, and you did something that took a lot of courage and a lot of mental and physical energy, especially as you're not used to it. You're allowed to rest. It's good for you. OK?'

I nodded my head against his and padded away towards the snug. He followed me and waited as I curled myself onto the sofa, whereupon he laid a blanket over me.

'I'll be back before long.'

'Are you sure you don't mind?'

'Not at all. I miss him too. Now get some sleep,' he said, giving me a smile before turning to the door.

'Jack?'

He turned back and I sat up a little, which prompted him to come closer. I reached out and he quickly accepted the hug, wrapping his own arms around me.

'What's this for?' he asked softly. 'Not that I'm complaining, I hasten to add. Just curious.'

'It's for everything.'

That seemed enough explanation and he tightened the hug briefly before letting me go and tucking me back under the blanket.

'We'll be back soon.'

I heard the door click closed and a few minutes later the sound of the car starting and heading off up the driveway. The house suddenly felt overwhelmingly quiet. I'd never noticed that before, in fact I revelled in the peace and tranquilly. But now it felt like something was missing. I knew that something was Clive, but I had a feeling that Jack was becoming more and more a part of that something as well.

* * *

The next few weeks found Jack and I spending more and more time together, often using Clive as an excuse to take a walk. Dinners in the evening saw us sitting longer and longer, talking about the past, the future, and every subject in between. We'd often decamp from the dining table to the sofa, or the snug, and Clive would happily plod alongside us and once we were settled, lie down across our feet and begin snoring happily.

My writing was flowing, and I looked forward to the evenings when Jack would be home to share dinner and conversation. Felix and Poppy had been round several times, often bringing the children, who would clamber all over their godfather and play with the dog until they wore themselves out, at which point Poppy and I would go and tuck them up in the bedroom I had made into their own. Quite often, Poppy would try to catch my eye and make gestures towards Jack, but I would either pretend not to notice, or laughingly blank them. I wasn't ready to be questioned, even with good intentions, about my relationship with Jack. I wasn't entirely sure what it was, or where it was going, let alone ready to try to explain that to somebody else.

'Have you…?' Poppy whispered one night as we closed the door on the children's bedroom.

'Have I what?'

'You know…'

I shook my head at Poppy, smiling. 'Clearly I don't know otherwise I wouldn't be asking. You are being exceptionally vague.'

Poppy let out a whispered sigh. 'Have you and Jack slept together?' she asked, still in a whisper, as we both knew how big little ears could be, even through a door.

I turned back, one stair down. 'No! It's not like that.'

'Could have fooled me.'

'It's not,' I repeated, although if I was truly honest with myself, I wasn't sure what it was like. I loved Jack's company and spending time with him had become one of my favourite things to do. From what I could tell, he felt much the same, but nothing physical had happened between us.

'It's not,' I repeated to Poppy. 'You know what Jack's like. If he'd have wanted anything more, he would have made a move in that direction and he hasn't. We're just friends. Close friends.'

'Have you ever thought that Jack might be waiting for you to make the first move?'

The thought hadn't crossed my mind.

'We both know that Jack's definitely an alpha male. He wouldn't be waiting for me.'

'We also both know that Jack now is not the Jack that he once was. He's matured, and he knows you've had a lot to deal with in the past. Maybe he's just waiting for a signal.'

'He's not,' I said definitively. 'And if the boys have eaten all the dessert while you've kept me up here nattering, I'm definitely going to give you a signal.'

Poppy laughed but put her hand on my arm to stop me as I headed back towards the kitchen.

'Just think about it.'

I nodded, knowing that it was the easiest way to close the conversation down. But I had absolutely no intention of thinking about any of it.

27

That truly had been my intention, but reality proved different. Once Poppy had brought it up, I couldn't *stop* thinking about it.

Surely if Jack wanted something more than a friendship then he would have broached the subject by now? He had never exactly been backwards in coming forwards before, and certainly not when it came to women. Yes, Poppy was right in that he had matured and was a much better man for it, but a leopard doesn't entirely change its spots.

'You look deep in thought.' Jack's melodic tones interrupted my musings as I crouched low and stared out over the wildlife pond that he'd been putting in, theoretically looking for creatures but in reality just daydreaming. I shot up at his presence and got a head rush, immediately looking for the nearest sturdy thing to hang on to as the blood rush settled. The nearest sturdy thing was, of course, Jack, and he laid an arm gently around me as I got my balance.

'Better?' he asked as I made to move away.

'Just didn't hear you come up.'

'Maybe just step back from the water a few paces.' Concern

creased his brow as he guided me. Did his arm linger a little longer than was necessary?

'I'm fine. I'll just go in and sit down.'

He nodded, looking a little confused as I marched off back to the house.

Bloody Poppy. Now she had me overthinking every little moment. I needed to just stop. Yes, Jack was gorgeous, and yes, I'd had feelings and sensations at times in his company that I hadn't experienced for a long time, but none of that meant anything. Any warm-blooded, heterosexual female with a pulse would be able to see that Jack was the epitome of tall, dark and handsome, with a strong, hard body gained from manual work and a love of being outdoors. As the weather had warmed, I'd had to close the blind in my office on occasion when Jack was out working in the garden, because the sight of Jack stripping off his top to wade into the pond and add rocks or plants or whatever else he was doing was seriously affecting my word count. On the other hand, he was damn good inspiration for writing a hero.

'Just came to check on you. Seemed a bit odd out there.'

'I'm OK, honest.' I held a glass of cool water to my head as I sat on the kitchen sofa facing the garden.

'How do you think it's looking?' He motioned in the direction of the pond with his chin.

I let my eyes drift up from his fitted T-shirt, over the strong jaw now darkened with a day's growth of stubble, and met the hypnotic eyes.

'It's gorgeous,' I said.

'Great! I was hoping you'd say that.'

'You were?'

'Yes. But what do you think about adding a fluffy diplodocus over on this side?'

Obviously that wasn't his exact wording, but as he was talking about plants and also using a Latin name, it may as well have been.

'Huh?' I snapped out of it.

He showed me a photo on his phone. 'One of these on the far side of the pond?'

'Oh. Yes. Looks nice. You really have free rein on this as I have no idea. I just like the idea of introducing more wildlife into the garden.' I looked down at the dog, who was now leaning against Jack's leg and getting a rhythmic head rub as he sat there. 'That doesn't include you though, mister. No more warnings.'

'Oh no, has he been in again?'

'It would be more accurate to say we both have, as he decided he was quite happy sitting in there and refused to come out.'

'So you went in?'

'Yes. Little sod,' I said, looking down at the now angelic face turned to the sun as Jack rubbed his head.

'I wish I'd been here for that.'

'If you had, it would have been you going in and not me. He's your dog and it's your pond when that happens!'

Jack threw his head back and laughed and I tried not to focus on the wave of happiness that always rushed through me at the sound.

'I'll do some more training with him over the weekend to keep him away from the pond. How's that?'

'That would be great, thank you.'

'No problem.'

'What were you thinking about earlier when I made you jump?'

'Oh... just how lovely it's all looking.' I smiled up at him.

Jack fixed me with a look. 'I see.' He was smiling, but I knew he didn't believe a word I'd just said.

* * *

'That smells good,' said Jack, coming up behind me as I was dishing up dinner.

Fresh from the shower, dinner wasn't the only thing that smelled good. As I turned around my eyes confirmed that, as usual, he looked even better than he smelled. I gave a quick smile of thanks, before gently moving him out of the way so I could busy myself with the final preparations for tonight's meal.

'Are you free for dinner tomorrow?' Jack asked, as I motioned for him to sit.

I mis-stepped in surprise as I began to bring the dish to the table. Jack was up and out of his chair, taking it from me within an instant.

'You OK? I've told you before if anything's heavy, I'll carry it,' he said, setting the dish on the table and pulling my chair out for me before pouring us each a glass of the fizzy grape juice I'd set there earlier. 'So, dinner tomorrow?'

I swallowed and began dishing us each up a bowl of the pasta puttanesca I'd made. 'What's the occasion?'

'There isn't one. I'd like to take you out as a way of showing my appreciation for all that you've done. And I just thought it would be nice.'

'So long as we go halves.'

Jack put his fork down on the side of the bowl and took a deep breath, letting it out slowly as he spread his hands flat on the table-top, stretching them before letting them relax.

'I have to admit this is absolutely the hardest I've ever had to work to ask someone to have dinner with me.'

I didn't know what to say so remained silent.

'OK. I'm going to try again. Lily, I'd very much like to take you to dinner tomorrow night, if you're free. And no, we would not be going halves.'

A swirl of emotions flooded through me. Did this mean

anything? Was it purely to thank me for hosting him? Did that mean that he would be moving out soon?

Jack rubbed the back of his neck. 'You're taking longer than I would have hoped over this decision. If you don't want to, then—'

'I do. I do want to.'

'You don't have to look quite so terrified. It's just two friends having dinner.'

'Ha! I'm not terrified. You're not that scary.'

Jack picked up his fork and made the motion of a circle around his own face before digging back into the pasta. 'Try telling your face that.'

'My face is fine. I'm just out of the habit of going out to dinner.'

Jack looked up at me. 'The place I've booked is really quiet, and I've asked for a table in a more secluded part of the restaurant.'

'You've already booked the table? There's confidence for you.'

'Not at all. In fact, this is probably the least confident I've ever been asking a woman out to dinner. And I was proved right. The table could always have been cancelled or, more likely, I'd have just gone there alone.' He looked down at the dog. 'Or maybe taken Clive as a partner.'

'Clive has a very busy social diary. We'd have had to see if he was free anyway.'

'Is that so?'

'Uh-huh.' I popped a forkful of dinner in my mouth.

He shook his head at me with a glimmer of a smile before focusing back on his own dinner.

'By the way, your face is a hell of a lot more than just fine.' He flicked the green gaze up and met my startled blue one before smiling again and returning to his dinner.

* * *

'I knew this was going to happen,' Poppy practically squealed when I spoke to her later on the phone.

'Nothing is happening. It's just dinner between friends. He said that himself.'

'He also said your face was a hell of a lot better than fine.'

'I knew I was going to regret telling you that.'

'Too late.'

'Yes. Unfortunately. Anyway, what am I supposed to wear?'

'What's the sexiest thing you own?'

'The dress that we bought for the premiere. One, he's seen it, two, I think it's a little dressy for the occasion and three, I don't want to look sexy. It's friends, remember.'

'I've got a feeling he's going to think you look sexy in whatever you wear.'

'Will you knock it off? It's not like that at all.'

* * *

The following evening, as Jack and I practically fell through the front door and he pushed me up against the wall, his lips exploring my throat as his hands explored other areas with an erotic growl of appreciation, I had the brief thought – very brief – that the next time I spoke to Poppy, I might have to eat humble pie. Apparently, it was very much like that.

'Oh God, Lily,' he whispered. 'I've been wanting to do this for so long, but I didn't want to rush you before you were ready.'

I'm not sure I am ready, I thought briefly, but I knew I wanted this. I wanted him. I'd known it for a while now but had kept talking myself out of it, convincing myself that my life was full enough, that I didn't need, didn't feel a desire for anything else, especially Jack. But I'd been lying to myself. I knew that too. The only thing I hadn't realised was that Jack had wanted more as well. But I was certainly in no doubt of that now.

We stumbled into the snug, both of us fumbling with the other's clothing. Jack hoisted me up, and I wrapped my legs around his waist as he made short work of the buttons on my dress and pushed it back off my shoulders, letting it fall to the floor, his mouth lowered, and my mind went blank of everything but Jack's hard body pressed against me and his gentle but confident movements as he laid me down on the soft rug and began to remove the rest of my clothes, each movement followed by a trail of butterfly kisses as he did so. All I could see was Jack. All I could think of was Jack, and all I could feel was Jack.

* * *

'We should have got Jack to come home a lot sooner if we'd known this was going to happen. Look at you, you're positively glowing!' Poppy laughed, giving Clive a head scratch after I'd made him sit and wait patiently for a square of cheese.

'I am *not* glowing,' I said, laughing. But I did feel different and not just because muscles I'd forgotten I even had now ached from the past month spent with Jack. I felt different inside – stronger, somehow. Jack and I had been out to a few places, and he was always encouraging but would never push me to do anything I wasn't ready for yet. Then again, I never thought I'd be ready to take another man to my bed and yet I had. It had felt right, just as everything felt right with Jack. This revelation had surprised me more than anyone. I knew I'd been blessed to have found a wonderful man in Mike who loved me and, when our time together had been so cruelly cut short, I'd never imagined I'd be so lucky as to find another with whom I felt so comfortable and cared for. But here I was, waking up each day next to a man who loved me entirely, a love that was so easy and natural to return.

Sundays had become a particular highlight, as Jack woke early, kissing me softly before he left the bed to take Clive out for a walk into the village to collect the papers while I snuggled back down in the warmth of the bed and dozed until they returned. As Clive ate his breakfast, Jack would prepare ours and bring it to the bedroom before hopping back into the bed I'd kept warm for him. Clive would trot in and settle himself in his upstairs bed as we read – Jack catching up on the news and me diving back into my latest book or occasionally a magazine. I'd move my legs so that they were against his, loving the feel of having his solid body next to me, each absorbed in our own things, but entirely together. It was blissful.

This morning, I'd spent a peaceful couple of minutes just watching him sleep, the dark lashes resting on his cheeks, his face tanned from the summer sun, and then he'd spoken, telling me with that hot, sleep-roughened voice I loved so much not to watch him. I'd stayed where I was and told him he'd have to make me stop.

'With pleasure,' he'd growled, suddenly reaching over and with one arm scooping me on top of him before rolling so that I was pinned below. We'd both been late for work.

28

'You're totally glowing.' Poppy leaned forward at the kitchen island and rested her chin in her hands. 'And now you have to tell me exactly why. All the details, please.'

I laughed and pushed the cup of tea towards her, alongside a slice of iced carrot cake that I'd made earlier. It was Jack's favourite and I got additional pleasure from whipping one up these days. He'd always been appreciative of my cooking, but now there were extra benefits to the gratitude.

'Come on,' Poppy said, through a mouthful of cake. 'I'm on tenterhooks here.'

I laughed and waved her away as I reached across to answer my mobile. I didn't recognise the number but swiped to answer it.

'Lily?'

'Who's calling?'

'It's Sanjid. I work with Jack.' I knew who he was. Jack had kept in touch with colleagues and friends from Kew and, when he was looking to take on more staff now that the business was growing, he'd put feelers out for an up-and-coming talent whom he could mentor. Sanjid had been one of the candidates. Jack liked him from the start. He had a flair for the work, enthusiasm, and an almost insatiable thirst for learning. Jack had told me that it wouldn't surprise him if the young man was exhibiting at Chelsea within the next five years. But why was he ringing me?

'Hi, Sanjid. Is everything OK?'

'Kind of.' The tone of his voice didn't match his words and I placed one hand on the cool quartz of my worktop to help the sudden rush of blood to my veins.

'What's wrong?'

'There's been a bit of an accident.'

I felt behind me for the kitchen stool and sat down, awkwardly and heavily. Poppy, having seen me change colour, was by my side asking in a whispered tone what was wrong.

'What exactly do you mean, a bit of an accident? Is Jack all right?' I forced myself to stay calm and keep my words measured and steady.

'Yes, but I think he needs some stitches and I'm not insured to drive the pickup.'

Oddly enough, Jack had just been speaking about this last night, and I knew it was on his to-do list for this evening. At least, it had been.

'Are you still at Mrs Dorsey's?' I asked.

'Yes.'

'I'll be there as soon as I can. Tell him not to move or do anything stupid.'

'He said he'll drive himself.'

'That's exactly what I mean by making sure he doesn't do anything stupid. Get several people to sit on him if needs be, but keep him there.'

We hung up and I turned to Poppy. 'Can you take Clive?'

'Of course,' she said, already grabbing his lead from the hook and calling him over to her. 'What's happened?'

'I'm not sure. Jack's had some sort of accident and Sanjid thinks he needs stitches.'

'You don't know where he's hurt?'

'No, I didn't think to ask.' My stomach was churning and my head was buzzing with a raft of emotions, some of which I didn't want to give way to at the moment. I would deal with those later. First, I needed to get to Jack.

'You go. I'll get the dog food and lock up. Just give us a call when you know anything.' Poppy gave me a huge hug then stepped back, holding onto my shoulders. 'He's OK, Lily. You know that, right?'

I didn't know that, but I nodded anyway.

'I'll see you later,' I said, hugging her back before bending down and giving Clive a kiss on the top of his golden head. 'You be a good boy for Auntie Poppy.'

The dog looked back at me with a slightly befuddled expression, as if he didn't know what was going on. That made two of us.

I pulled up outside Mrs Dorsey's house and hurried out of the car around towards the back where there was a plethora of builders, building materials, and in amongst it all was Jack, sitting on a low wall with blood pouring down his face. I pushed back the wave of nausea that threatened to overwhelm me and headed towards him.

'I told them not to call you,' he said with a mixture of tiredness and spikiness.

'Well, then, I'm glad that your apprentice has more sense than his mentor and ignored you. What have you done?' I asked, bending down in front of him and gently pulling away his hand, which held a cloth soaked red with blood. A large, deep cut on his forehead showed underneath, still bleeding profusely. I quickly put it back and told him to apply pressure.

'You should have called an ambulance,' I said, getting Sanjid to help me get Jack to his feet. The young man was a much slighter build than Jack, but between both of us, and with one of the burly builders standing behind him in case he tipped backwards, we managed to get Jack to my car.

'Sorry again, mate,' one of the builders said, as we settled Jack inside the vehicle. 'Bit of a freak accident.'

I put my hand out against the side of the car and closed my eyes for a moment as the words reverberated around my brain. A freak accident...

'You OK, love? I'd have taken him myself, but he was kicking up hell of a stink about it all.'

'It's fine,' I said. 'And yes, I can imagine he was. Thank you anyway.'

I took a deep breath and hurried round to the driver's side, got in and pulled away towards the hospital.

'Why wouldn't you let them take you to the hospital?'

'Because they've got work to do,' said Jack. 'As have you. You shouldn't be here.'

I pulled the handbrake on at a traffic light and turned to him. 'And what exactly were you planning to do with that?' I asked, gesturing at his bloody face.

'It will stop in a minute. Everybody is just overreacting.'

'Don't be so bloody ridiculous. There's a damn great gash in your head. Stop being so stupidly macho about it all. What happened?'

'I was walking under the scaffold and one of the blokes tripped over something. His foot caught a hammer that he'd just put down and knocked it off the edge of the scaffold. I looked up at the shouts, which is when it clocked me straight on the bonce.'

'Why didn't you have a hard hat on?'

'I did. Well, I did have until the second before. It's so hot, the sweat was running in my eyes, so I'd just taken it off to wipe it away. Bad timing.'

Another flash of memory ripped through me, and I pushed it away to deal with later.

'Jesus Christ. Did you lose consciousness?'

'Not that I remember,' he said with an ironic smile.

I was failing to see the humour in the situation at this moment. I instructed the Bluetooth in my car to redial my phone's last number. Within a couple of rings, Sanjid's voice was on the other end.

'Hi, it's Lily. Does anyone know if Jack lost consciousness? The hospital will want to know.'

'Oh, for God's sake, Lily,' Jack snapped. 'I just told you I didn't.'

I ignored him, waiting for Sanjid to reply. 'I don't think so. He certainly fell down and it is a hard surface there, but he was already sitting up by the time I sprinted across the garden, which was less than a minute after it happened.'

'OK, thanks, Sanjid.' I hung up and could practically hear Jack seething next to me. Right now, I didn't care. The most important thing was to get him checked out properly. If he chose to be angry at me for that, then so be it. Some things were more important.

Several hours later, I was walking up and down the same patch of corridor that I had been wearing out for the last couple of hours. I'd sat occasionally in the waiting area, but I couldn't focus on anything and probably got my day's ten thousand steps in within the first hour.

'Are you Lily?' A nurse was walking towards me.

'Yes,' I said, moving quickly to meet her. 'How is he?'

'He's fine. We did a full scan as he had quite the impact at the front, and we don't know for sure whether he lost consciousness when he fell to the ground. It's better safe than sorry in these circumstances.'

'Absolutely.'

'But the scans were all clear and you can see him now,' she said, pushing open a door and allowing me to go through to where Jack was sitting on a bed in a hospital gown, a row of dark stitches down his forehead above his right eye. Despite all that, he still managed to look sexy as hell.

He raised a hand and gave a slightly sleepy smile.

The doctor attending him introduced herself, then explained that the gash was too deep to use the butterfly stitches, so they'd had to sew it.

'We used local anaesthetic to do that and he's had some quite strong painkillers now. It's going to be pretty painful once the anaesthetic starts wearing off. I'm afraid it's going to leave a scar and there will be some substantial bruising, but that will obviously fade.'

'Do you still love me now I've lost my looks?' Jack asked. His eyes, although sleepy and clearly rather drugged up, were mischievous.

I turned to the doctor. 'Are you sure he doesn't need any stronger drugs? You know, ones that might knock him right out for a few hours?'

She laughed as she placed the dressing over the stitches and began to secure it to his head. 'We did tell Jack about how to care for the wound but it's all here, just in case some of it is a bit fuzzy with the medication.' The nurse handed me some paperwork.

I stood waiting, trying to keep back all the thoughts threatening to rush into my mind. Suddenly, I felt Jack's fingers wrap around mine.

'I'm OK, Lily,' he said, for a moment seemingly totally lucid.

'I know.' I squeezed his fingers gently and fixed on a smile that felt one size too small.

* * *

Jack took the next few days off, thankfully, although I had a feeling it was more to satisfy and pacify me than from any real desire to on his part. I encouraged him to rest as much as he could, agreeing that he could take the dog out for a gentle walk, knowing that staying inside all the time would drive him mad.

Logically, I knew that the hospital had given him the all-clear, but my mind kept flashing back to seeing his face smothered with blood and the gaping wound in his head. I wanted him to at least give it a chance to start to heal and get a bit of rest before he was back at work. Sanjid had been by to see how he was doing, and had assured me that he would be keeping a close eye on Jack when he did return and ensuring that he didn't do anything that seemed like a bad idea. I was relieved that Jack had employed someone so level-headed and thanked the young man for his help and reassurance, before waving him back off in Jack's pickup, which he was now insured for.

* * *

I hadn't written a word all day. Normally I could switch off from the world around me and lose myself in my stories. It was, after all, once the initial shock was over, how I had coped with Mike's death. But right now, I couldn't switch off. I couldn't stop seeing Jack's face covered in blood. I'd even woken up last night crying in terror, as an image of him lying bloodied on the floor permeated my dreams, but when Jack asked me about the nightmare, I told him I couldn't remember. He'd wrapped his arms around me and we'd laid back down together. His breathing soon became deep and even but I'd been unable to sleep any more that night, fearing the return of images I couldn't bear.

29

Jack walked through the open back door, the air scented with blossoms, lavender and honeysuckle drifting in. He made his way towards me, smiling as though he hadn't seen me in ages, as he always did. It gave me the most wonderful feeling of contentment. Except tonight was different.

I took a step backwards and he halted in his tracks, the smile fading.

'What's wrong?'

'I can't do this.'

'Do what?' He asked the question, but his face told me he already knew the answer.

'This. Us.'

'Since when?' His voice took on a hard edge and the green eyes I loved so much lost their warmth.

'I think we both got caught up in something. The premiere, living on top of one another... we just got carried away. I think we both know that.'

'I don't know that at all. I think it's entirely the opposite. I think we both waited until we were absolutely sure.' He took a step towards me. 'You know this is right, Lily. I know you do.' He took my hand. 'I know the accident freaked you out and I'm so sorry about that, but I'm fine. The hospital confirmed it with scans. I don't know what else to say.'

'This time,' I said, pulling away from him and putting more space between us. If I didn't do that, I couldn't carry on with what I knew needed to be done. 'You were all right this time.'

'There won't be a next time. It was just an accident.'

'A freak accident!' I cried, repeating the phrase I'd not been able to shake from the moment the builder had said it. 'A freak accident, just like Mike's death was a freak accident, and yours could have been just as serious. You were lucky this time. I can't deal with having to hear those words again – there's been an accident. Next time, it might...' I couldn't finish the sentence.

'You don't need to think about that, Lily. You can't think about that all the time. None of us would do anything if all we considered were the risks. I thought you were happy?'

'I am happy. So happy, but don't you see? That's the whole point. I can't risk it again. I can't risk losing this happiness.'

'Lily, I'm not going anywhere.'

'You can't say that! You don't know! It's not up to us, is it? Mike told me the same thing. He promised he would never leave me and then I lost him. You shouldn't make promises you can't keep.'

'Lily.' Jack took a step towards me and when I tried to step back, I bumped into the countertop. He was close now. Too close. All I wanted to do was wrap my arms around him and never let him go. To feel safe, pressed against his solid, reassuring bulk and feel cared for and loved like I had in the past few weeks, something I'd never thought I would feel again. But I couldn't. I knew the longer I was with Jack the harder I would fall, and I was already well in over my head. It would be painful to stop this now but having it ripped away at some point down the line was too unbearable to even consider.

'Jack, I know you have good intentions, but you can't make a promise to be there because there's always a possibility that for one reason or another you might not be. Some things are beyond your control. And I'm sorry, but I'm just not prepared to risk it.'

He took a step back, his body tense now and his eyes dark with anger as he crossed his arms across his broad chest.

'There's more than one way to lose somebody, Lily. We've both been given a second chance at happiness here, and I can't speak for you, but I know I'm happier than I've ever been. And you're prepared to throw that all away?'

I looked away from him out to the garden that I'd always loved and that he had made even more beautiful. I couldn't bear to see the hurt in his eyes. I hated the accusatory tone in his voice because I knew that everything he said was true. But I couldn't change how I felt and could only hope that one day he would understand and forgive me.

'So what happens now? You're just going to spend the rest of your life living in the shadows for fear of what might happen? You were spared that day, Lily. And if I could change the past for you and bring Mike back, I would, even though it would mean I'd never have had any of this with you, so believe me, that's not something I take lightly.' He flashed me a black look, his eyes like cold green emeralds.

'I haven't taken it lightly either.'

'You could have fooled me.' He strode across the room to the threshold, staring out at the garden. The dog hurried over to him and rested against his leg, a small questioning whimper the only sound to break the tension.

'It's all right, boy.' Jack crouched down, making a fuss of him and soothing his upset.

'None of us knows how much longer we have on this earth, Lily.' Jack spoke, his back still to me. 'That's why we have to make the most of it. Every day could be our last but spending the whole time thinking about that means you never do anything and waste your life. I'm so, so sorry that you had to go through what you did, but you were spared, and you should be celebrating that, not hiding away. Not everyone gets this sort of chance for happiness so when it comes you need to grab it with both hands and not let go, no matter what.'

I stayed silent, my hands behind me gripping the cold, hard edge of the worktop to stop me running across the kitchen and into Jack's arms. He didn't understand, and I didn't expect him to. I didn't blame him for being angry. I was just as furious with myself, but the fear of losing him further down the line was more than I could bear.

When I didn't reply, Jack turned and watched me for a second, then pushed his hands roughly back through his hair. 'I was under the impression that this, us, meant as much to you as it did to me. I can see now that I was mistaken.'

'You weren't.'

He gave a cold, hollow laugh, so unlike his warm, rich regular one. 'Yes, Lily. I was. I love you with everything I have, and there's absolutely no way that I would ever, could ever, walk away from you. I know I didn't go through what you did, and I can't even pretend to understand that pain, but I'm here now and so are you. And yet you're still throwing it all away.'

'Jack, please try to understand.'

'I'll never understand, Lily. Never.' He snatched up his keys from the bowl and walked out of the house without another word. Moments later, I heard the rumble of his pickup engine starting and the tyres crunch through the gravel as he left.

Clive padded over to me, confused by the fact that Jack hadn't taken him with him. 'It's OK, boy. He'll be back later. I'll take you out now, how's that?'

Ordinarily Clive would be bouncing about, dancing on his paws at the prospect of going out but, sensing something was wrong, he was currently walking between me and back to the open doors of the house, clearly looking for Jack.

I went upstairs to close the windows and change into some shorts. Through the open door, I heard the soft, unhappy whine of Clive. I did my best to push all the emotions to the back of my mind and changed my clothes but suddenly the reality of the situation overwhelmed me and, the next thing I knew, I was sitting crumpled against the bed, sobbing like I hadn't done for years.

Ending our relationship was the right thing, the only thing, to do, but if it was, why did I feel so awful? A warm, furry body rushed in and pressed itself against me and I wrapped my arms around the solidness of the dog and buried my head in his golden fur until all the tears had been spent. I sat up and stroked his now damp coat. Eventually, I pushed myself up and headed downstairs to take him out. Hopefully the fresh air would do us both some good and help me convince myself that I hadn't just made a huge, horrible mistake.

Two hours of tramping around did not bring the hoped for respite from the anguish and emptiness that resided within me. When we returned to the house, Jack's truck was still gone, and I wondered where he was but then told myself I had no right to. Jack had come to the house as a lodger and that had worked well until I had allowed emotion to cloud the situation. I'd never intended to spend as much time as I had with Jack, even when we were just friends. He'd been talking about finding his own place a little while before we got together. I realised that both of us had been finding excuses for him not to, but now there was nothing to stop him. Still, that was bound to take a little time and I hoped that, given that space, Jack would forgive me and that we could at least part as friends. Clive scampered into the house and went zooming off to check it out as he always did. Coming back, he had another sniff around and then went to his water bowl and began lapping away. Hanging up the lead, I bent and undid my trainers and pushed them off before heading upstairs to shower and change. As I passed Jack's room, I noticed the door was ajar, but I was sure it had been closed earlier.

'Jack?' There was no reply, so I pushed the door open a little more. It was empty. All his things were gone and the room once again looked like just another guest room instead of Jack's room. The duvet was folded on the end of the bed and it was then I noticed a note, together with the keys to the house and the studio.

Lily, have made other arrangements, think that is best. Sheets etc in washing machine. Look after yourself and Clive. Jack.

I read the note three times before sitting heavily on the bed, staring out of the window across the beautiful countryside, not seeing any of it.

30

With Jack gone, each twenty-four hours seemed to stretch for far longer, the days and nights dragging out without the distraction of his company, his smile, his love. I went to bed early in an attempt to shorten the long days, but all that succeeded in doing was to lengthen the nights.

I looked down at the dog, who was now ensconced in his upstairs bed, snoring contentedly, completely oblivious that he was the one thing that kept me from tumbling back down to the absolute depths of sadness, despair and loneliness I once had before.

Summer turned to autumn and, although I took Clive out for his daily walk, I couldn't appreciate the changing season, the burnished gold and bronze leaves fluttering to the ground and collecting around our feet. Clive had finally stopped looking for Jack every time we came into the house, but he'd become more clingy to me since Jack had left, as though afraid I would disappear too. If my heart hadn't already been shattered, the fact that I'd hurt this beautiful, innocent animal would have destroyed it again. All I could do was reassure him that I wasn't going anywhere, just as Jack had tried to reassure me of the same thing. The dog would look at me with big brown soulful eyes and then rest his head on whatever part of my body was nearest with a big sigh. I wasn't sure if he understood any of it, but I hoped he at least got the gist. Felix and Poppy had tried to help, but both they and I knew there was nothing to say. I'd made a choice and had to live with it. One time, when I couldn't stop myself, I asked them how Jack was doing. Poppy had looked unusually grave and shook her head.

'Not great. He's working every hour that he can. The children and I have barely seen him either.'

'I'm so sorry that I put you all in the middle of this. That was never my intention.'

She laid a hand on my arm. 'We know that and I'm sure Jack will come around when he's able. He adores his godchildren too much to stay away for long, but I think he just needs to get his head in the right place.'

I thought I had been saving myself from hurt, but the pain of losing Jack, even by my own volition, was still as raw now as the day he'd left. I'd hurt him badly, but I'd also hurt my family and even my dog. Time heals all wounds, so they say. I wasn't so sure about that but could only hope that in this case it would be true.

* * *

'You're still coming to the wedding, though?' Felix was wolfing down a piece of the Victoria sponge cake I'd just set out on a plate.

'What wedding?'

'William's. You RSVP'd that you would months ago. You can't cancel now.'

William was one of the village boys made good. He'd risen through the ranks of the law to become a top barrister in London and was getting married in the local church to a girl he had gone to school with. They'd dated as teenagers but drifted apart, and both had been through several relationships as adults. A chance meeting had set them back on the path to love and now they wanted to celebrate that in the place where it all began. The whole village was invited and I knew that included Jack.

'Don't even think it, let alone say it.' Felix was unusually sharp.

'What?'

'Whatever excuse you were coming up with to not go. Faith and William are really excited that you said yes, and they'd be hurt if you didn't turn up now.'

'I wouldn't just not turn up! Obviously I'd let them know.'

'And you think that makes it all better?'

'Felix…' Poppy's voice was soft, but her tone had a warning to it.

'What?' He turned to her. 'I thought she'd got over all this.'

'Got over all what?' I said.

'This whole bloody recluse thing.'

'I'm not doing it out of choice!'

'Of course you are! Everyone understood at first, of course we did. You went through a horrible experience, but you refused to get help and instead shut yourself away, missing out on events, special moments in the children's lives, in our lives, in your own life…' He shook his head. 'And now this with Jack? You were happy, Lily. Why on earth would you throw that away? He was so good for you. He got you out of this bloody mausoleum!'

'It's not a mausoleum!' Oddly enough, I was more offended at him criticising my house than the other things he was saying, perhaps because I knew the other things were true.

'OK, fair enough. But you're still locking yourself inside as though it was one. You started going out, Lily, you went to a bloody premiere, for God's sake, and you survived. I'd even go so far as to say you enjoyed it. You started having a life again, Lily. And you were happy.'

'I'm still happy.'

My brother scrubbed his hands up and down his face. 'You are so not happy! You are the complete opposite of happy, and that's all your own doing!'

I felt the tears burning down my cheeks. 'Are you finished?'

Felix pushed the cake away. 'Yeah. I'm finished.' He stepped off the bar stool, gave the dog's head a quick rub and left without saying goodbye. I jumped as the heavy front door slammed shut behind him. Poppy and I sat there for a moment in silence. My brother and I had argued before, but never like this, and he'd never once left without saying goodbye.

'I'd better go,' she said, and I realised her eyes were full of tears.

'I'm so sorry, Poppy, I never meant to hurt anyone.'

'I know you didn't, Lils. It just makes him so sad when he thinks of the things that you have missed out on and he was so happy when you began...' She spread her hands. 'Living again. It's just hard for him to see you so unhappy and retreating back into yourself. He's worried and sad for you and unfortunately it's come out as anger because he's frustrated.' She gave me a hug before bending and ruffling Clive's fur and placing a kiss on top of his head.

'Felix is right about the wedding, though,' she said, turning at the front door. 'It's this weekend so too late to cancel on them and, as he said, they are looking forward to seeing you. You were all such great friends growing up. I think it would be rude to cancel now.' With that, she gave me a quick kiss on the cheek and crunched off across the gravel to the car in which Felix sat waiting. Neither of them looked back as they drove off. I had never felt so alone. The click of toenails made me look down.

'Come on, boy, let's go for a walk.' It was the last thing I felt like doing but I'd upset people close to me and right now it felt like Clive was the only good thing I had, and he asked for so little.

* * *

The golden blaze of sunrise melted into a clear sky of cerulean blue, the temperature generously staying at a mild level considering the time of year. I hadn't heard from Felix since the argument and unusually only received one text message from Poppy saying that she hoped I was OK, followed by a hug emoticon. I knew now that, despite trying to fool myself for the past couple of months, I was far from OK. I hadn't been from the moment I told Jack it wasn't going to work. I'd hurt people including those who had supported me at a time I needed it the most. Felix was right. I should have got help but refused to see the need for it, instead shutting myself away and thinking that closing myself off to everyone and everything would protect me from hurt. In the end, it hadn't, and had only spread the hurt to other people, good people, something I would struggle to ever forgive myself for.

Parking the car in the playground car park, I walked up to the village. Had I had my hiking boots on I could have walked, but the church was a little far for me to go the whole way in heels.

Approaching the church, I could see the crowds of people, and wondered if we'd all fit in there. There were whispers behind hands but there were also waves and smiles and I did my best to keep my head held high. I could have rung Felix, apologised and gone in with them but I knew I needed to do this alone, to prove to him and to myself that I could do it. Jack had been right when he'd said I was living in the shadows and I had been for far too long. It was time to step into the light, no matter how scary and bright it felt right at this moment.

'Auntie Lily!' Ruby's little legs carried her along until she ran into my arms and I crouched down and swept her up. 'I didn't know you were coming today! I miss you!' She gave me a big kiss on the cheek and I willed myself not to cry. It had taken me over two hours to try to replicate Jemima's beautiful make-up from before, trying to remember the tips she'd given me as she'd done it, explaining every stage. Thankfully the mascara was waterproof as I cuddled Ruby's little body to me and she hooked her legs around my waist as we walked on towards the rest of my family.

Freddy, seeing me, ran out to join us and I bent down to give him a kiss, which he then shyly turned away from, seeing a couple of boys from school. Still, he searched for my spare hand with his and held tightly as we headed through the lychgate and into the grounds of the church.

'You look beautiful,' Poppy said, kissing my cheek as we exchanged a look that said so much more than words.

'Thank you. So do you. I love the hat!'

I turned to my brother. 'Hi.'

Felix wrapped me in the most enormous hug, encompassing his daughter within it as her little arms clung around my neck. 'I'm sorry,' he whispered.

'Nothing to be sorry for. It's me who should apologise for so much.'

He shushed me and kissed my temple.

We separated and Poppy tactfully took Ruby off me and led her and Freddy to a little bench where she took a couple of treats out of her bag to distract them for a moment or two, leaving Felix and me alone.

'I shouldn't have spoken to you like that. I'm sorry. I wanted to apologise before now, but Poppy thought it might be wise to give us both some time to calm down properly.'

'That wisdom is another reason why I have the best sister-in-law and you have the best wife.'

'I think you're right.'

There was silence between us for a moment, but it wasn't uncomfortable. We walked until we were far enough away from others not to be overheard. 'I never meant to hurt anyone, least of all you.'

'I know you didn't,' said Felix. 'You were dealing with something awful in the best way you could. I shouldn't have exploded like I did the other day.'

'Maybe you should have. I've had a lot of time to think over the past couple of months and the other day just confirmed some extra things for certain. I've missed out on so much and I don't want to miss out on anything else.'

Being in a public place my brother kept his face stoic, but the tight hug he wrapped me in said everything it needed to. We both glanced over to where their children and Poppy were and, through that silent communication that husband and wife often have, Poppy allowed the children to hare back over to us as she followed at a more sedate pace. Ruby retook her position on my hip as Freddy leant against his dad's leg.

'Uncle Jack!' Ruby called over my shoulder as she began to wriggle with excitement. A fluttering sensation filled my stomach as we turned to see Jack walking up the church path towards us. He wasn't alone.

'Hello, chickpea,' he said, taking the little girl who was reaching out towards him as far as her arms would stretch. Our hands brushed as we transferred our goddaughter to his arms. My breath caught, as though I'd touched a low volt electric fence, but Jack barely looked at me. The tall, elegant woman next to him removed her hand gracefully from his arm in order to allow him to take the child properly and placed it across her other one, which held a delicate Chanel clutch bag with a large gold clasp. As her hand moved, the late autumn sunlight flashed off the huge solitaire diamond on her left hand.

'We haven't seen you for aaaaages!' Ruby pointed at him, big blue eyes looking imploringly – she was going to be a heartbreaker when she grew up.

'I know, sweetheart. I'm sorry. I'll try and do better, OK?'

'Promise?' Her fingers toyed with the white carnation in his buttonhole.

'I promise.' He held up his free hand and hooked his little finger. Ruby did the same and linked them before cuddling against him, his arms wrapping her tighter.

'So sweet,' the stranger in our midst commented. 'Clearly Jack's forgotten his manners, so I'll introduce myself.' She smiled warmly. 'Cecily Fullington-Beck. You must be Felix and Poppy. I've heard so much about you, it's wonderful to finally meet you. And what's your name?' she said crouching down on a level with my nephew.

'Freddy,' he said, his hand sneaking up to Felix's.

'That's an excellent name, and don't you look handsome, all smart in your nice suit.'

'Thank you.' His other hand snaked up to take my left one and I wrapped my own around it.

'And you must be Lily.' It was a statement rather than a question.

'I am,' I said, offering my right hand, which she shook, smiling pleasantly.

'It's so nice to put faces to names, don't you think?' Cecily said.

My gaze flicked to Jack and unexpectedly locked with his. He immediately looked away.

'Excuse me a moment, I just need to check on something.' I let go of Freddy's hand and headed around the corner of the church towards the back in the old part of the cemetery before sinking onto a bench. The peace of the area contrasted with the screaming that was currently going on inside my brain, telling me what an idiot I'd been to push Jack away. I'd been lucky enough to find one man who loved me and then, years later, been given a second chance at happiness. Instead of being grateful and grabbing the opportunity as I should have, I'd thrown it away, pushing the man I loved into the arms of Lady Cecily. As Jack had said at the time, there was more than one way to lose a person and this time I'd helped the process. My heart felt like it was in shreds as I dialled the number on my phone.

Perhaps this was for the best for Jack – this was the woman his family had wanted him to marry and, so long as he was happy, perhaps their marriage would help heal the rift between him and his parents. I could only hope something good came out of it, because Jack deserved that.

'He's absolutely fine, dear,' Mrs Dorsey said, laughing, before I'd had a chance to say a word down the line. 'Clive and I had a chat when you left and I told him you'll be back later, and he seems quite happy with that now. Busy playing with his friends, he is, zooming around the garden at the moment.'

'Thank you, Mrs Dorsey.'

'Oh, none of that Mrs Dorsey lark. Call me Pearl, dear. Have you seen the bride yet?'

'No, not yet. I should think we'll be going into the church shortly, though.'

'Would you take me some photographs, dear? I'm more than happy to look after everyone's pooches today, but it's always nice to see a lovely wedding, isn't it?'

'Of course I will.'

Judging by the massive rock on Cecily's hand, Pearl might just have the chance to go to another big wedding in the village before long.

'Thanks again, and I'll see you in the morning.' I hadn't been sure what time I'd be back, so we'd arranged for me to collect Clive tomorrow.

'Have a lovely time!' she said cheerily before hanging up. I sat with the phone in my hand and stared out across the carefully tended cemetery.

'There you are. We were wondering where you'd gone.'

I smiled. 'It's OK. I haven't chickened out and gone home.'

Poppy sat down next to me. 'We didn't think you had.' She placed her hand over mine. 'You all right?'

It would be easy to pretend I didn't know what she was talking about but that would have just been a waste of breath for both of us.

'Did you know?'

'No. But we haven't seen him much since you two broke up. I have to say I'm a bit surprised. He was absolutely devastated at losing you.'

'He's known her for a long time. He mentioned her once when we were talking about things. Apparently, their parents have always wanted them to marry, but she got fed up with Jack not asking her and married someone else. She was widowed a few years ago so the old hopes had once again been raised between the two families.'

'He can't love her.'

'He must do.'

'Not like he loves you.'

'Loved,' I said, putting the emphasis on the past tense. 'I blew that one well and truly. He must love her, anyway. He wouldn't be marrying her if he didn't, he wouldn't hurt her by committing himself to something he didn't believe in.'

'You're right. But I don't understand it. It just seems so quick.'

'Yes,' was the only response I could make. My stomach churned and my head pounded. Right now, the last thing I wanted to do was attend a wedding knowing that the man I loved would soon be marrying someone else and that it had all been my own doing. Today was William and Faith's day. I'd looked inward for far too long. It was time to look outward and today I would watch them marry and look for the joy, for once not thinking about all the things that could go wrong. I'd see only the love that had brought them together, full circle, where they were meant to be.

'Clive OK?' Felix popped his head around the corner, pointing at my phone. 'I'm guessing that's what you went to check on.'

'Where are the kids?'

'With Jack and Cecily,' Felix replied to Poppy before glancing back towards me, awaiting an answer.

'Yes, he's fine. Having a great time apparently.'

'Sounds good. Come on. Let's see if we can get you to have a great time too.'

Poppy and I both looked up at him and he sighed. 'Yes, all right. I saw the ring. Let's see if we can get you to have a half decent time, at least.'

I stood and linked arms with them both and headed back towards the church.

31

Jack and Cecily were on a different table to us for the reception, which made things a little less painful. Jack was sitting with his parents, although I was surprised not to see his brother in attendance. They were with a few others that I didn't recognise from the village, perhaps friends of William's from London. I tried not to look too often but it seemed that there was less of a strain between Jack and his parents now than there had been at the social gathering I'd attended with him earlier in the year. As I watched, Jack put his arm around his dad's shoulder and leant in to say something, both of them laughing at the joke. Even his mother looked more relaxed. Perhaps this marriage was for the best, healing a divide that had been difficult for everybody involved. That didn't mean I would ever not regret letting Jack go. Seeing him walk up the church path with Cecily on his arm, the huge engagement ring flashing in the sunlight, had felt like a physical blow.

I was nowhere near getting over Jack Coulsdon-Hart and knew I wouldn't be for a long time to come, but I wouldn't be closing myself away this time. Yes, that left me open to hearing gossip, and I imagined Jack would get married in the village church too, bearing in mind his ancestors had once owned the entire area, and I wasn't quite sure how I'd cope with that – but I would. I was stronger than I thought, and I had my family and the wonderful gift that Jack had given me in Clive. Together we would find our way.

* * *

'Looks beautiful all lit up at night, doesn't it?' The deep tones wrapped themselves around me and squeezed my heart.

'It really does,' I replied, without looking around.

'Are you having a nice time?'

I wasn't sure which was worse. Not speaking to him at all, as in the churchyard, or this inane small talk.

'Yes, thank you. It was a beautiful wedding, and the food was delicious. I hope you're enjoying yourself too.'

Jack moved closer, resting his hands on the stone balustrade surrounding the terrace that looked out over the landscaped gardens of the five-star hotel where the reception was being held. I gave an involuntary shiver, just as much from the chill of the evening as from the proximity of Jack's warmth, once so familiar and now achingly missed.

'You're cold.' Jack slipped off his jacket and made to put it around my shoulders, but I stepped away.

'I'm fine, really,' I said, pulling up a smile. It was definitely colder now, but I didn't think Cecily would appreciate her fiancé putting his coat around another woman's shoulders, especially one he had recently been in a relationship with.

'Lily, you're shivering. Just take the jacket.'

'No,' I said, 'but thank you for the offer. I'm going back inside in a moment.' As I moved I saw Cecily through the open doors, watching us.

'Why the hell are you so stubborn?' The question had a

controlled but wary tone to it, and I looked up, meeting his eyes for the first time since the churchyard when he had looked away so quickly.

'I'm learning.' I smiled sadly at him, inwardly cursing the tears filling my eyes. 'I'm going to head in now.' I glanced again at Cecily. 'Perhaps you should too.'

Jack frowned at me for a moment and then glanced in. 'She's fine. Cecily's superpower is always being able to find somebody to talk to.'

'That's not exactly the point, though, is it?'

The dark brows knotted. 'What is the point then, Lily?'

He really was going to make me spell this out for him, wasn't he? 'The point is that you should be with your fiancée rather than trying to be chivalrous to your ex-girlfriend, as much as she appreciates the gesture.'

He stared at me and then that smile that I loved so much began to show on his face. He picked up his jacket from where he'd thrown it over the balustrade when I'd refused it and wrapped it around my shoulders before I could protest.

'God, I miss you.'

'Jack...'

'Do you love me?'

'Jack, you can't ask me that.'

'I just did. It's a simple answer yes or no.'

'How can you do this to me?' Tears began streaming down my cheeks.

'Because I love you. I've always loved you and I always will love you. I knew I wasn't worthy of you when I was younger and, although I was probably seen as callous and likely was to more women than I care to think of, I knew you were different. Special. I knew you didn't deserve to be treated that way, but I wasn't sure how to deal with anything more. When I heard you were getting married, it was like someone had pierced my heart – but when I heard about the accident, it was even worse, because I knew how destroyed you were. I'm not the man I was back then, but I had to wait until you realised that, even though I knew I would love you until the end of my days.'

I pulled away from him, staggering a little as my heel caught on the paving. I reached out to steady myself, but Jack was already there, wrapping his arms around me. Pushing against his broad chest I shook my head. 'You can't say that. Not when you're marrying another woman. It's not fair to her or me.'

'I'm not.'

I gave a snort of disbelief. 'I'm pretty sure the astronauts on the International Space Station can see Cecily's engagement ring with the size of that diamond. It is an engagement ring, right?' I said, folding my arms across my chest.

Jack took a deep breath and let it out slowly. 'Yes, it is an engagement ring.'

'Exactly, so you can't just go around telling other women you love them and—'

'But it's not from me.'

I opened my mouth, closed it, then stared at him for a while. 'What?' I said quietly, when I found my voice again.

'Cecily's engagement ring isn't from me. I'm not marrying anyone. Not yet, anyway.'

'But you're... together. You came together and your parents seem so happy.'

'I am Cecily's escort for the day, and yes, my parents are happy as our two families are finally uniting as they'd always hoped.'

'I don't understand.'

'Cecily is marrying my brother. Edward fell off a horse yesterday being a stupid arse, and he's laid up in bed with a bad back. So I am escorting my sister-in-law-to-be to the wedding.'

'But I thought your parents wanted you to marry her.'

'I don't think they really minded which one of us did, and a few months ago, she and Edward were chatting together at a party and for the first time in her life, Cecily realised she was madly in love. Luckily, Ed felt the same.'

'And how do you feel about that?'

'Couldn't be happier for them.'

'So why has she been watching us ever since you came out here?'

Jack didn't take his eyes off me. 'Because Cecily is no fool. She knows I'm still crazy about you, and apparently she could read something in you in the churchyard that made her think you might still have feelings for me. She told me to come out here and bloody well do something about it before I lost you again. You were right before. I can't promise to be there for you forever.'

I made to step away and he caught my hand, continuing. 'But I promise that I want to be there for you forever and will do absolutely everything in my power to keep that promise. So I'm going to ask one more time. Do you still love me?'

'More than ever,' I whispered through my tears.

'I was hoping you'd say that.'

Jack crushed me against him as his lips came down on mine, one hand at the back of my head, cradling me against him as though he never wanted to let me go. Behind us, a barrage of whoops and clapping and catcalls came from the ballroom.

'At bloody last!' A cut-glass accent made herself heard over the noise.

Jack released me just enough for us to turn and grin rather stupidly at the audience we had amassed, including Cecily, who stood at the front.

'Obviously I'll be taking all credit for this reunion,' she declared.

'Of course you will,' Jack said, laughing, before kissing me again.

EPILOGUE

Eighteen months later, there was an heir to the Coulsdon-Hart name, with Cecily and Edward the enormously proud parents and Jack clearly already a favourite uncle. With the pressure off to marry the 'right' woman, and a very frank and what had, surprisingly to Jack, turned out to be emotional meeting with his parents, when all the pent-up feelings of years gone by poured out, there had been a clearing of the air and finally a fresh breeze had swept through the family home.

Jack had agreed that, when the time came, he would accept the title, but that Edward and Cecily would take over the family home and he would continue to live at his own marital home, Meadow Blossom House.

Whilst initially we'd planned for a small wedding, when Jack had proposed on my fortieth birthday with a breathtakingly beautiful ring to match the necklace he'd given me for the premiere, the plans had grown. To our surprise, we had both embraced them, finally accepting that after years of us hiding in our own ways, we wanted to celebrate our hard fought for love with as many people as wanted to be a part of it. I'd had a couple of wobbles at the thought of all those people focusing on us, but when it came to the moment of walking down the aisle, Felix beside me, all I saw was the man I loved waiting for me, looking far too handsome to be standing in a house of God.

Jack's business had gone from strength to strength and the gold medal he and Sanjid had gained at the Chelsea Flower Show recently only cemented its reputation. He still worked from the garden studio, and I still worked in my study, but, when he was home, we would meet up for lunch and then walk Clive together in the evening.

Clive was still our soppy, smiley, beautiful companion. I didn't know now how I'd ever managed without him and knew I didn't want to. So, instead, I focused on what I had, and what I had was perfect.

ACKNOWLEDGMENTS

This is a book that had been planned for the previous year, but due to personal circumstances, I was unable to focus on it, so my thanks first of all goes to the incredible team at Boldwood Books. They allowed me to just write the book as and when I felt ready with absolutely no pressure which was just what I needed. Best. Publisher. Ever.

Special thanks goes to my lovely editor, Sarah Ritherdon, for her comments upon reading the first draft which made my year, let alone my week. Thank you! And also for her insistence on having Clive on the cover. Perfect call.

Thanks to all my writing pals who understand what this mad, brilliant, frustrating and rewarding writing life is all about from the inside. Also massive hugs to those special non-writing friends who know who they are.

And thank you, of course, to James, for all the stuff. LYLM.

MORE FROM MAXINE MORREY

We hope you enjoyed reading *You Only Live Once*. If you did, please leave a review.

If you'd like to gift a copy, this book is also available as an ebook, digital audio download and audiobook CD.

Sign up to Maxine Morrey's mailing list for news, competitions and updates on future books.

http://bit.ly/MaxineMorreyNewsletter

Explore more uplifting reads from Maxine Morrey.

ABOUT THE AUTHOR

Maxine has wanted to be a writer for as long as she can remember and wrote her first (very short) book for school when she was ten.

As time went by, she continued to write, but 'normal' work often got in the way. She has written articles on a variety of subjects, as well as a local history book on Brighton. However, novels are her first love.

In August 2015, she won Harper Collins/Carina UK's 'Write Christmas' competition with her first romantic comedy, 'Winter's Fairytale'.

Maxine lives on the south coast of England, and when not wrangling with words loves to read, sew and listen to podcasts and audio books. Being a fan of tea and cake, she can (should!) also be found out on a walk (although preferably one without too many hills).

Instagram: @scribbler_maxi (This is where she is to be found most)
Facebook: www.Facebook.com/MaxineMorreyAuthor
Pinterest: ScribblerMaxi
Website: www.scribblermaxi.co.uk
Email: scribblermaxi@outlook.com

Boldw☺☺d

Boldwood Books is an award-winning fiction publishing company seeking out the best stories from around the world.

Find out more at www.boldwoodbooks.com

Join our reader community for brilliant books, competitions and offers!

Follow us

@BoldwoodBooks

@BookandTonic

Sign up to our weekly deals newsletter

https://bit.ly/BoldwoodBNewsletter

Printed in Great Britain
by Amazon